B – ZONE
A NOVEL OF THE GUN

We are all tested.

Al Voth

BY
AL VOTH

TRIGGER PRESS INTERNATIONAL
SPRUCE GROVE, ALBERTA, CANADA

This book is a work of fiction. The characters, incidents and dialogues are products of the author's imagination and are not to be construed as real. Any resemblance to actual persons, living or dead, is entirely coincidental.

Copyright © by Alan J. Voth
First Printed in 1999
Second Printing 2001
Third Printing 2002
Printed in Canada

THE PUBLISHER

Trigger Press International
Box 3713
Spruce Grove, Alberta, Canada
T7X 3A9
Website: www.triggerpress.com

Canadian Cataloguing in Publication Data
Voth, Al, 1953 –
  B-Zone

  ISBN 0-9685050-0-7

  I. Title.
PS8593.O84B19 1999   C813'.54   C99-910545-0
PR9199.3.V67B19 1999

Cover Photo: Jordan Photographic
Cover Design: Penny Waite
Printing: Jasper Printing

AUTHOR'S NOTE

As the sub-title indicates, this is a novel of the gun. By that, I do not mean this is a novel about a gun but instead that it is a novel set in the world of the gun. The world of the gun is not a place but rather it is that community of people who share a common interest, professional or hobbyist, in firearms. The people who make up that world are those men and women who are the serious students of the gun. These are the people who are hunters, collectors, competitive shooters, dealers, gunsmiths and some who wear a uniform. It is them that this book is about.

Choosing to study the gun and live in its world means a person abandons the lies, myths and misconceptions about guns that exist among the uninformed and embarks on a search. It may be a person's search for the skills that will aid in survival, a collector's search for historical knowledge, a competitive shooters search for his limits or a hunter's search for a means of testing himself.

Some students of the gun, especially those that wear a uniform, have embarked on their studies by the nature of their profession but the vast majority have done so as hobbyists. Contrary to popular opinion, most of those who wear uniforms and go armed do not choose to study the gun at all. It is their loss. Those who do wear a uniform and have chosen to enter the world of the gun have often done so seeking knowledge on how to survive in the dark places, but invariably have found much more.

Professional or hobbyist, to those that live in the world of the gun, it is a safe and familiar place where one can be assured of encountering other people who share strongly held values of freedom, trust, responsibility and honor. There are people there who share the dream that everyone would embrace those values but who also share the fear that they are slowly being eroded.

To those not familiar with the world of the gun, it often appears to be a frightening place and the people in it dangerous. That is as understandable as it is incorrect since their perception is inevitably based on television and the movies which, as we all know, exist to create illusions. As a work of fiction this is also an effort at illusion but it is my hope that those aspects of the world of the gun that it portrays it does so accurately and that it reflects well on the men and women who inhabit it.

I trust that those well-versed in the world of firearms and especially competitive handgun shooting will be able to identify strongly with many of the people, places and events portrayed here; that this book will fit them like a custom rifle stock or a finely crafted handgun. There certainly is little fiction currently available of which that can be said. To those readers unfamiliar with firearms, it is my desire that you will be transported by the story into a world you are not acquainted with, someplace unique to visit and exciting to learn about. After all, isn't that part of the reason we read – to discover new worlds?

All who open these pages are cautioned that this is not a training manual but a work of fiction. Whether or not it is a worthy effort, I leave to my readers to decide.

Al Voth

ACKNOWLEDGEMENTS

My sincere thanks to the numerous people who gave selflessly of their time and energies to help me with this seemingly endless project. With friends and family like these I have something extremely valuable. For help with the manuscript, I am indebted to Paul, Jim, Ken, Sharon, and Kathy. For design work and advice my thanks to Rueben and Penny. For encouragement and faith I owe my two daughters, my wife and our "small group" of friends. And ultimately, for the wisdom to allow a young boy to follow his passion and become a student of the gun, I thank my parents.

*If you do that which is evil, be afraid,
for he does not carry the sword in vain.*

Romans 13:4

THE INTERNATIONAL PRACTICAL SHOOTING CONFEDERATION (IPSC) TARGET

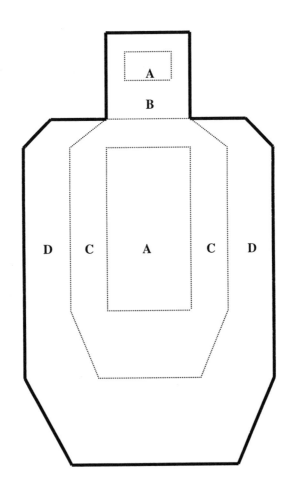

CHAPTER ONE

Nathan Burdett sat on the late fall grass at the edge of a small meadow, his back against the trunk of a poplar tree. The tall grass had started to bend downwards as its summer life departed and now his body crushed it flat to the point where it would not rebound upright again this year. He peered upwards through the branches of an overhanging dogwood and scanned the cloudless sky. Two crows rode the wind, using it to lift themselves higher in banking circling formations. He could see they were searching now. Their heads swiveled down, constantly watching the ground below. Nathan suspected that from their vantage point they could tell if he was being hunted yet.

He was right about the crows. The scenario unfolding under their watchful eyes was as timeless as the mountains, in whose shadows it was being played out. Predators hunting their prey. In this case, Nathan was the prey and the hunters believed him to be injured and weakening fast.

He was as conscious of the wind as the crows. For in these, the Alberta foothills, the wind and its use can mean survival or death to the hunted. The wind lives in these hills and is as much a part of the landscape as the mountains to the west and the vast plains to the east. The foothills form the transition from the Canadian Plains to the western mountain ranges, and in the same way as the mountains and the plains, the wind defines the land. Without the wind the land could not exist in its proper form, it would become something other than what it was made to be.

B-ZONE

The people and creatures of the hills accept the wind as part of their daily existence and allow for its influence in what they do and how they do it. When the Indians lived with the wind they called it *Chinook* which means snow eater. They hunted on the wind. Their prey escaped or fell to them on the wind.

The hunters already knew where their victim was. He lay ahead, at the edge of a row of tall poplar trees arrayed like a line of soldiers on parade. These sentinels, however, offered only a symbol of protection to the prey. They couldn't see him yet but they could clearly hear the occasional cries of his pain. It was going to be an easy kill.

The wind rose in a brief strong gust that brought with it the taste of snow. None fell yet but it would be only days before it did. At this elevation the leaves were just beginning to drop, transferring their fall colors from the branches where they clung, onto the ground where they would fall and rest. Once there, they would begin to contribute to the heavy humus smell unique to the late fall, and which filled Nathan's nostrils.

Overhead the crows worked the wind and swooped ever lower as they gained confidence, like a pair of dark suited lawyers anticipating violent death and sensing the opportunity to profit from it. The prey gasped in agony again and the hunters crept closer, ever cautious. They emerged from the brush that concealed them fifty yards from where their keen senses indicated the injured victim had sought refuge. Without cover now and the wind not entirely in their favor, no sound passed between them as they made an instinctive decision. They were a team, a unit of two that hunted as one and their killing record proved they were considerably better at it than most of their kind. The larger of them moved to the right in a sweeping circle, a flanking movement, while the other crept slowly ahead. He stayed low and quiet as he closed in, creeping directly to the clump of dogwood from where the last noises had come.

Nathan Burdett saw them both as they left cover. He had continued to watch the crows and a change in their flight patterns had told him five minutes ago that he was being actively hunted. When they revealed themselves by emerging from the trees and the larger of the two began to circle to his left he guessed their plan and began to calculate his options. They were obviously confident in their abilities and their two-to-one advantage.

Nathan's thumb moved to the safety of his rifle, ready to shoot and salvage the situation as best he could if his camouflage and the illusion he had created didn't hold. Both held however, and when the nearest of them had closed to within twenty yards Nathan shouldered the Sako .223 in one smooth movement and shot the circling coyote broadside through the left shoulder. Nathan saw him go down hard with nothing more than a twitch from his tail. He worked the bolt and refocused his attention. The second coyote had realized the ruse and was sprinting the short distance to the protection of intervening brush. Death was in the meadow and now he was racing it to survive. His tail streamed out behind him and his paws clawed for traction as he pushed his muscles to the limit. Even his ears were laid back as the body instinctively strove to make itself more aerodynamic. It was in vain. Within two strides of entering the safety of the trees, a Hornady V-Max fifty-five grain bullet caught him at a raking angle behind the right shoulder, disintegrating inside his chest cavity. Momentum slammed him into the base of a tree, there was a twitch from his tail and then he too lay still.

Nathan stood up slowly, appearing like some strange apparition rising from the earth. His camouflage making him invisible until he started to move and then his form separated from the grass and bushes, as he rose. He was ready for a follow-up shot but none was required.

Within a half-hour he had both animals field skinned and was walking back toward his truck with two prime coyote pelts in hand. As he left, the ever opportunistic crows swooped down on the carcasses. It wasn't what they had anticipated but they accepted it with relish nonetheless. Out of the empty sky more dark suited crows appeared to take advantage of the two coyotes' misfortune. None of them cared what had died or why it had happened.

Nathan was about to throw the furs into the back of his truck when the farmer who owned the land on which he was hunting, drove up. He was Jim Gates, a man Nathan had known since he was a boy and who had once helped Nathan's family with meat and garden harvest when Nathan's mother had been laid off. Like a lot of the farm or ranch trucks in this area Jim Gates' pick-up was a wondrous device, held creatively together with baling wire and spit. Rust had attacked it like a cancer and the fenders and body seemed to flap as he drove down a rough road. At one time it had been blue but the paint was slowly yielding to the unrelenting attack of the brown rust. Nathan's truck, while only slightly newer than Jim's and starting to show its age mechanically, looked pristine in comparison.

Jim Gates always had a three or four-day growth of beard and wore a battered baseball cap given to him by either a fertilizer company or a farm equipment dealer. The hat's beak was especially dirty and greasy on the right side because that's where he would grab it to take it on and off. And Jim's hands were never particularly clean. When you saw him take the hat off, a mostly bald head was revealed and a tan line that ran around its circumference made it appear as if he were wearing a white skull cap.

4

Jim didn't get out of his truck but just leaned out through the open window. "I heard two shots," he said looking at the pelts, "I figured that meant you got them both."

"I got lucky," Nathan said, walking over to where Jim sat and putting his left elbow up on the large side mirror. "I worked the area you suggested. It's a good bet these are the killers who were giving you the trouble."

"Good job kid. Thanks for the help – and that's from me and four of my lambless ewes. These guys and their buddies even worked their way around Pedro." Pedro was a donkey Jim pastured with his sheep. Donkeys have an extreme dislike for anything canine and end up acting as guards for the flock. "Pedro has worked out fairly well but you know I think the coyotes are learning how to get by him regularly. At first I thought they were just lucky but that's not it, they're smart and they've learned."

"That doesn't surprise me at all, but you know if you raised beef like everybody else you wouldn't have as many coyote problems," teased Nathan.

"Now don't you be starting on me too," countered Jim looking pained while grinding his truck into gear. Nathan stepped back. "As far as I'm concerned, everybody should eat mutton – after all," he shouted over the revving engine, "a hundred thousand coyotes can't be wrong." And with that and a wave he roared off in a cloud of dust.

Nathan drove home leisurely, taking time to enjoy the scenery of the country he had come to love. The road builders had tried to make the gravel road he followed as straight as the roads on the nearby prairie but the land had not allowed it. The varying contour of the hills, the rock outcroppings and the small lakes ensured each stretch of road had its own character just as each hill or nearby mountain did. He counted himself fortunate to have grown up in the beauty of the leeward shadow of these western mountains. It had always appeared to him as if the hills and mountains were beautiful only because of the prairies which lay stretched out flat to the east, as if they had given their all to make the mountains and now could only lie there, empty and wasted by the effort.

With winter not far away he could see the snowline creeping down the mountains like a growing bald spot on the head of an aging man. Nathan wondered if he would be plagued with that curse of nature that came to some men at middle age when their hairline like a high country snowline started to move. At twenty-six years of age he was a long way from that point yet, he hoped.

If he had known his father, he supposed that perhaps he may have been given a clue as to what would transpire on his own head, but his father had not seen fit to stick around and a few short years after Nathan was born had left his young family. Nathan's mother spoke about him sometimes. She said he looked liked his father but she was never specific or particular about that statement. She told him that his father had stayed in touch with her for about a year or so and then gradually all contact was lost. Nathan wasn't interested in learning much more than that. His father had left and cut his ties with the family. That settled it for Nathan. He was gone and there was no need for anyone, especially himself, to go looking for him. He told himself he wasn't even curious.

His thoughts returned to the land. The elk, deer and other big game would be traveling down those mountains ahead of that moving snow line, drifting toward their wintering areas where their respective predators would be waiting for them, be they man or beast. Nathan hoped to put a deer or two and maybe even an elk into the family freezer this fall. He enjoyed the hunting experience as a welcome break from his high stress job as an Emergency Medical Technician. His mother would welcome all the meat but his sister and her husband in Calgary would take some only if it was elk. They didn't care for the distinctive taste of deer. Within sight of Nathan's home was Bob's Gunsmith Shop and Nathan pulled in as confidently and comfortably as if he lived there – which his mother often accused him of, joking with him that he spent so much time there he should use *it* as his home address. Bob's shop and Nathan's home were both situated in the country on a main county road, a fifteen minute drive northwest of the small town of Cochrane, itself only ten miles northwest of the metropolis of Calgary. Bob's shop was across the road from the Burdett house and a little more than a quarter mile further to the west. They were both in a small valley that was one of those particularly beautiful spots made up of steeply rolling grassland interspersed with dense patches of poplar and aspen. Behind Nathan's house the valley rose steeply and within three hundred yards disappeared into an outcropping of stone that was a geological precursor of the Rocky Mountains. The gray rock formed the spine for a longer ridge that ran westward and upward.

After taking an early retirement from the military, but before the Burdetts had come to live in the valley, Bob had bought the property on the downhill side of the road. It had a modest house on it and he had added a shop, attaching it to the existing home. The house was one of those that from the front appeared to be a single floor residence but from the back looked like a two story. No basement was visible from the road but the downhill slope of the land exposed the basement at the rear. Also at the back, a large deck Bob had added at the main level provided a place from which to enjoy the view.

The shop itself had a separate entrance and a small frontal area where customers could gather. They weren't fenced

7

off from the machinery and equipment by a counter as in most shops, but they were limited to the sitting area. There weren't any signs to this effect but any customer who strayed out of the appropriate area without an invitation was quickly reminded about where he belonged. The sitting area had three worn wooden chairs arranged around a coffee table strewn with heavily thumbed gun magazines. It was quite all right here to put your feet up on the coffee table, boots and all, and as a result it was in atrocious condition. A decade of heavy boots and spilled coffee had left it deeply scarred. A small high counter against one wall held the obligatory coffee pot.

It wasn't a retail shop and as such Bob carried very little stock to sell to customers. He took pride in the fact that he was a gunsmith and a gunsmith only. In fact the doors were open only from 1:00 p.m. till 4:00 p.m. The rest of the time the shop was closed so that he could work without interruption. There was no concern here about growth or expansion or market share. Bob had advertised for a year when he first opened and after that was proud of the fact that he hadn't spent a dime on advertising and was never short of work. His reputation had grown simply by word of mouth among satisfied customers.

In Nathan's opinion his own life really had not started until the day twelve years ago when he first wandered into the shop and met Bob Coombs. His mother had bought their small place in the country to try and get her son away from the bad crowd he had started hanging around with in town and they had been in this new house a couple of days. There had been no way to get to town to hang out with his friends and so boredom had driven him to make the walk down the road to the 'gunsmith's shop.' Even then Bob's hair had been white. It had looked out of place on him, white hair on a middle aged man with a six-foot frame and a strong looking body; white hair belonged on older, grandfatherly type men. Bob had added glasses since then and he showed more age now. He was starting to look the grandfather part, thought Nathan. Too bad he had no kids.

At the time, like any boy, Nathan had been curious about the shop's firearms but what he found was a man who took an interest in a troublesome fourteen-year-old kid with a mother too busy trying to make ends meet to be more than a part-time parent. It was Bob Coombs who had gone out of his way to take him hunting and fishing and do the things fathers did with their sons. Bob had introduced Nathan to the sporting world of the gun and Nathan had taken to it like the proverbial duck to water, at the same time turning his back on the drugs, booze and crime that were claiming many of his old friends. Nathan could still hear his mother saying that as far as she was concerned, Bob Coombs had saved her son's life.

Today, Nathan noticed an unfamiliar car in front of Bob's shop. At least it was unfamiliar in the sense that he didn't know who owned it, and he knew virtually all of Bob's local customers. From the Budget sticker on the rear bumper he recognized it as a rental, probably from the airport in Calgary. Bob occasionally had what he called 'special customers' who would fly in to see him and a rental car in front of the shop meant just that.

When Nathan walked in, he saw a fit-looking stranger talking with Bob. The man was probably a couple of inches shorter than his own five feet ten inches and like Nathan his hair was short though slightly darker. Nathan guessed him to be about midway between his own age and Bob's fifty-six years. He was well dressed, no jeans or camouflage. They wouldn't have suited the expensive looking tan colored leather jacket and the polished shoes anyway. A businessman or perhaps a professional of some kind thought Nathan. Bob and his customer were seated at the coffee table involved in an animated discussion and Nathan detected an awkward pause in the conversation as he entered.

"Hi Nathan. What are you doing here?" asked Bob. That startled Nathan. Bob had never asked him that before, he had never needed a reason to be in Bob's shop.

"Afternoon Bob. I just took care of a couple coyotes that were snacking on Jim Gates' lambs." Walking over to the counter against the wall, he reached for the stained coffee pot. "There's a lot more than two around his place but it should take some of the pressure off for a while. Thought I'd stop for a mug of your terrible coffee is all."

"Well you might as well come over here," said Bob, "there's someone I want you to meet." Bob pointed to Nathan and said, "Nathan Burdett." Then he pointed to the customer and said, "Danny Forbes." That was how Bob introduced people, short, to the point, with no pleasantries. His assumption being, if you both were in a gunsmith's shop you already had enough in common and just needed to know names.

The man stood up and the two shook hands. Nathan read an expression of surprise and discomfort on the newcomer's face. He sat down but Nathan remained standing. There was a nagging feeling he had seen Danny somewhere before.

"I . . .uh . . . you said you shot a couple of coyotes?" Danny Forbes was struggling.

"Yeah." Nathan wasn't helping.

"Nathan calls them in." said Bob, trying to assist.

"Really," said Danny starting to get it together. "How do you do that?"

From that question Nathan knew this guy was not a hunter and that perked his interest even more. What was he doing here then? "I just sit in the bush and make a noise like a rabbit," said Nathan. "Mr. Coyote hears that and it sounds like a free lunch to him, so he comes running."

Danny's interest was genuinely piqued now. He frowned. "Really! What kind of a noise does a rabbit make? I can't ever say I've heard a rabbit make any kind of sound."

"Well," Nathan said, "it sort of sounds like this . . ." Setting down his coffee cup he glanced over at Bob and cast him a stern look. Then he began making a show out of puckering his mouth a certain way and holding his fingers interlaced just so, making a megaphone with his palms.

Bob had seen this before and was biting his lip and turning away in his chair as Nathan made three little munching noises in a row and in his best nasal voice called out, "Nnn-yeah - what's up Doc?"

Bob exploded with laughter, pounding his knee while Nathan just stood there smiling smugly. Danny Forbes turned pink with embarrassment and chuckled good naturedly. "I guess I walked into that one," he said.

Nathan noted the reaction and decided this guy just might be okay. He could laugh even when the joke was on him. He felt sorry for him now and fished a coyote call out of his jacket pocket. "Really Danny, this is how we do it. This little call, properly used, makes a noise like an injured rabbit or small animal. By using it the right way a hunter creates an illusion and the deception he creates gets the response he wants from a predator. Here let me show you." He popped the diaphragm call into his mouth and belted out a series of animal cries with all the feeling and soul of a blues musician. In the back yard Bob Coombs' dog immediately howled in response.

"Good grief!" said Danny, "That sounds awful! And I mean you, not the dog."

"Yeah it does, doesn't it?" said Bob. "The first few times you hear that, it makes the hair on the back of your neck stand up. But there's a lot more to it Danny, than just sitting down and blowing on the call, especially if you're trying to fool a coyote. They've got to be the smartest predators on the face of the earth. Nathan does pretty well when he sets his mind to it," he teased.

Nathan had extracted the call from inside his mouth. "Only because I learned from you," he replied.

"From what I hear, you're a fast learner Nathan," said Danny.

Nathan directed a questioning look at Bob who avoided eye contact and just pointed with a grease-stained finger at the other empty chair in the sitting area. Nathan sat without questioning, the respect for Bob was obvious to Danny. Bob walked around and opened the windowless shop door, it was still fifteen minutes to four but he changed the sign outside to *CLOSED* and then locked the solid door. "Danny's an old friend of mine but he's here to see you Nathan," said Bob, as he took up his usual chair. "Not me."

Nathan's face looked as puzzled as his mind was.

"You kind of walked in on us here Nathan," said Danny, leaning forward in his chair. "I was going to call you tomorrow and get together more formally, but since you're here we might as well talk now." Nathan saw an intensity enter his brown eyes.

"First, I guess you could say that I'm sort of a talent scout at the moment. However, the talent being scouted is not the usual sort. What I'm looking for is a talented pistol shooter and that's why I'm here to see you. My employer is a major corporation that is looking at getting into sponsoring someone in the competitive action pistol shooting circuit."

Danny leaned into his pitch. "I don't need to tell you that pistol shooting is a growing sport internationally and the people I am working for are looking to get in on the ground floor with a shooter that can carry their colors for them. You know some of the guys that are pro shooters now. Well, they're being sponsored largely by companies involved directly in the firearms industry in some way, primarily gun, holster, sight or ammunition makers. But this is different. The company I represent is not firearms related. All they want is exposure. Just like some of the companies who paint their colors on a race car, they have nothing to do with cars but by sponsoring the driver, they get exposure."

"Well, this is really flattering," said Nathan, taken slightly aback. "I love competition shooting enough to have allowed myself to dream of being a professionally sponsored shooter some day but I'm realistic enough to know that I'm not in that class yet, and I may *never* be."

"Don't sell yourself short," interrupted Bob, pointing an accusing finger at Nathan. "You've been shooting IPSC and USPSA matches for what, around seven years now? This last year you made it into the top 16 at the US Nationals and at the North American Championships. You've progressed faster than anyone I've ever seen, your accuracy is great and your speed is uncanny. You've already learned everything about competition that I or any of the locals can teach you. The only thing holding you back is an advanced teacher and more high level match experience."

Nathan didn't reply, he looked down at his coffee mug, examining it intently.

Danny, jabbing a thumb in Bob's direction, said, "That's the same line he's been giving me over the phone. Nathan, I'm not saying I'm here to offer you a sponsorship contract here and now. All I want is to talk to you about this and then do some basic testing. I'll tell you right now, up front, that I'm doing the same thing with several other shooters. This is a field trip for me, to develop a short list and that's all. If you want to participate in this we'll get you to do some shooting against a timer and if you make the short list then we'll move on to the next phase."

Nathan's mind was spinning. He interrupted. "Hold it. Hold it. Who are these people you represent? What company? I've been around long enough to know that firearms are not exactly politically correct these days. You're trying to tell me there's a non-firearms related company out there that wants to sponsor a pistol shooter? This sounds like a fairytale to me. How do I even know you're legit?"

Bob quietly interjected. "Danny's legit because I say he is."

Danny blushed with embarrassment. "I understand your concerns Nathan. At this stage of the project, I'm not allowed to tell you who the sponsor is but as we get further along you'll be given all that information."

Nathan glanced over at Bob, uncertainty and skepticism visible on his face. Bob just nodded at Nathan.

Danny caught the nod. "Here is what I'd like from you now," he said, holding up two fingers and then ticking them off as he went. "First, I would prefer that you keep this little proposal to yourself as much as possible. Talk it over with Bob here if you want but no further than that at the moment. Second, let's get together at a range somewhere nearby and let me run you through a couple of basic exercises with a timer. You bring your match gun, holster and ammo and do some shooting for me. That's all I'm asking of you now."

"I have a short range out behind the shop here with a few target stands and a set of Bianchi plates," offered Bob. "Will that do?"

"It sure will," said Danny. "What about it Nathan, meet you here tomorrow morning?"

Nathan avoided the question as he ran a hand through his light brown hair, deep in thought. "You look vaguely familiar Danny. Have I seen you somewhere before?"

14

Danny smiled. "You have a good memory for faces. I was in the gallery at virtually all of the big national handgun matches this year, the U.S. and Canadian Nationals, the Bianchi Cup, The Masters and the big steel shoots. I know you weren't at all of them but I was. I was scouting for talent all summer. I started on this project this spring when the competition season began."

Nathan nodded slowly, studying Danny. "Yeah. Okay. That's probably it."

Silence dominated the room, the same way the smell of solvents and oils usually did. Bob fidgeted with a short section of bulged shotgun barrel that he kept lying on the table in the sitting area as a reminder to his customers to check for bore obstructions before shooting.

"Okay," said Nathan. "Let's do it. Nothing to lose I guess and I've certainly gone shooting with a lot poorer excuses."

Danny looked pleased and said so.

Bob got up, walked to the front door and let his dog in. He spoke only to the dog, ignoring Danny and Nathan as they finalized their plans for tomorrow.

When Nathan got home, his mother had already gone to work. She worked as a dispatcher/receptionist for the local RCMP detachment and that required the usual shift work. After tossing the coyote hides into a plastic bag and then dropping them into the freezer for later delivery to a trapper friend, Nathan busied himself preparing his gear and finding something to eat. Checking his gun out and locating some ammo was the easy part; he was in his element. It was the kitchen that had him floundering. When his sister had still lived at home, she'd been a big help to their mother, especially in the kitchen. She enjoyed cooking and was good at it. When she married Todd Jenkins, it had left a hole in Nathan's life and especially in his stomach. He managed to find some leftover meat loaf and rice and made do with that.

He cleaned up the kitchen when he was done and tried to watch TV. It was no good, the programs on the tube were all too far detached from where his thoughts were. Giving up, he went back to his equipment, rechecking both gun and ammo. He cleaned his magazines and even emptied his shooting bag and housecleaned it. When there was no equipment left to clean, adjust or tweak he practiced drawing and dry firing, especially weak handed, and he did reloading drills. It helped, this was where his mind was.

When he ran out of things to do, he was faced with trying to go to sleep. Well before finding himself staring wide eyed at the dark ceiling he knew that would not be an easy task. His career as an Emergency Medical Technician for the local ambulance service was an enjoyable one, at least usually. But here was someone offering him a chance at a career as a professionally sponsored shooter and he didn't just like shooting, he loved it. His mind churned, turning over and over the possibilities like a brass polisher grinding at a load of fired cartridge cases.

Action pistol shooting was his sport. He had known that ever since participating in his first match as a teenager. The challenge of controlling a powerful handgun, to find the right balance of accuracy and speed, while strategizing his way through the constantly changing courses of fire was a task he loved. His lean body craved the action and physical demands of sprinting over, around or under obstacles while the mental discipline required to maintain complete control and deliver precise shots in the midst of the effort challenged his mind. Not lost on him either was the position by some proponents that this sport was the birthplace of the next martial art. The Asians had mastered the empty hand, but when the hand was full the mastery of it belonged to Nathan and those like him. And this was only the first generation.

Nathan had relentlessly pursued improvement ever since starting in the sport and each year he had done better. This had been his best year ever. But was he good enough to go professional? How good could he become if allowed to shoot and travel and compete without the restrictions of a full-time job? How would it change him? The torrent of questions made him restless enough that at 1:00 a.m. he was still awake. Reaching over he reset the alarm for an hour sooner than necessary, determining to go for a run before he saw Danny. With the same discipline he used to improve his shooting skills, he concentrated on going to sleep and eventually drifted off.

When the alarm sounded Nathan got up groggily, put on his running gear and stepped outside. The wind was there to greet him. It was gentle at this time of day, as if it too had rested all night. After some preliminary stretching he started down the road at an easy pace. The sun was still about ten minutes from coming up and it was cold. The fog of his breath puffed out in front of him like the steam from an old locomotive. Running down the road past Bob's shop he saw the light on in the kitchen of the house. That told him his timing should be about right. There was a small grade beyond the house that led up to where the trees hung over the road making it look like a tunnel into a wall of yellow and gold and he labored up it. When he turned the corner at the top he saw her about one-quarter mile ahead of him, out of the trees and into the open fields. She was striding purposefully like someone on a mission. She referred to herself as a 'power-walker.' Nathan increased speed enough to catch up, it took a serious effort. She was walking while he ran, but her pace was fast and she could probably walk him into the ground.

Frankie Coombs turned as she heard Nathan puff up beside her and slow to a walk. Frankie was Bob's wife and the nickname came from Francine, a remnant of French heritage somewhere in her past. There were people in the area who had known her for fifteen years but had no idea what her real name was. She was Frankie to everyone that knew her. Nathan thought of her as sort of a surrogate grandmother, someone who had retained all the wise things she had ever learned and was willing to share them with you when they were needed. He realized a lot of other people thought of her like that too, it was her gift. When Nathan wanted to talk to someone, he usually found Frankie. As much of a friend as he considered Bob to be, he could talk more easily with his wife. He didn't know why that was.

"Good morning Nathan," she said, flashing the disarming smile that always told him she was genuinely glad to see him. "Nice morning isn't it?"

"Yeah, looks like its going to be a good day." Nathan picked up Frankie's rhythm and stepped out walking and swinging his arms as he matched her speed.

"I heard you're going to do some shooting today," Frankie said, getting straight to the point.

"So Bob told you about Danny Forbes and what he wants."

"Oh, I've known Danny almost as long as Bob has. He's a good boy. He likes my sausage soup."

Nathan chuckled, "He's hardly a boy Frankie, he's got to be close to forty."

"Nathan when you're over fifty like me anybody who's under forty is a boy."

"Okay. Okay."

"He wasn't married when I knew him but he is now. And they even have a little girl. He showed me her picture. She looks like a real sweetie."

They were out over a mile from their homes now. The sun, starting to rise, was painting the tops of the hills with its yellow brush. They headed up another short steep grade toward the line of sunlight that was inching down toward them.

Frankie swung her arms smoothly and rhythmically as she walked. "You're worried about where all this might lead and especially what it might do to your career as an Emergency Medical Tech." It was a statement not a question.

"I've worked hard to get into this career Frankie. I'm not sure I want to give that up to go chasing after some pie in the sky. Even though it seems to be an unbelievable opportunity. Maybe that's just it. Maybe that's what's bothering me. It's just too good to be true."

"Are you a good EMT?" she asked.

"Sure, I got good marks in training and everybody tells me I'm doing a good job. I usually like the work and I like the people I work with. It's great to be helping people in need as well. Too often the drunks, the druggies and those people who seem to be trying to commit suicide in increments get you down. But when I go to an accident where innocent people are injured and I get to help them out, it makes me feel good and helps keep me going when I get to feeling I'd rather be somewhere else; like on a range shooting."

"Think you can be the best EMT in the world?"

"Oh come on now, I doubt that," Nathan scoffed. "There's a guy in Calgary who's an M.D. but works as an EMT because that's what he enjoys. I'll never be in that league."

They walked on silently for a short while, the only sound the crunching of gravel under their feet. As they approached the line of sunshine Frankie said, "Bob thinks you can be the best action pistol shot in the world."

"Oh he just says that to try and build up my confidence. It's the old positive mental attitude thing," replied Nathan.

"No you're wrong about that Nathan." Frankie had switched to her scolding voice now and she shook her index finger at him as she spoke. "He really believes that. How much stock you put in his opinion is up to you, but he really believes you can be the best in the world."

Nathan was quiet. He'd just been what Bob called "finger wagged." When Frankie unholstered her finger and shook it at you it was time to pay attention. And whatever you do, don't contradict her.

They met the line of sunshine creeping down the hill and strode on into its orange warmth. Nathan continued walking for a moment and then abruptly stopped as he looked at his watch. Frankie stopped too and Nathan squinted into the sun as it came up behind her. "I might never get another chance to find out how good I could really become."

Frankie nodded. "And one of these days soon you may find a girl you want to settle down with and then it'll be even harder to go chasing dreams."

Now Nathan nodded in agreement. "It's time for me to head back, I've got to get ready to go shooting." He turned and jogged back down the hill into the gloom of the shadow. Frankie never spoke but watched as he crossed from the sunlight into the darkness below. She prayed it wasn't an omen.

The agreed time had been 9:00 a.m. and that was when Danny Forbes and Nathan Burdett both arrived at Bob's shop. By that time Bob had already done a couple of hours work and he set aside a Winchester 1897 shotgun to go out back and watch the proceedings. Nathan knew his way around Bob's range and busied himself setting the steel plates and stapling some targets to mobile frames. He set them up as directed by Danny. Nothing unusual, all quite straightforward thought Nathan, when he was done.

Next he dug out his equipment. His match gun was a Para-Ordnance 38 Super with all the usual tricked out features and a Tasco optical sight. Bob had helped him put the gun together about three years ago and it had turned out accurate and reliable. The multi-port compensator Bob had machined worked well and it shot with little muzzle rise. This last season it had served him well. The gun instilled confidence, a good solid piece of workmanship that always performed for him. Nathan velcroed his gun belt to the liner belt he already wore, inserted loaded magazines, holstered his gun and declared himself ready to Danny.

From a briefcase Danny retrieved some eye and ear protection as well as a clipboard and timer. He passed the timer to Bob and asked him to run it. "Want to do any warm up Nathan?" he inquired.

Nathan replied in the affirmative, did a few practice draws and then faced the bank of Bianchi steel plates. Bob had built the plate rack himself, setting the six dinner plate sized disks about four feet above ground level and building a reset mechanism so that all a shooter had to do was pull a rope to reset the targets after knocking them over. Nathan drew and hammered all six down in a burst of gunfire. A reload, pull the rope to reset the hinged plates and he did it again. "Everything seems to be working," he declared, as he strode over to Danny refilling a magazine. "Let's get on with it."

For the next thirty minutes Nathan performed an assortment of simple drills at Danny's direction. They included drawing and firing single shots, double taps, multiple target exercises, speed reloads and a short stage with partial targets and a no-shoot. Danny recorded times and scores on his clipboard. Nathan was happy with the numbers he was racking up for Danny. He had some exceptional runs and some that were average but overall it was as good as he could deliver. The fact

21

that this little exercise was happening at the end of the competition season meant he was at the peak of his performance. He had pushed himself to improve all summer and he was pushing himself even now, but not to the point where he was losing control. He was shooting only as fast as he could get good hits.

Anyone not familiar with the sort of accuracy and speed that a top action pistol shooter could be capable of would have stood in awe as they watched Nathan drawing and firing. The movements a blur and the gunshots so rapid as to be impossible to count, each bullet launched at a target and once there either punching through paper or slamming over a steel plate with relentless authority. To the uninitiated this would have been an incomprehensible feat of arms unless personally exposed to it. To the three men engaged in this exercise, however, it was nothing more than the type of good solid performance that any of several hundred people in the sport were capable of.

"One last thing Nathan," said Danny, "I want you to assume your firing stance and point your loaded gun downrange into the backstop. When you hear the timer beep, fire a single shot as fast as you can."

"OK, but what's my target?" asked Nathan.

"There is no target," replied Danny. "This is just to test reaction time. You hear the beep and then you fire the shot as fast as you can, don't try and hit anything other than the backstop."

"Whatever you say," shrugged Nathan.

Bob, still running the timer, gave the ready commands again and when the sophisticated electronic clock beeped it was tough to tell where the beep ended and the gunshot began. Bob tilted the timer for Danny to see. Danny raised his eyebrows and wrote down the numbers. They did that nine more times and Nathan's times crept lower as they went.

"Nathan, have you ever done this exercise before?" asked Danny.

"No," he said, his blue eyes conveying a puzzled look behind the safety glasses. "It seems kind of meaningless to me, especially since the gun is already out and I'm not even trying to hit anything."

Danny tapped the side of his timer with his knuckles. "Do you happen to have a timer in your shooting bag? I'm not sure this one is working right."

Nathan fished it out and threw it to Bob. "Want to do it again, Danny?"

"Yeah let's. Load ten more and get ready, same drill."

Ten repetitions later Danny had essentially the same numbers as the first time. In fact Danny thought that the average might be a couple of hundredths of a second lower. He didn't comment further about that. "Good job Nathan. That wraps it up."

"Gentlemen," said Bob "I think it's coffee time and Frankie mentioned she was going to bake cinnamon buns this morning. If you'll follow me into the house, I'll bet we can talk her into giving us some." He received no argument from anyone, but then he hadn't expected any.

CHAPTER TWO

Opinions on the character of Earl Raymond Radmer differed considerably depending on whose opinion a person might be soliciting. His mother thought of her son as a fine young man who just hadn't quite grown up yet. He liked to ride around on his motorcycle and didn't really hold down any kind of a steady job, but he was basically a good boy. However, because of his friends and the clothes he wore, the police were always picking on him. They even made up lies about him and planted evidence in efforts to frame him in various crimes. She knew all this to be true because Earl himself had told her it was so. There was that especially bad episode in which the police had planted a large bundle of cocaine in a car he was driving and then had arrested him for trafficking in drugs. He had gone to jail for two and a half years for that. In her mind it was a disgrace the way the law enforcement community was conspiring against her son.

The law enforcement community that Mrs. Radmer was so upset about had quite a different opinion about her little boy. Besides the drug matters, which concerned them greatly, he was their leading suspect in two separate murders. Interestingly enough there were no minor matters such as assaults or robberies that were known to be outstanding on Earl. For those police officers that made it their business to know Earl, and there were several, this was entirely in keeping with his position.

Those same officers would have been interested to know that this particular sunny afternoon Earl was driving back into Calgary with another man named Lee James. The mode of transportation was not their favored Harleys but instead a rental car acquired in Vancouver. Keeping a low profile had been

24

important because of the 'business' that had required their attendance in Vancouver and besides, the fall weather was too cool to be travelling through the Rocky Mountains on bikes anyway. Today their clothing was low profile as well in that they had taken pains to wear garments that covered their numerous tattoos. Even hair had been shaved and trimmed as necessary. Befitting his position, Earl occupied the passenger side of the car while Lee drove.

Most of the people traveling into the million soul city of Calgary from the west were using the freeway known as Highway 1 but Earl and Lee had elected to use the quiet, winding, secondary Highway 1A. While Earl and Lee were driving east anticipating their return home to their respective girlfriends, Todd Jenkins was westbound on the same stretch of road in his mobile welding truck. He had just finished working a full day welding steel at a local school construction site in Cochrane when a call from a customer came in. The man needed a rush job done where a pipeline crossing was being built across an environmentally sensitive river. Todd had considered telling him to hire someone else but the pay would be good and with Louise pregnant he would definitely need some extra money soon. Starting out for the pipeline crossing and pushing his truck up over the speed limit he left Cochrane behind.

Todd's enthusiasm for hard work, however, was not tempered with an equal amount of good judgement. If it had been, he may not have been trying to place a cell phone call to Louise to tell her what had happened, change the station on the radio and drive the truck at the same time. Predictably, he dropped the phone to the floor and when he came up from retrieving it found the narrow two-lane road had made a right turn – but he hadn't. His truck crossed the centerline directly into the path of Earl Radmer and Lee James.

B-ZONE

If Lee had been even close to being as good a driver as he thought he was, avoiding Todd's truck may have been a possibility. Since this was not the case, a crushing impact resulted. The groan of flexible metals folding, bending and twisting was compressed into the single crashing noise of high speed impact, while fragile safety glass shattered into a million twinkling droplets that sprayed outward in a lacerating shower.

Lee and Earl detested wearing motorcycle helmets and seatbelts. Their only reason for not wearing them was that the law said they had to. Like all of their associates they were rebellious by choice and it didn't really matter if the law was good, bad or indifferent. If they could get away with defying it, they would. In this case they were once again able to avoid legal sanction but not the sanction of elementary physics.

As laminated windshield glass flexed dramatically, it cracked but stubbornly held together until it could no longer withstand the forces acting upon it – Earl being one of those forces when he exited the vehicle through the windshield. He did not survive the journey. As one Highway Patrol officer later commented to a second officer, an open casket would not be an option at this man's funeral.

On impact, Lee's driver side air-bag deployed properly and while it saved his life it did not save him from serious crippling injury. Of the three, Todd fared the best. The combination of a large heavily built truck and a faithfully worn seatbelt, meant his injuries were serious but not life threatening. A helicopter ambulance service known as STARS, an acronym for Shock Trauma Air Rescue, transported the living to hospital and left the Highway Patrol to investigate and remove the dead.

* * * * *

B-ZONE

Nathan said goodbye to Danny Forbes that morning and went home to clean his gun and begin the waiting. He already knew he wasn't going to like the waiting part. He also knew more certainly than ever that he was prepared to give up his EMT job. This was his chance to chase a dream and he wasn't going to let it pass him by. Normally he would have scaled down his practice routine at this time of year, but Danny's proposal had ignited a fire in him and instead he found himself planning how to increase his range time. He thought that he might have to give up some hunting to do it, but that was okay. This was something worth sacrificing for. Danny had told him that it could be up to a month before he was back in touch to tell him anything concrete and he had suggested to Nathan the obvious, that he get on with his life in the meantime. Nathan's impression was that there had been a positive note in Danny's voice and he now found himself cautiously optimistic that when Danny did call it would be with good news. He knew that until Danny did call, every time the phone rang his stomach would tighten as he reached to answer it.

That evening Nathan sat at his small basement workbench with a Smith & Wesson model 10 in pieces on the table in front of him. It was recently purchased from an acquaintance who no longer wanted it. Nathan didn't need the revolver either but the price had been right and he thought perhaps it could be sold or traded at a profit for something he really could use. While in the process of checking out the gun he had found a timing problem that probably explained the good price. When the trigger was pulled straight back in double action mode the cylinder would not rotate far enough into a fully locked position before the hammer dropped. This meant the cartridge when it fired wasn't completely lined up with the barrel and it caused inaccuracy and lead spitting as part of the bullet shaved off on the rear edge of the barrel. Bob had given him a new 'hand' – the part that would correct the problem – and explained to him how to fit it properly.

He was repeatedly assembling, stoning and reassembling; trying to get the hand to work properly and in the process for the first time that day forgetting about Danny. One more time, he thought, as he tried to remove the trigger's rebound spring again just as the phone rang. It startled him into losing control of the partially removed spring, which immediately sailed off into the clutter on the other side of the room. His mother upstairs answered the phone as he mentally kicked himself for being so jumpy and started looking for the part. She was speaking to someone and while he couldn't make out the words he heard the tone in her voice and it told him something was wrong. He left his search for the spring and went upstairs to find his mother just hanging up the phone in the kitchen.

"Something wrong Mom?" he asked, already knowing the answer from the look on her face.

"That was Louise. Todd's been in an accident. He's hurt and in the Foothills Hospital in Calgary . . . but he's going to be all right. She's going to him now and wants us to meet her there." Emily Burdett's face had lost its color and her voice trembled but she was in control. She hadn't raised two kids on her own without developing the inner strength she needed now. On the outside her experience as a police dispatcher took over. "Nathan would you go get the car ready and I'll meet you outside in a minute?"

Nodding he asked, "Sure, but what happened? Where was the accident?"

"I'll tell you everything I know on the way to the hospital and what I don't know we'll find out there, but for now let's get going."

"Okay, come out when you're ready," said Nathan as he grabbed his coat and ran outside.

28

B-ZONE

Nathan drove his mother's car and on the way to Calgary she told him the known sketchy details, reminding him several times not to push the speed limit too much. They wouldn't do anyone much good if they were in an accident themselves she told him. She was trying to be professional but Nathan knew she wasn't nearly as calm and collected as she sounded. A fellow shooting competitor and friend, Paul Simmons worked for the local Cochrane RCMP detachment where his mother did administrative work and dispatched and he had often ridden with Paul on night shift. It had been there on a particularly bad night amid the flashing lights and screaming sirens that he had heard his mother on the radio as a cool dispassionate voice who could co-ordinate resources and people in a crisis. He recognized that same professional person emerging in her now but he also saw a mother in the tremble of her hand and the paleness of her face. Todd Jenkins was not her son but his wife was her daughter and that was close enough for the mother instinct to take over.

Nathan thought about Todd. He liked him, he was a good guy who treated his sister right. They didn't have enough in common to be anything like best friends but Todd was 'good people.' Nathan had genuinely celebrated at their wedding, something he would not have done if Louise had ended up marrying one of the zeroes she had gone out with over the years. As he pulled into the hospital's emergency ward parking lot, he found himself praying Todd would be all right.

Both Nathan and his mother were visibly relieved when they eventually found Louise standing over Todd's bed holding his hand and talking to him. Todd was talking and even smiling but Nathan could see it was strained. If he guessed right Todd was putting on a painless front for Louise' benefit. When Louise saw her mother the two women embraced, shedding tears together and drawing strength from each other.

Nathan clasped the hand of Todd's that Louise had dropped, "Hey man, you've looked considerably better."

"Yeah I know," Todd said, "I've felt better too. But from what the Doc tells me, I'll be okay. They might even let me out in a few days. I was pretty lucky."

"What happened?"

Todd sighed heavily as he shifted in his bed and Nathan felt his grip tighten in response to pain. "I was on my way to a job and got distracted by trying to do too much and drive at the same time. I crossed the centerline on 1A and hit an oncoming car."

"What about the other car," asked Nathan's mother, "was anyone else hurt?"

A shadow came across Todd's face. "I think worse than that." His lower lip quivered and he bit it, looking away to avoid their eyes. He took a deep breath and turned his head back in Nathan's direction. "I don't remember much after the accident and you can't get anything out of the people around here but from what I've overheard, I think somebody's dead."

There was an awkward silence and Louise took back Todd's hand. She used a tissue to dab at the tears running down from the corners of his eyes to the white hospital linens.

"Nathan, will you try and find out for sure what's going on?" asked Todd. "Like I said, nobody here is telling me anything. Can you see if you can find somebody who'll talk? I need to know. There was a cop here a while ago and he had the Doc take some blood samples from me and I told him what I could about what happened before the accident, but he wouldn't tell me about the people in the other car either. I think I saw two people in it, but that's all I know. Can you find out for me?"

"Yeah, no problem," said Nathan, glad for an excuse to leave such an emotional scene. He felt unsure here. He was good at first aid to the body but not to the emotions and he

30

welcomed the chance to escape. He left his mother and sister with Todd and started prowling the corridors of the hospital.

The cafeteria was usually a good place to find cops in a hospital and he had been in this one enough to know where it was. He took the stairs down a level and there, alone at a table, found an older highway patrol officer busily writing in his notebook. Nathan recognized the man. He had been transferred into the area recently but he couldn't remember the name, if he'd ever heard it. The cop wouldn't know him by sight, but he knew it didn't matter if he introduced himself as Emily Burdett's son, it was all the reference he needed.

"Oh yeah. Sure, you're the kid who's the EMT and the hot shot pistol shooter. I've seen you around the office a couple of times. You hang out with Paul Simmons right? Nice to meet you. Emily's always talking about you. You don't look like you're working, so what are you doing hanging around this dismal place?"

On the table was a blood kit, used to collect blood samples from suspected impaired drivers. The label on the exterior of the box had been filled in and it had Todd Jenkins' name on it. Nathan tapped the box in reply, "Todd's my brother-in-law, married my sister," he said, sitting down across the table.

"Really? Too bad about his accident. It looks like he'll be okay though . . . " A light seemed to come on. "Hey, you mean Todd Jenkins is Emily's son-in-law?" The cop swore and slammed his fist down on the table in answer to his own question. He swore again.

"Easy," said Nathan holding up a hand. "It's no big deal, I understand you have a job to do. It doesn't matter whose son-in-law Todd is, you just do the job. I'm not here to get anything other than a little information for the family."

"Sorry kid but this isn't about Todd. It's about something else all together."

31

When Nathan confirmed to him that he knew nothing about the accident details the officer took the time to fill him in, validating Todd's fears that one man had been killed and another seriously injured.

"Your family needs to know as well, Nathan, that these two are a couple of bad characters. If it was my choice I'd go up there right now and pin a medal on your brother-in-law." He glanced briefly to his left at two nurses occupying a nearby table and leaned forward as he lowered his voice. "You see, the guy he killed is the vice-president of Calgary's resident outlaw motorcycle gang, the Satan's Riders!"

Half an hour later Nathan had learned as much as the officer could tell him, both about the accident and the two gang members that had been in the other car. His mind was reeling with both the implications this had over the long term for Todd and Louise and with the short term problem of how he was going to go upstairs and tell his family. He had to get back to them soon, they would be wondering where he was. He finally just started moving in their direction, his body taking him to his family but his mind resisting, and with no idea what he was going to say. Nathan determined to himself once again that he really did not like hospitals. They were places of pain and suffering and not of healing and good news. Maybe his career as an E.M.T. wasn't such a good idea after all. He would spend his life taking people to places like this, where their families could gather to receive the bad news and have their lives changed forever. He was being bitter and pessimistic and he knew it. Yesterday he had been on a high because of Danny's visit and now chance had dealt his family a problem of unknown dimensions.

Returning to Todd's room he had no plan or strategy about how to tell them, so when he walked in he just let it all out. The image of a Colt 1911 with a worn sear that goes full auto till the magazine is empty flashed through his mind and he accepted the image as one he could understand. He talked till his magazine was empty. When he was done there was the same kind of stunned silence he'd seen on the range when the malfunctioning gun finally runs dry and everyone checks their body for leaks.

After the silence came the gasps and the crying and, worst of all, the uncertainty. The uncertainty of Todd's recovery, of what court action would eventually be brought against him, of what any penalty might be and especially of what the reaction would be among the outlaw bikers to the death of their vice-president.

They were in a dark forest that had to be negotiated and there were no paths. They talked about it for what seemed like hours and eventually Nathan felt them emerging from that darkness to a place of decision making, into a place where there were trails and paths that could be followed to a destination. It was decided someone should call a lawyer to represent Todd, Emily would do that. Nathan would use some contacts his mother gave him to try and learn more about the bikers and determine if there was anything to be concerned about in the way of retaliation from them. Louise would stay with Todd and look after him.

It was the next day that Nathan met Paul for breakfast in Calgary. Paul had been transferred to the Cochrane RCMP two years before and in the professional contact they had with each other Nathan had soon learned that Paul was also a student of the gun. That was all it had taken to start a friendship, one that grew as they pursued their sport by reloading, practicing and competing together.

They were in the usual sort of greasy spoon breakfast joint that Nathan had often observed cops seemed to prefer, at least when there wasn't a donut shop available. With them was a detective who was introduced to Nathan as 'Jim,' and when no last name was offered none was requested.

They were at a window booth at the back of the place and outside the sun shone as if there was nothing wrong with the world. The view was bright, clear, the sunlight bounced off the cars in the parking lot and the wind blew leaves in swirling patterns on the pavement. Of the two at the table, Nathan observed, only Paul looked like a cop, even in the jeans and blue western shirt he was wearing today. He was about the same height as Nathan but stronger and therefore heavier. Additionally the requisite short hair and the acquired self-confidence of an experienced street police officer were evident. Jim on the other hand, looked like an armpit with eyeballs, a walking hairy beer belly with a large man attached. His jeans were filthy and he wore a stained *Grateful Dead* T-shirt. His hair was long and on his face flourished a full growth of beard. And, Nathan noted, he smelled bad. He wondered if that was part of the disguise or if Jim had become so absorbed into this lifestyle that he had adopted certain aspects of it unconsciously. Jim had been specifically sent to the family to provide them with information about the Satan's Riders and to help evaluate the risk they might be to Todd.

"Nathan," said Jim, "the first thing you have to do is shake any image you have of outlaw bikers being a bunch of beer swilling, brawling, lecherous thugs who ride around the country on their bikes terrorizing people. That may have been true at one time but it isn't anymore. Today's outlaw biker gang is a sophisticated professional criminal organization with ties to a worldwide network. They have a tight cohesive structure with a well-defined code of behavior and strict discipline. Their objective is not to ride around on Harleys and party, it's to make money through criminal labor and make a lot of it. And they do that very well. They're especially into the drug trade, prostitution and smuggling but will settle for anything that will make them a buck."

"Like robberies?" volunteered Nathan. He decided that everything about Jim was planned and deliberate. There was no hint of gutter type street language when he spoke, he sounded like a college graduate. No doubt he could turn it on at will when he wanted to, now he chose not to.

"Not at all," countered Jim. "There was a time when the outlaw gangs liked to do that sort of 'macho' crime, but today's organizations are too smart for that. They don't want the kind of heat that brings down on them. As a rule, bikers prefer the cleaner less visible sort of crimes that I mentioned."

Nathan nodded, trying to ignore the bits of breakfast nestled in Jim's beard. "But how does that relate to what kind of threat they are to my brother-in-law?"

"Simple, they don't like heat from the law because it cuts into their 'business' and believe me, they understand bottom lines. If there's no profit in going after your brother-in-law then that tips the scale towards leaving him alone. And don't worry about some rogue element going after him even though the leaders have decided it's not worth it. Remember what I said about their strict discipline? If the president says to leave the guy alone, that's it pal. He's safe." Jim slapped his substantial hand on the table for emphasis.

"So we don't have to worry then?" asked Nathan, sounding unconvinced.

"No, I'm not prepared to say that," replied Jim thoughtfully. "It's true that hassling your brother-in-law is not going to make them any money as such. They do however have a certain code of brotherhood and an eye for an eye philosophy that can override the bottom line in some circumstances if they feel violent revenge is needed to solidify their position of authority on the street."

Nathan's face showed his confusion. "I can see what you're thinking," said Jim, stroking his beard and combing out the eggs in the process. "So far I've probably sounded like a politician to you. I told you he might be completely okay and also that he might be in big trouble. Well, it could go either way Nathan. I really don't know for sure but judging from what is happening at the moment I would say he's safe. We busted some of them on pimping charges last month and as a group they're laying low at the moment trying not to draw any attention. Your brother-in-law is no threat to their profit line and there is nothing happening on the street at the moment to challenge their authority. My best guess is your family won't have a problem from them. Now remember, that's just a best guess, not a guarantee."

Nathan looked visibly relieved. "That's good news Jim. We'll be careful and we'll try to be smart and if you'll let Paul know if you hear anything he'll pass it on to us. Maybe we can put this behind us yet."

"No problem there," said Jim. "Say, are you going to eat the rest of your toast?"

CHAPTER THREE

Two weeks later Todd was out of the hospital. The two day forecast he had originally been given had been far too optimistic, but his long term prognosis was good and included a return to his welding profession. The charges which had been laid against him were the less serious ones he had been hoping for and his lawyer was confident that they could do well in court with them. The Satan's Riders had been as well behaved as a troop of boy scouts and the world was starting to look like a better place for the Burdett family.

Nathan had heard nothing from Danny Forbes over these two weeks and had been too busy helping Todd and Louise to think much about him. Several trips to the range had been squeezed in as he tried to keep his handgun skills sharp, but it hadn't been enough to suit him. Well, he thought, family came first – no matter what.

Because of Todd's accident, hunting season was going to be a wash out too. Nathan had reluctantly resigned himself to that fact. His eyes wandered though, to the line of mountains visible in the distance and his thoughts lingered there in the high meadows and the heavy timber, in the places that took your breath away, the rushing rivers with their power and the quiet still places with their beauty. Places where he could pit his skills against an animal that had better senses, was stronger and faster, possessed by nature, superior camouflage and knew more woodcraft than he could ever hope to learn. It was part time hunter versus full time animal but that was how it was supposed to be, the way it had always been, thought Nathan. The quiet challenge of the outdoors and the hunt was what he longed for now. All year his shooting had been focused at the intense pressure cooker level of international competition and now was the time when that fell off like a heavy weight and he moved to the silent intensity of the hunt. But not this year.

* * * * *

Loading cartridges into a rifle magazine makes a distinctive ticking sound. As the round is forced in on top of the previous one, it moves clear of the magazine lips and a sturdy spring snaps it into position. The stolen Ford van reverberated with that sound. There was no conversation as the four men in it went about their business. The van's interior had been stripped bare and the ticking sound rattled around inside like a clock measuring the remaining seconds of someone's life. It finally stopped, but was replaced by the louder click of magazines being locked into place in their respective firearms and then the slam of bolts and slides being driven forward by powerful springs as chambers were loaded. The driver spoke, to check everyone's readiness, and having that confirmed, the van started to move slowly forward.

If Jim had known all of the dynamics that were occurring within the criminal world occupied by the Satan's Riders, he would have anticipated they were going to seek revenge. But since outlaw bike gangs are notoriously difficult to obtain good intelligence on and even more difficult to infiltrate, he could not know what Lee James had told his friends from his hospital bed. Once he had come out of the anesthesia, and had what the doctors considered to be sufficient time to come to terms with the loss of both his legs, they let his friends in to see him. The rules said only family, but in this case no family came.

"That guy in the welding truck took a deliberate run at us," Lee had told his friends. "At first I thought he was just trying to play chicken with that big truck of his but I think I've run into him before. Remember when Mack and I went into that cowboy bar last year and a bunch of those horse lovers put the boots to us? I think he was one of 'em. The only reason he smashed up too, was that I was too fast for him and when he came over the center line I almost got away from him. He had to come over way further than he figured and he couldn't pull it back in time."

That and seeing the living reminder of what Lee had become made it hard to control the club members. Jim also had no knowledge of the pressure the president was feeling because of accusations he was getting soft on the club's enemies. The pimping charges Jim had spoken of were commonly viewed as being the result of going too easy on a pimp who had crossed the club and when he hadn't been taught the appropriate lesson he ratted them out to the cops. Earl had been well liked and when the bikers heard that Todd was not going to be charged under the Criminal Code but rather with a lesser offence under the Traffic Act it had been the last straw. The president had given in to the pressure and sent these men to deliver a message, one that would not be forgotten.

Two well-directed phone calls to the Calgary Police Service had pulled those patrol cars that might have been in Todd and Louise's neighborhood to other areas chasing non-existent incidents. One had been a sobbing almost incoherent female reporting that an intruder armed with a knife had just kicked in the door to her house. She had grabbed her cell phone she said and locked herself in the bathroom and now the man was trying to break *that* door down. She had no idea who he was but would they please hurry. The other was a man who lived around the corner from a neighborhood bank. He reported he could see two men waiting suspiciously in a parked car in his alley. He had caught glimpses of a long barreled gun being

passed between the two of them and he thought that maybe –
yes, he could see for sure now – they were definitely pulling on
masks.

That left it clear for the white Ford van to pull onto the
Jenkins' street in the semi-darkness of early evening. It attracted
no attention as it eased to a stop at the curb in front of the house.
The driver scanned the street for pedestrians or vehicles and
when he was satisfied signaled the men crouched in the back.
The sliding door slowly eased open to its full width and death
poked four muzzles out of the opening, a Mini-14, an AR-15 and
two 7.62X39 Chinese Kalashnikovs. No one got out. On
command, triggers were pulled and hammers fell.

The roar of the gunfire was so foreign to the tranquil
domestic suburbia of the street that its residents didn't really
understand what they were hearing until the bikers had
completely emptied the first of their magazines. In the short
pause after all four shooters ran their guns dry and during which
they stopped to reload, reality arrived for the Jenkins' neighbors
and they began to run for their phones or windows depending on
their personalities. For the Jenkins, reality had already arrived
with the first bullets.

Todd was in the living room at the front of the house
watching TV and longing to go back to work. Louise snuggled
beside him knitting a baby blanket. As the guns started to roar
and bullets began to pour through the windows and walls they
both knew immediately what was happening and why. A lack of
aimed fire and an instinctive dive downward saved them both
from being hit during the first volley, but their tranquil world
fractured into a blizzard of broken glass and flying lead as they
clung to each other on the floor. Louise screamed over and over
while Todd's mind raced. The lull in firing occurred then and he
grabbed his wife by the arm and dragged her violently to the
corner of the room and tried to shield her with his body.

Nathan, if he had been there, would have recognized the pause as a group reload. Then the bullets came again, shattering their world, breaking it into little pieces as surely as if it were a fragile ornament on a shelf. Splintering wood, falling plaster and cracking bullets was all that existed. Another lull, more ragged than the first and Todd wished he'd taken up Nathan's offer of a gun. He had trusted in being able to call the police if he needed help and he knew now that had been a mistake. If the men out there came in after them they were both dead and he had no way to put up a fight. Then more bullets came. And more still. The TV exploded in a shower of sparks as one smashed into the picture tube. Louise screamed again and began sobbing uncontrollably. A few more scattered shots and then the bullets stopped. In the frightening stillness he heard a shout, a door slam and squealing tires. Todd lifted his head from the floor then and looked up into the perforated, dust filled room as he realized they were leaving. At least they were still alive, he thought, they had survived – this time.

The shattering of Todd and Louise Jenkins' world was not yet complete. The bikers had come to kill. They really didn't care if it was Todd or Louise, as long as someone died and they fulfilled their own desire for revenge. A short time after that bullet filled evening they did in fact kill someone. Louise Jenkins miscarried her baby.

Nathan had found both Todd and Louise in the hospital. It was a scene he had already participated in but this time it was Louise on the emergency ward gurney with Todd standing over her holding her hand. She had been crying uncontrollably and the sight of his emotionally broken sister and the news of the miscarriage Todd gave him had brought tears of pain and sympathy to his own eyes. He fought back at the pain he felt and tried to suppress it, to tell himself that at least his sister and husband were alright. They could always have another baby, they were still young enough to have lots of kids. He'd be an uncle many times over yet. It didn't work, there was too much pain here. Someone had died, it was an unborn baby but it felt the same as if it had been a living child. The pain was as real as the death and it refused to be banished until he allowed a black rage to rise up and replace it . . . that numbed it.

The sense of darkness returned to the Burdett family. The police of course suspected who had committed the attack, but as they explained to the family, knowing and proving were two different things. Their investigation would continue. In the days that followed, with police assistance, Todd and Louise disappeared into hiding in another city and Emily took time off work to be with her daughter. She was the strength that Louise needed in her time of personal darkness.

Two weeks after the attack Frankie found herself needing to talk to Nathan. Bob was gone on a week long hunting trip with friends and she had a message for Nathan and was concerned about his well being. She called him midmorning, when she saw his truck was home, and invited him for coffee. He needed little encouragement to make the short drive and Frankie got the official business out of the way as she poured his coffee, "Danny Forbes called looking for you yesterday. He said he's been trying to reach you for days but could never get an answer."

"Did you tell him what was going on?"

"No. I just told him that your Mom was out of town and that you hadn't been home much. He asked me to have you call him." Frankie sat down at the table.

"That's all he said?"

"That's all. Be sure and call him though, okay?"

"Yeah sure," said Nathan looking out the window. "I'll call him." Outside a snow squall had found the valley and was unleashing a hail of mushy flakes against anything unprotected. Frankie took off her glasses and laid them carefully on the table. "How are you holding up Nathan?"

"Oh I'm surviving I guess."

"Surviving is an achievement," acknowledged Frankie. "Especially considering what's happened. There are different levels of surviving though. I don't mean physical survival Nathan. How's the rest of you doing?"

Silence filled the kitchen. Nathan looked down at his coffee and then out the window. He had been trying to bury this and now Frankie was digging it up. Well, that's what she did wasn't it? She ferreted it out of you. What did you expect her to do if you came here, he asked himself?

"How do you feel Nathan?" she tried again.

"Oh, you mean other than wanting to kill every single one of that group of collective pond scum who call themselves Satan's Riders? Besides that I guess I feel just fine. They killed my sister's unborn child and chased my family into hiding. I'd like to return the favor. I feel like looking at some of them over the barrel of a 12 gauge." He felt like saying something more graphic but Frankie wouldn't have appreciated it. He left it at that.

"Nathan, it's natural to feel the way you do and no one is going to condemn you for being angry with these people, I'm angry too. But don't get caught in a revenge trap yourself, that's what *they* are doing. It would mean you're just stooping to their level. Let the police finish their work." She reached across the table and touched his hand but he pulled it away.

"Don't worry about me Frankie," said Nathan. There was ice in his voice now. He wanted to leave this alone. "I'll be okay. What have you heard from Bob? How's the hunting trip going?"

Frankie gave up, letting him change the subject and making small talk until he said it was time to go. The snow squall was dying as she watched Nathan walk back to his truck and drive off down the road. There was a level of anger there that concerned her. The snow was melting as it hit the ground. She doubted his hatred would melt that easily.

By this time Nathan had already made a decision to do something. There was no longer any question. Exactly what was not yet determined but he would do something. The bikers would pay. Following the attack on his sister's house he had spent the nights lying awake, staring at a dark ceiling imagining all sorts of things he could do to the Riders. In his imagination most of them turned out bad – for him. He wondered if he was a pessimist. These people wanted to bring violence to his family and since the law could do nothing to stop them, it was up to him. Nathan determined his response would be measured and he would make sure they understood why it was happening. More than that he didn't know yet. It was a forgone conclusion that it would come from the muzzle of a gun.

Three days later he had made more decisions and he had a plan. He now had a place as well as a time. Most of the information originated from Paul and Jim, if that really was his name, even though they were unaware they were giving it to him at the time. In another meeting that Paul had arranged for the three, Nathan had learned the Riders liked to party and they especially liked to party outdoors away from prying eyes, in a place where they could make noise. Toward this end the gang had six years ago bought a three hundred and twenty acre parcel of land in the hills southwest of Calgary, where they had built a simple shack. They had moved in a couple of outhouses as well as building a firepit, but that was all. It had no electrical service, it was a party spot, pure and simple. Most people didn't know it existed and the Riders kept it that way to stay out of the public eye. The property had a long private access road complete with a gate keeper on any night when a party was on or even all weekend for a long weekend like the one coming up. Nathan had scouted the spot on foot and found it suitable. Hunting season was on again after all.

The evening after the scouting trip found Nathan in his basement workshop with his most recent rifle project on the bench in front of him. When the wildcat 7mm STW first started getting some publicity as a long range hunting caliber, Bob Coombs had seen potential in it. He had talked Nathan into converting a Ruger Number 1 he owned, into the potent 7mm cartridge. The two of them had worked on it together and as usual Bob had taken no money from Nathan who had purchased the necessary parts but that was all.

Since long range capability had been the chief goal of this rifle project the custom barrel the gun now wore was twenty-eight inches in length. It made for a long rifle but not excessively so, which it would have been if the action had been anything other than a short falling block. To squeeze out even more velocity Bob had specified gain-twist rifling in the RKS barrel. A muzzle brake had been added to reduce recoil, as had a Decelerator recoil pad. All of Bob's refinements on the trigger and action had also been carried out and they had installed an adjustable tension device between the barrel and the fore-end hanger. It allowed tuning of the barrel's harmonic vibrations to squeeze the last drop of accuracy from the rifle.

Nathan usually referred to the gun as his 'Thunderbolt.' It occurred to him as he worked, that a name change might be in order. In a magazine article he had recently read, a long range hunter had built a similar rifle and called it 'The Fist of God.' A good name, he thought. It fit here.

B-ZONE

The scope was wrong. The Ruger wore a Leupold 4-12X variable but he needed more magnification now. He removed it and mounted the 8-24X Bausch & Lomb from his Remington 700 varmint rifle. When that was done, the ammunition got his attention. The accuracy load he had developed for the Thunderbolt drove a 150 grain Nosler Ballistic Tip bullet at 3570 feet per second. His hunting load was similar but instead used the Nosler Partition bullet. For this trip he would go with the former. He would need accuracy and violent expansion more than the bone crushing penetration of the Partition bullet. The targets weren't that thick skinned. Accuracy averaged a little over one half minute of angle for five shots and while Nathan's blueprinted bolt-action 22-250 would do better than that he needed the extra power here. Especially considering the distance he would be working at.

The next morning at the local gun club's outdoor range the big Ruger lay action open across sandbags while Nathan set up his spotting scope and other gear. The club's range went to an official five hundred yards but the land sloped uphill quickly past that mark and by climbing the hill beyond with a portable target frame he had managed what was needed, a clear seven hundred yard shooting lane at a slight uphill angle. After setting up his target he paused to look at the nearby mountains. The snow line was getting lower and would envelop the hills any day now. Not much of fall left. As always, he noted the wind at this end of the range. It was a light morning breeze, seven o'clock at about five miles per hour, the same as at the firing line. Shouldn't be a problem compensating for that, he thought. On the walk back he considered the uphill angle, when it came time to do this for real the angle would be about the same downhill but he reminded himself that in determining point of impact, shooting uphill had the same effect as shooting downhill. Therefore, no adjustment would be necessary.

46

He fired the big gun slowly and analytically. Twenty rounds later he was confident it was zeroed. While cleaning the rifle's bore and waiting for it to cool a red four wheel drive Chevy pick-up with two camouflage clad men in it pulled up. Nathan finished wiping out the barrel as the two set up at another bench. When one of them looked ready to hang a target he walked downrange with him.

"Any luck hunting so far?" asked Nathan.

"Some," said the man, the older of the two, "all of it bad. Gary back there missed a nice buck yesterday evening. He doesn't usually miss so we figured we had better stop and check out his rifle."

"Good idea," agreed Nathan. He could see the man's curious looks at the large pumpkin under his arm but he didn't ask about it and Nathan didn't volunteer anything. He left him at the two hundred yard mark and carried on up the hill where he retrieved the target frame and left the pumpkin in its place.

When he got back to the shooting benches, the two hunters were waiting there for him. The one who had walked downrange with him spoke first. "That's a long way friend. I can't hardly see that far let alone hit anything at that range."

"Well I'm not sure I can either," said Nathan. "I'll definitely need some luck. Tell you what. Would you mind watching through my spotting scope while I shoot? You should be able to see my bullet strike on the ground if I miss and at least tell me which way I'm off."

"No problem," the man replied. He had his own spotting scope and brought it over to the bench beside Nathan, set it up and settled in behind it. "Let 'er rip," he announced.

Nathan dropped one of the large cartridges into the open chamber and snuggled in behind his rifle. He levered the action shut and began to concentrate. Wind, mirage, his contact with the rifle at cheek, shoulder and trigger, all would influence where

47

the bullet went. With finger lightly on the trigger he shut out the world. To him only the rifle existed. Wait for the wind. A deep breath in – a third of it expelled and send the bullet into its mark by sheer anger and force of will . . . more trigger pressure. Check the wind. Increase the trigger pressure.

With a roar the rifle fired and nine-tenths of a second later the pumpkin exploded in an orange mist as the bullet slammed into it. The man spotting let out a whoop and then, two seconds after impact, the loud plop of the bullets' strike came drifting back to the firing line. As Nathan removed his hearing protection his spotter slapped him on the back.

"I ain't never seen shootin' like that," he said. "Friend, I figure whatever you shoot at this season ain't got a chance."

"Yeah," said Nathan quietly as he opened the action and slid the empty cartridge case into a green plastic box. "That's the idea, no chance at all."

In the days leading up to the long weekend Nathan had rarely watched the weather forecast on the six o'clock news with more interest. The forecast had been for a good weekend and for once the weatherman got it right, the sky was clear and it was warm for this time of year. How similar this was to dozens of other hunting trips he'd taken, only this time his trip wasn't ending in the evening, it was starting.

It was fully dark and 8:00 p.m. when Nathan coasted his truck into a heavily wooded area off an old logging road and killed the engine. He rolled down the window while waiting for his eyes to adjust to the darkness and inhaled the smells of the night. While waiting he felt for the cab's interior light and pulled the bulb to insure darkness when the door opened. Ten minutes later, once the individual trees on the other side of the trail became visible, he slipped out the door pulling his rifle with him. He loaded the Ruger before pressing the truck door closed with his hip. The clack of the latch springing into place interrupted the stillness and Nathan waited a moment to see if the night would react to it. Nothing moved. Holding the rifle in a ready position, he stalked quietly along a game trail leading to a hillside vantage point overlooking the Rider's party spot. A harvest moon was coming up near the horizon giving him enough light to move by. Stars winked at him like fellow conspirators.

Nathan was not in a winking sort of mood. The anger he had felt initially had ebbed somewhat and an icy calm determination had replaced it. Now there was something else there too, it was anxiety. There were questions rattling around in his mind. Listening to the questions, though, was something he chose not to do, he let his anger suppress them. Moving faster along the trail helped too, it meant he was noisier but he accepted that risk because it kept his mind focused.

When he had reached his predetermined destination his heart was beating faster than it should have been and he felt too warm even though the night was cool. Looking out over the scene below, he tried to calm himself. To the northeast, Calgary's glow could be seen washing out the stars near the horizon. It highlighted the skyline in that direction making the hills and trees stand out starkly against the night sky. In the opposite direction the line between sky and earth was harder to discern, just two different shades of black. Between the two extremes lay the broad open bowl, which formed the bikers' party spot.

He bellied down beside his bipod-supported rifle and could see a large bonfire below him in the distance. The light gathering ability of the large scope was impressive. People moved about near the fire and he could hear the pounding bass of the music, though neither the words nor the tune were decipherable at this distance. He scanned the area to learn as much as he could.

The wind where he sat was nonexistent and judging from the way the fire's sparks swirled straight up, this was the case on the valley floor as well. People stood around or danced in a broad circle close to the fire, but not too close because of its size. He allowed himself a small smile as he remembered one of Bob's early camping lessons delivered in a Tonto impersonation. "White man build big fire, sit far away. Indian build small fire sit close."

Tonight Nathan was thankful for the big fire, it served to light up the area below him. Beyond the people gathered near the fire, in a somewhat larger semi-circle, were half a dozen large wooden picnic tables stacked with cases of beer, coolers and assorted bottles. And beyond that, near where a shack stood, a line of about twenty Harleys. The number of four-wheeled vehicles there surprised him. He could see half a dozen cars and perhaps two vans parked out beyond the bikes, and then only barely visible to him because of the fire's reflection off their windshields.

Nathan felt himself beginning to calm inwardly as he studied the scene below. He felt the adrenaline flushing out of his body and he tried relaxing alternate muscle groups to speed the process. It would come rushing back when the time came, like an unwelcome house guest, but he would control it then, just as he always did when competing, he was confident of that. Now he had to wait.

Waiting meant time to think and he wasn't at all sure he wanted to do that just now. He wanted to act. To act and in so doing set the world right again. It surely wasn't right now, with his sister's baby dead and Todd and her cowering in fear for their lives. He knew that wasn't right.

Today, after the post office had closed, Nathan had mailed a letter addressed to the Satan's Riders. They should receive it sometime after the weekend. Words he'd cut from a newspaper and glued together had formed a short message: 'You should have left Todd Jenkins alone.' Sending a letter like that left Nathan with a hollow cowardly feeling inside but he wanted them to know without a doubt why tonight was happening. He speculated that these guys probably had lots of enemies and he wanted no guessing. It was important they know.

Below, at the party, a Harley started up. He heard the motor roar first and then saw the headlight come on as the driver cracked the throttle and spun the rear tire taking off in a rooster tail of dirt and debris. The bike made a circuit around the tables and then headed south out of the campsite. Nathan lost sight of its taillight as it disappeared down the winding access road among the trees. Probably a run for more drugs or booze he thought.

The faint smell of wood smoke hung in the air as he waited and fifteen minutes later he heard another bike. He was sure it wasn't the same one, this exhaust had a sharper crack to it. This one was coming in. A shift in position allowed him to pick up the headlight in his scope. The front end of the bike, and therefore the headlight as well, was bouncing up and down as the driver negotiated over a rough stretch of the access road. It looked like it was nodding in agreement saying "Yes, I'm the one, take me."

Once in the campsite, the driver parked at one end of the row of bikes, the end furthest from Nathan. As he began to realize this was the bike he had been waiting for, he felt the adrenaline surging back. His chest tightened but he willed himself to relax as the years of competitive training, discipline and practice kicked in. Nathan's mind had made the decision to

51

act and now his learned skills and reflexes took over. Slipping electronic muffs over his ears was the last necessary step. As always, they would allow him to hear normal sounds but protect him from the vicious muzzle blast.

Three cases of beer stood stacked on a picnic table and it was these Nathan had selected to check his zero. He centered the scope's cross hairs on the light colored cardboard, checked the wind one last time and began his trigger squeeze. The Ruger roared. As the rifle came back down from recoil, Nathan made no attempt to reload. He watched the stack of cases, intent on observing if at all possible where the bullet would strike.

If he had been able to actually see the bullet, he would have observed its entry into the middle case where the polymer tip caused it to immediately expand and displace liquid in all directions, as a shock wave at the speed of sound blasted out from the point of entry. The non-compressible liquid, with no place else to go, literally exploded out of its containers in a shower of beer and glass. The biker standing next to the table, was drenched by the exploding case and didn't fully understand what had happened until the sound of the gunshot arrived a full second after the bullet. That *was* something he could comprehend and people began scrambling in all directions. By the time the echo of that first shot bounced off the hills and came rolling back over the campsite like a distant thunder predicting a coming storm, there was no visible human presence.

Nathan meanwhile focused his attention on the recently arrived bike and when the Ruger bellowed again, it sent a bullet screaming toward the bike's gas tank at three times the speed of sound. On impact the tank came apart at the seams and the filler cap was launched upward like a piece of shrapnel. Vaporized gasoline droplets from the ruptured tank hung in the air, but only until they started to settle downwards where some of them contacted the hot exhaust. They ignited with a flash and the remaining air-fuel mixture caught and erupted into a rolling fireball.

Confident he had the range now, Nathan put the rifle to work. Load, acquire the target, squeeze off the shot; load, acquire the target, squeeze. The succession of vaporizing gas tanks turned the row of bikes into an inferno. He heard gunshots from down below but doubted they even had any idea where he was. The rifle's muzzle brake, as well as reducing recoil, was acting as an effective flash hider. Probably just shooting blindly at shadows. He doubted there was anyone down there who could even comprehend what a good rifleman was capable of, let alone have the skills and equipment to be a threat to him at this range.

There were still bikes untouched. Five more shots would do it. Load, acquire the target, squeeze. Keep it up. More fireballs. There was no movement down there, everyone had found a hole and crawled into it. Tires were starting to burn on some bikes, one exploded like a huge popping balloon. Load, acquire the target, . . . someone ran up to the bike he was sighting on and tried to drag it out of the line. Was he crazy? A gas tank blew from the heat of the fire and he saw the man knocked backwards by the blast. His long hair burst into flame and then his clothes caught fire as well. Leaping to his feet he fought blindly against the flames. Was that screaming Nathan could hear above the racket of the still booming music or was he imagining it?

As Nathan watched, he came to the realization that the scope's cross hairs were centered on the struggling man's back and that his finger had taken up at least two pounds of weight on the three-pound trigger. He had no intention of shooting but something within him had taken all the steps necessary to complete the task. Would he have fired if he hadn't caught himself? A chill ran through him. He hadn't come here to kill.

Nathan refocused again on the scene in his rifle scope, conscious now that his finger was completely off the trigger. The man had given up on the bike. He was rolling on the ground and two other people were trying to help him. Nathan turned back to the bikes. The Ruger roared and recoiled and another bike was consumed in a fireball. Satan's Riders eh? He'd give them a taste of what hell would be like. One more shot, the final roar of the fire breathing dragon and the last Harley erupted. Finished.

He took a minute to survey the scene. To the naked eye the original bonfire was hardly noticeable next to the blaze consuming the bikes. Black smoke and fierce orange flames rolled skyward from what had once been polished petrochemical machines but were rapidly becoming charred wreckage. The campfire looked like a younger sibling of the larger fire, its yellow flames meek and mild by comparison, as if trying not to anger this sudden monster lest it too be swallowed up in the destruction. The night's sweet smell of wood smoke had been overcome by an acrid black odor rolling off the flaming debris. Nathan could see no one moving below so he scooped up and pocketed his brass, snapped the rifle's Harris bipod back into position and started to slip quietly back the way he had come.

He realized for the first time that he was soaked in sweat. Walking back, moving carefully down the hill in the darkness the perspiration evaporated and cooled his adrenaline fevered body, it felt good. But by the time he arrived at the hidden truck his mind was relentlessly replaying the image of the biker with the upper part of his body engulfed in flames. Framed by the scope, the image of the duplex crosshair centered unwaveringly on the man's back was now indelibly etched in his mind. The realization that his finger had been an instant away from sending a bullet to finish the job the flames had started was imprinted on his conscience. He leaned against the front corner of his truck and threw up, retching until nothing was left, shaking and oozing what was now a cold sweat. After ten minutes he pulled himself together enough to drive, he had to get out of here. He'd failed. Sure, every Harley he had seen was destroyed but the rage was still there, the flames hadn't destroyed that. It hadn't even been dulled. Instead, a new thought had taken up residence with it, flirting with the edges of the anger, dodging in and out, teasing it and coming back repeatedly to taunt it. It echoed repeatedly in his mind, 'What have I done . . . what have I started?'

CHAPTER FOUR

Three days later Nathan, planted in his usual chair, was in Bob's shop listening to the details of the gunsmith's hunting trip. Like any hunter with a lot of miles on his boots, Bob judged the success of a trip not by the number or size of the game taken but by the quality of the hunt. Intangibles like the friendship and camaraderie in a camp, the challenge of tracking, the woodcraft of the stalk and the never ending beauty of nature were what mattered. If pressed, Bob would have conceded the need for good weather as well.

By his enthusiasm Nathan could tell this hunt had indeed been a good one. As Bob started in on the first story he already knew it would end with him filling one of his deer tags. Nathan listened while thinking about the excellent jerky that would, therefore, soon be available.

"I was still-hunting my way through a patch of old growth timber," Bob was saying, "when I heard what sounded like another hunter doing some horn rattling to try and call in a buck. I was going to veer off and work in the opposite direction when I thought to myself 'Hey, what if it's not a hunter? What if it's the real thing?' The rattling had stopped by then but I kept working towards where it had come from and found a small clearing in the trees where the ground was all torn up. The sign was so easy to read even I could do it, two bucks had been fighting alright."

"So what did you do then?" asked Nathan.

"Well, I didn't have any good idea which way they had gone, so I just sat down where I had a good view of the area and waited to see if anybody came back."

"And . . ."

"I'd been sitting there ten minutes when Mr. Monster Whitetail came trotting back into the clearing. I figure he was the winner of the fight, had chased off the loser and now was coming back to his territory. It wasn't exactly a tough shot, about fifty yards."

Nathan shook his head. "So that custom 7X57 deer rifle you spent all summer tuning wasn't exactly required to do any tack driving. What you're telling me is you could have done the job with a rusty old 30-30?"

Bob scowled, trying his best to look offended – but not succeeding. "My rifle served me very nicely wise guy."

"Okay, okay, so how big *was* Mr. Monster anyway?"

"Six points on a side," said Bob, waiting for the reaction. He got it as Nathan let out a whistle.

There were more stories and Nathan let Bob tell them all while he worked. A gunsmith who takes holidays during hunting season can expect work to pile up while he's gone. And there are always those customers who need work done immediately, so Nathan started to give him a hand with some of the simpler jobs like scope mounting and cleaning.

"Have you heard from Danny?" asked Bob eventually.

"Yeah, I phoned him a couple of days ago when Frankie mentioned he had called here looking for me. I've made his short list and he wants me to spend the winter in sunny Arizona shooting guns and eating Mexican food. How about *that?*"

"Well, that's great but I think you know I'm not surprised."

"I guess you've always had more confidence in my abilities than I have," said Nathan. He pushed another solvent saturated patch through the barrel of a 300 Winchester Magnum. The blue colour on the patch indicated there was still copper fouling in the bore. "I guess it might be a good time to leave town anyway, the rest of my family has."

"How's your family doing?" asked Bob. "Anything new happen in the last week?"

"Not much," replied Nathan. "Todd and Louise are still in hiding and Mom's helping them out. I'm just kind of holding down the homestead here."

Bob finished re-crowning the damaged muzzle of a rifle barrel and shut off the lathe. "Frankie told me someone shot up the Riders party spot on the weekend. Pretty much destroyed a whole pack of Harleys. Even put one of the members in hospital with some bad burns. That's how she found out about it, from a nurse friend of hers over at the hospital."

"Is that so?" said Nathan. He didn't look up as he twisted a new patch onto the cleaning rod's jag.

"It is indeed," replied Bob. "You wouldn't know anything about that would you?"

"Nope." Nathan intently worked the new patch through the rifle's bore.

"I didn't think so," said Bob. "It's just that whoever did that should probably leave town for a really long time. I can imagine that if those boys find out who that was, things could get pretty hot."

"Yeah," said Nathan, "pretty hot."

* * * * *

By the end of the week Nathan was pushing a cart, loaded with luggage and shooting gear, out of the baggage area of the Tucson airport looking for his ride. He had left Calgary as quietly as he was arriving here. Only his immediate family and the Coombs' knowing where he was going and what he was doing. Everyone else was simply told he would be out of circulation for a while looking after family matters. Recent events allowed this to be accepted at face value with no questions asked.

Nathan had been in Arizona before, always for shooting matches, and the prospect of spending a winter there now appealed to him. A gray haired man was holding up a piece of cardboard with "Burdett" scrawled on it and Nathan introduced himself. His name, Nathan learned, was George and he was an employee of the ranch they were going to be using. George, Nathan guessed, was probably in his mid fifties, his body lean for a man of his age and the face weathered, each line in that face suggesting it had a story to tell. His hair had grayed to the point you couldn't tell what it had been originally and he walked with a noticeable limp while leading the way to a Suburban.

George rebuffed all of Nathan's attempts at starting a conversation so he had plenty of time to think during the drive. Danny had told him earlier they were going to use the facilities of a private ranch, which had a small but adequate range complex and a classroom and accommodation on site. For three months he and half a dozen others would live, eat and breathe handgun shooting. According to Danny they would have most weekends off and get back home once for Christmas. That was just fine with Nathan. He had closed off his life as an EMT and had come to shoot. There was a dream here to chase and, by God, he was going to run after it as hard as he could.

An hour later they turned off the pavement and drove down a short access road into what was obviously their destination. This looked like it may have been a working ranch at one time, thought Nathan, but it wasn't one now. He'd grown up in ranching country and thought he knew a little about them. There were too many people buildings on this ranch and not enough animal ones. George drove up to one of those people buildings and showed Nathan his room. The ranch's guest accommodations were set up in modern cabins that had been finished with a brown wooden siding to match what he guessed were the original buildings. His cabin looked much the same as the others, two separate bedrooms, one at each end of the building, with a full three piece shared bathroom in the middle. The rooms were twice as large as an average motel room and had the usual closet, table, chairs and bed. Each of the two rooms had its own entrance that opened onto a covered porch that ran the full length of the front of the cabin.

Standing on the porch he viewed two rental cars in the gravel parking lot near what appeared to be the main ranch building. Nathan presumed, at least, that was what it was. The flagpole out front with the desert type rock garden was a dead give-away. Before leaving Nathan to unpack, George explained that the cars were for use by the students, but they had to be signed out at the administration desk. Waving toward a building he called the classroom he grunted out instructions about a meeting at seven o'clock that evening with Danny and all the candidates.

When he had emptied his bags, Nathan checked the time and left the cabin with just enough time to take a short walk and explore the grounds before the meeting. A warm dry breeze stirred the flag in front of the office as a friendly black and white dog of no identifiable breed wandered up to him. He scratched its head and it stayed with him as he walked in a loop around the main buildings and saw what looked like berms for shooting ranges about two hundred yards to the south. Nathan followed a dirt road in that direction and found a row of three small neat ranges there, all facing east and each capable of about fifty to seventy-five yards. Beside the last handgun range was a rifle range with what appeared to be a three hundred yard capability. The handgun ranges had an assortment of props and targets stacked neatly in a common area while the rifle range had ten shooting benches under a sheltering roof. A couple of temporary trailers, the kind seen as offices at construction sites, watched over the ranges from the other side of the dirt track.

The dog had left him to root around at the far end of the middle handgun range, and now came trotting back to Nathan with a broken piece of wooden target stand clenched firmly in its teeth. He dropped it at Nathan's feet and stood there expectantly wagging his tail. Nathan picked up the wood and sent it twirling back downrange with the dog in pursuit. A puff of dust showed where it landed. The mutt came back with it proudly and offered it to him once again. Nathan obligingly repeated the exercise.

"He's getting you trained fairly well."

Nathan started, turned around and squinted into the low sun to see the source of the comment. He shaded his eyes and liked what he saw. An attractive young woman stood in the doorway of one of the trailers. As she stepped out of the trailer's shadow the sun fell on her shoulder length red hair and Nathan couldn't decide which he liked more, that red hair or her smile. The smile reminded him of Frankie's. "I said, it looks like Radar is getting you trained fairly well," she repeated a little louder.

"Oh . . . yeah . . . right," said Nathan. "Radar. Is that his name? Radar?"

"Yes that's Radar. He's the resident rabbit chaser around here." She walked up beside Nathan and Radar brought the stick over to her this time.

Nathan guessed her to be a year or two older than him but his inspection of her stopped at the SIG P229 she wore on her right side in what was obviously a serious carrying scabbard and not just a range holster. She tossed the stick out and Radar ran after it.

"Are you one of Danny Forbes' people?" Kim asked, already knowing the answer because she recognized him from the file photos. This was the Burdett whiz kid. But then they were all supposed to be whiz kids weren't they.

"That's me. I'm Nathan Burdett." He held out his hand as he looked into the brown eyes that were a couple of inches lower than his. She didn't have the complexion of a redhead, no freckle laced cheeks and her skin was too dark. Nathan guessed the hair color came out of a bottle.

She took the offered hand. "I'm Kim Corel, nice to meet you."

Nathan found her handshake firm and sensed a confidence that came from more than the 9mm on her hip. She carried herself like someone who was in excellent physical condition. She looked like it too, there was no extra weight to be seen and the bare arms visible from the edges of the T-shirt sleeves showed muscle. "Is Radar your dog?" asked Nathan.

"Oh no," she said. "I'm not sure that Radar belongs to anyone in particular. As a matter of fact, I think he figures this ranch belongs to him and he just lets us use it." Burdett's accent wasn't as strange as she had expected it might be. But then she wasn't really sure what to expect, having never met a Canadian before. He seemed pleasant enough too, maybe a little awkward, but then young men often reacted to her like that.

"That's really good of him," said Nathan as they walked back along the road to the main buildings playing fetch with Radar, who always brought the stick back to Kim. He noticed she never just threw the stick, she always heaved it as far as she possibly could. There was an aggressiveness in her that he suspected could be intimidating if you let it be. "This looks like a great little range set up here. Who uses it when guys like Danny aren't renting it? Who even owns this place? The driver who picked me up at the airport wasn't exactly a sparkling conversationalist."

"That would be George," Kim threw the stick for Radar again. "And you're right about him not saying much. He'll open up more once he gets to know you. I've talked to him enough in the short time I've been here to know he's a good guy even though he comes across kind of gruff most of the time. He's paid his dues." Which you, my blue eyed pupil have not, she thought.

"That's good to know but it doesn't answer my question."

"You're right," said Kim. " This is a shooter's dude ranch. It caters to people interested in shooting and firearms training. Primarily we run courses in the defensive use of firearms. It's owned by a small group of investors and the Mullins', who live in the main house over there, manage the place."

"What about you?"

"I work for the ranch as an instructor and help out in other areas wherever I'm needed."

An instructor, thought Nathan. Interesting, but what was she supposed to teach people like him and the others who were supposedly coming? He doubted she could teach *him* much, at the same time conceding she might be good with beginners, especially other women. They were within sight of the classroom and as it was nearly seven o'clock, Nathan angled in that direction while Kim continued along the road. "Maybe I'll see you around," said Nathan. "I have a meeting to go to."

"Oh I'm sure you will," said Kim. "Probably tomorrow morning," she added, her smile indicating there was something about that she found humorous.

Nathan was the last one into the classroom, a simple room with a whiteboard on the wall at one end and eight long narrow tables instead of desks. The tables were set in two rows so there was an aisle down the middle and the chairs all faced toward the front. The room could probably hold twenty people but there were only Danny Forbes and five others gathered at the front. As Nathan took in the faces he stopped in surprise. The number of people was right but the faces were not the ones he had anticipated. He knew all of the top action pistol shooters in the country either personally or by sight and not a single one of them was in the room. Three of these guys were familiar to him from the competition circuit but they were all definitely second string material like himself. The other two he couldn't recall ever having seen before.

Danny jumped up from the table he was sitting on. "Nathan, there you are. We've been waiting for you. Come on in."

Nathan waded into the group and greeted the three men he knew, Joey Baines and Bruce Pollock from California as well as Aaron Crantz from Washington State. Danny introduced Nathan to the other two men, Dave Kimmler from New Hampshire and Brian Edwards from South Dakota.

"You're a long way from home," Dave said to Nathan.

"Yeah, and I'm really going to miss that Canadian winter," came his reply.

Danny interrupted them, directing everyone's attention to the whiteboard. He sketched out a plan of the ranch layout as he spoke, detailing where to find everything from washrooms to meals to the ranges. When that was done, he repeated what he had told Nathan before about a corporate entity that wanted to sponsor a competitive shooter. Nathan looked around at the other candidates in the room as Danny spoke and the nodding heads suggested to him they too had heard this spiel before.

When Danny stopped for questions, it was Aaron, who spoke up first. "Danny, just how many of us are looking at getting a sponsorship out of this little exercise once we are all done here?"

"Only one," said Danny, pausing briefly. "Someone is going to get the brass ring gentlemen, and the rest of you will go home without it. I'll be brutally honest with you. This is a contest. There will be one winner and five losers. But that's no different than it is in competition, is it?"

"Where are the big guns?" asked Nathan. "Where's the Super Squad?" He didn't mention any names. He didn't have to. In this crowd everyone knew who he was talking about and the murmur from the other candidates told him they were thinking the same thing.

Danny smiled and sat down on the table top he had occupied before. He pointed a felt marker at the group as he spoke. "Well, they certainly aren't here, are they?" The put down wasn't even subtle and he let it hang for a moment. "Yet," he added. Six pairs of eyebrows rose. "They *are* coming though, one at a time. Over the next three months most of them are going to be here. You guys didn't really think that I was going to be your instructor did you?"

"I didn't even know that there would be any instruction. I thought we were just going to be 'evaluated.' Whatever that is," said Dave.

"You are going to be evaluated . . . continually," said Danny. "Your ability to learn and how you progress through instruction is one of the criteria you'll be evaluated on. Additionally, we will be asking your instructors who they think can go the furthest in head to head competition."

"So why not just hire one of them?" Dave wasn't letting Danny off the hook.

"Those shooters are already accepting sponsorships. Although they could all probably get out of them, our sponsor wants someone fresh and clean who will be theirs alone. Also, I have assured them, and I believe it, that there is sufficient talent and hunger present here to progress to a level significantly beyond what the so-called Super Squad is capable of doing now."

As he spoke, Nathan saw a fire come into Danny's brown eyes. He got the distinct impression that he had made this same speech before, probably more than once.

"The limits, gentlemen, are not where we think they are. You guys look at the top shooters and long to shoot as fast and as accurately as they do. But let me tell you that I passionately believe, you cannot only do as well as that but you can move beyond them to set new limits we can scarcely imagine now. There was a time when the four-minute mile was considered impossible but we've surpassed that limit by so much, we laugh about it now. Action shooting is only in its infancy and the standards that the first generation of top shooters have set for us in terms of speed and accuracy are nothing more than a good start. And, as good as they are, the Super Squad are not going to be the ones setting the new limits. It's going to be people like you, shooters who believe they can progress beyond what we think is possible and who are willing to do the work and the training to take them as far as their abilities allow them to go. Remember this, it is going to become your creed for the next three months . . . The limits are not where you think they are."

The room was silent. Nathan didn't know whether to applaud or sing the National Anthem. He did know his opinion of Danny had gone up a couple of notches.

Danny stood up and reminded everyone they had been told to bring exercise gear with them. "In front of the classroom at seven tomorrow morning. Be ready to go for a run," he said, walking past them out of the room.

The group in the classroom didn't disperse for another two hours as the shooters compared notes and speculated on who the mysterious corporate sponsor might be. In the process they all began to learn about each other.

Nathan discovered his cabin partner was Aaron and that pleased him. He knew him from twice having been on the same shooting squad, which was more than any of the others in the room. His shooting ability had impressed Nathan as had his open and outgoing personality. After the group broke up the two returned to their cabin and sat on the porch talking. Nathan learned Aaron had just finished a University degree in Psychology. He had applied to several Washington police forces, most notably Spokane and the State Patrol but they had so far failed to come up with an opening for him. Working a dead-end job at a car dealership had been his livelihood when Danny found him and offered this reprieve. The talk naturally turned to guns and equipment and it was midnight by the time they let that subject go and wandered off to bed.

CHAPTER FIVE

The next morning Aaron was up first, pounding on Nathan's door when he heard no sign of life from the other side of the cabin. "Hey, Canuck! Let's go," he yelled. "The sun's up."

"Yeah, yeah, I'm coming," came the groggy reply.

Aaron was stretching out his hamstrings on the porch when Nathan finally came out. "Nice morning isn't it?"

"If you say so. I'm not much of a morning person," replied Nathan scratching the back of his head with both hands and stretching at the same time.

"Come on Nate, let's go find Danny and the others." Aaron led the way toward the classroom with Nathan stumbling along behind.

The two walked around the corner of the building and stopped. Kim was there, dressed in Nike shoes, shorts and T-shirt. Her hair was tied back in a pony tail and her presence, like a drill sergeant's, towered over the other four candidates who were on the ground in front of her. She was leading them in a series of warm up exercises. "So that's what the joke was," muttered Nathan.

"Wow! Who's that?" asked Aaron, suddenly breathless.

"Bad news for anybody who can't run, is my guess," quipped Nathan.

Kim had seen them by now and called out. "Nice of you two to join us. We're just finishing stretching so you're going to have to run cold. Let's go." Collective groaning filled the morning air but everyone fell in behind as she ran down the dirt road that led past the ranges.

68

"Watch out for snakes and stay together," she called over her shoulder. Radar appeared from somewhere and took the lead.

"Watch for snakes?" blurted Aaron to Nathan as loudly as he dared. "*She's* going to run in front of us dressed like that and she wants *us* to watch for snakes? What does she think we are, queer?"

"It'll be distracting," agreed Nathan. "But think of it as an opportunity to practice your mental discipline."

With the breeze in their faces and the rising sun starting to feel warm already, the wise cracks flowed freely for the first mile until everyone realized they should be saving their breath if they wanted to keep up. Nathan settled in at the rear of the pack and observed the others as they ran. Bruce Pollock looked like he was going to have trouble with this. He was carrying too much extra weight on his six-foot frame and if Kim really pushed them he'd never make it. Except for Aaron, everyone else looked like they were going to survive. Aaron looked like he could outrun Radar. Probably going to be the jock of the group, guessed Nathan.

So far things were looking just great, thought Nathan sarcastically, a jock female for a fitness instructor and a jock roommate. He was doing fine so far, this was no more strenuous than his own runs, but he feared the future. These two would feed off each other and, as a result, life would become painful in the mornings. Oh well, just keep running, he thought as he paced himself, we'll get to shoot eventually.

They had been following Kim's bobbing red pony tail for a mile and a half when she stopped the group. "Eat dirt! Let's do pushups." More groaning. "Make it thirty," she yelled. Some could and some couldn't. Kim did every one. Nathan barely managed his. Aaron looked like he could do another thirty as he helped up Bruce who was sprawled like a victim of the Arizona desert in a patch of loose sand.

They reversed course and ran back to the ranch. They'd finished the cool down routine and dispersed to shower and change when Nathan, walking back to his cabin, caught a glimpse of Kim running back down the road. It looked like she was going to do the route again – only faster. She had taken it easy on them, for that he could be thankful. By the end of breakfast Kim had been dubbed 'The Amazon Queen.'

After breakfast Danny Forbes appeared for the first time that day.

"You're looking well rested this morning Danny," prodded Bruce, whose face was still red from the morning's exertion.

Danny ignored him. He handed out a schedule for the remainder of the week. "Every weekend I'll put out one of these, it will tell you what's going to happen in the coming week. Read it and prepare yourself accordingly. As you can see, the remainder of this week is going to be taken up with various administrative, preparatory and familiarization functions."

Still no shooting, Nathan thought to himself. I thought this was a shooting ranch. We're going to be here a week and not shoot. His face betrayed none of his thoughts however, as he accepted more paper from Danny who was handing out forms on personal and medical history, liability waivers, and insurance. When they were completed to his satisfaction he led the shooters to the temporary trailers across from the ranges.

Entrance into the first trailer elicited a series of low whistles. This was a reloader's dream come true. Dillon 1050 reloaders were the centerpiece of each of six work stations. These were complimented by the usual support equipment such as electronic scales and brass cleaning equipment. Bins for brass and bullets and shelves for powder and primers were an integral part of each station.

"You'll be responsible for loading your own ammo," said Danny. "I've laid in a basic stock of components but I want a list from you as to any specific stuff you want. Give it to me by tomorrow and we'll have it for you in a couple of days."

Nathan had already guessed what would be in the other trailer when Danny led them into that one. It was a combination gun cleaning station and minor gunsmith shop. George sat at a desk sorting some small parts into a compartmentalized box.

"One of George's many talents is gunsmithing," announced Danny. "He's got some basic replacement parts in stock as well as some spare guns and sights. If you have any equipment problems see George. We don't have any machine tools here but if it can be fixed with hand tools he can do it; or if you prefer, provide you with the tools to do it yourself. If you want him to stock parts or equipment, let him know."

"Don't be expectin' me to clean your guns, though," growled George. "You get 'em dirty yourself and you can clean 'em yourself."

"You heard it here," said Danny.

Aaron nudged Nathan and whispered, "Ever meet a gunsmith who wasn't grouchy?"

"Yeah, in a dream. I'd died and gone to heaven."

They spent the rest of the day unpacking, setting up and checking out personal guns and equipment as well as the tools and materials they found in the trailers. Order forms for reloading components were filled out – generously. By late afternoon everyone was checking the zero on their guns and plinking at two banks of steel targets.

With six competitive shooters on the same range it was only a matter of time before one of them proposed a contest.

In this case it was Dave. "Listen up guys. How about this . . . a rack of six steel plates with a popper on each side. Take them down in any order. Fastest time wins."

"Wins what?"

"How about a date with the Amazon Queen?"

"I think I just sprained my trigger finger. I won't be able to shoot."

"OK, then how about the slowest two guys have to pick up the brass?"

"That's it. You're on."

"Ready to get on your knee's Canuck?"

"Eat my comp smoke Yankee."

"Who are you calling a Yankee? I'm from California."

Dave scratched a line in the dirt with his toe at about fifteen yards. "Three runs each. Two of which are throwaways. Who's first?"

"I'm your Huckleberry," said Joey, in his best Doc Holliday drawl as he moved to set up the targets. Two plate racks were a permanent fixture on this range so he and Nathan merely added one of the lollipop shaped steel targets known as pepper poppers to each side of the left hand rack. Once they had confirmed the three and a half foot high target's trip mechanism worked properly, allowing the target to fall when hit by a bullet, they set them in the upright position and moved back to where the rest of the shooters stood.

This was their first opportunity to test themselves against each other, to determine if someone was markedly better than the rest, or as this contest might indicate, to discover if someone was significantly worse than the others. It was a time to feel each other out as everyone approached the steel with a similar strategy. The first run was relatively cautious and deliberate and if it was clean, each successive run pushed for more speed. When the last piece of brass hit the ground and the last steel target had fallen Dave examined his clipboard, circled each shooter's best time and numbered them one through six.

"Aaron's the winner. Joey and Brian – you two have a nice time picking brass."

The winners cheered and the losers groaned but they picked up the brass while the others put away the targets.

The remaining days of that week were not much different from the first. Except for the morning runs with the Amazon Queen the pace was slow and relaxed. Nathan felt himself getting fidgety and was anxious to be working harder. He had come here ready to push himself as hard as he could and now he felt like he was spinning his wheels. Nothing was ever what you expected, he reminded himself. Take it easy, be patient, the time will come.

The opportunity to shoot came the following week when the first of the instructors arrived. A four time National Champion and a full fledged member of the 'Super Squad' he had an established reputation as a gifted teacher as well as a shooter. Only the two Californians, Joey and Bruce, had ever received any formal training in pistol. For the others it was a new experience but one they accepted with relish. He started by having them shoot slow groups at fifty yards and then fast ones at five yards, trying to get a handle on their abilities. Once he had that, he addressed some problems and started in on the remedies. Before long Nathan picked up a pattern . . . evaluate the skill level, diagnose any problems, prescribe a correction and then practice what you've learned. The pattern was applied to their reloads, movement, shooting around obstacles, every skill they needed and it was repeated over and over. They spent two weeks with their first instructor. By the time they were done everyone was starting to feel there was little else to learn and even less that could be done to improve their abilities.

Their first day off the ranch came after the instructor had finished and Danny's schedule announced medicals for all of them. George chauffeured them to a large modern looking clinic in a Tucson suburb.

They were processed individually. The initial tests consisted of familiar poking and probing and specimen donation that all had encountered at one time or another. After that came the hearing tests, the wires, the computers and the X-rays. The medical staff only spoke to instruct, "sit here," "hold this," "breathe in" and "relax." Nathan was able to identify the reasons for most of the tests; agility, strength, reflexes, endurance and Nathan was sure, even though no one said so, that one of the tests was for IQ.

"I have never been so physically assaulted in my life," said an indignant Nathan six hours later to a like-minded Aaron in the waiting room. "That was flipping ridiculous."

"I hear you," said Aaron. "Those bums didn't even feed me lunch and it's almost dinnertime. My stomach thinks my throat's been cut."

Over the next half-hour the others joined them, with similar tales of woe. When George arrived shortly thereafter and once he had them all loaded in the Suburban, he was summarily told to head for the nearest pizza joint. George didn't like pizza and said so. The ensuing chants of 'Kill the Driver' did nothing to sway his opinion of where they were going until Bruce found a rope under one of the seats and it was pointed out to George that he could find himself tied to the roof rack. That resulted in a change of destination to conform with the wishes of the majority.

The second instructor had been at the ranch a week when Kim found Nathan working late one evening in the gun cleaning trailer. Pieces of his Para-Ordnance were spread out on the table.

"Will it live?" she asked.

"Yeah, it'll live," said Nathan, brushing crud out from under the extractor claw. "It's just time for a detailed strip and clean, that's all."   .

"That's good." She paused for a moment with her hands in her jean pockets. "Danny wants to talk with you. Would you mind coming with me?"

Nathan looked up. Danny hadn't been around all week. Now he wanted to see him at ten at night? "Sure. What's up?"

Kim shrugged and her red nylon windbreaker rustled as she moved towards the door. "He's waiting for us in the classroom."

"Hang on. I'll go over with you," said Nathan, hurriedly wiping his hands. "If you promise not to run."

Kim laughed. "No running. I promise."

Radar was outside the door waiting for Kim and the three of them walked toward the classroom. Kim hadn't been around much after hours and Nathan had found little opportunity to get to know her better. The 'Amazon Queen' jokes he shared with the rest of the shooters were just that, jokes. He suspected it was the same for the rest of his friends, they all joked about her and the pain she caused them but . . . there was no doubt about it, she *was* attractive. A personality, other than the drill sergeant one, had peeked out occasionally and if it really was there he'd have to do some digging to find it.

"So, where are you from Kim, around here?"

"No."

"Ever been to Canada?"

"No."

"Have you . . . ?" .

Kim cut him off. "Listen Nathan, I'm kind of a private person, okay? Find something else to talk about."

That went really well thought Nathan, as they now walked on in silence. The night was cool, the air still and he saw that Radar's ears would perk up and his head swivel toward the night noises the two people couldn't hear. He didn't run off to investigate but stayed beside Kim.

"How come Radar stays so close to you all the time?" he asked. "Is he protecting you from what's out there or is he counting on you to protect him?"

"Are you suggesting I might be meaner than anything that lives out there?"

Nathan rolled his eyes. "No, just tougher," he said in resignation.

"Never fear the night Nathan. Only fear what hunts at night."

In the darkness Nathan didn't see the smile that passed briefly across her face. He missed the joke because the comment had dragged up an image he was trying to forget, an image from his own recent night hunt. A burning man seen through a rifle scope that had begun appearing regularly in his dreams.

They walked the rest of the way to the classroom in silence and Kim opened the door for him to enter. Danny was there with an open file folder spread out on the table in front of him. Nathan could see his name on some of the papers as he sat on a chair across from him.

"Hi, Danny. What's up?" There was concern in his voice.

"Evening, Nathan. It turns out it's time for a little chat. It's about your medical so that's why the after hours privacy."

Nathan looked over at Kim who had taken up a position leaning against the wall behind him. Some privacy, he thought. She caught his questioning look and ignored it.

So did Danny. "The doctors found something interesting in your test results. They tell me they aren't quite sure what to make of it."

"Interesting in what way?" His anxiety level had gone up a notch but he tried not to let it show.

"Well, let me reassure you, it's not interesting in a bad way. It does explain some things though. Remember that exercise we did at Bob's range, where I asked you to fire a shot as soon as you could after the timer's beep? Your reaction times were so low I wasn't sure my timer was working, so I borrowed yours and . . . well . . . the results I got were the same."

Nathan nodded warily, remembering but still not sure where this conversation was leading.

"When we gave your file to the medical clinic, I asked them to check out your reaction time a little further. They did that for us. Their findings confirm what I saw that day. Nathan, your reaction time to an external stimulus is half that of anybody else's here."

Nathan leaned back in his chair, "Well . . . that's encouraging . . . I guess . . . isn't it?"

"Let me explain this a little further," said Danny. "You displayed exceptional reaction times to visual, auditory and tactile stimuli. Actually, according to the doctor who briefed me, exceptional is not the right word. His term was 'freak of nature'." Danny paused to let that sink in.

"After doing the tests the Doc did some further research. He told me of two other recorded cases where individuals have displayed reaction times at your level. I've seen the numbers and it's unbelievable."

Nathan's mind was reeling. "I've always known I have good hand-eye co-ordination but reaction time was something I never considered as an explanation for it. Did they find a reason for this . . . this . . . difference?" he asked.

"The Doc told me they really don't understand why, they can just make educated guesses. There were some unusual readings on a brain scan they did and he threw a bunch of medical mumbo jumbo at me but I didn't understand any of it. Their best explanation in laymen's terms was they suspect you have a short circuit in your brain that in some way allows this to happen. It's a good short though, not a bad one, and there is no problem anticipated as a result of it.

"Somewhere out there Nathan," said Danny, waving his arm in a sweeping motion, the enthusiasm in his voice growing, "is someone who's the tallest person in the world. There's also the shortest person in the world and the one with the best hearing and the best eyesight. But sitting across the table from me is the person who could very well have the shortest reaction time in the world. A pretty good position for an action pistol shooter to be occupying wouldn't you say?"

"I don't know what to say," said Nathan. "I guess maybe this explains some of what I've always thought of as natural abilities. But beyond that I just don't know."

"So far you've been performing well here Nathan," said Danny. "As you get more professional instruction and come to understand and exploit this natural ability you have, who knows how far you can go. But I'm not convinced this short reaction time is enough for you to come out on top here. There's a lot more to a good action pistol competitor than a fast reaction time, you know that too. Even with this ability you could still end up on the bottom of the pile when it's all over."

"Sure, I understand that," said Nathan.

"The limits are not where you think they are." It was the first time Kim had spoken.

Nathan smiled "Yeah. I guess that takes on new meaning now."

"Now get out of here and get some sleep," said Danny. "I want you alert for class tomorrow. And Nathan, I want your solemn word that you won't tell any of the other candidates about this. I'm serious, you tell anyone about this and you're out of the program. Period. It would be discouraging to them and that's not fair. This goes no further."

"Okay Danny, I understand." Nathan rose and walked past Kim on his way out the door. "See you in the morning," he said to her.

"Sure." Kim watched him leave, made sure the door was shut and then took his vacated seat across from Danny. "That went well," she said.

"So? What's not to go well?" answered Danny as he reassembled Nathan's file.

Nathan went to bed but not to sleep. Replaying his life he tried to find places where his reduced reaction time had manifested itself. He believed they could be plucked out.

As a grade schooler, when playing dodge-ball he was consistently the last one to be hit. As a teen playing sports and catching the occasional passes or line drives that amazed his team mates, and as a beginning pistol shooter when he skyrocketed past the abilities of his peers and experienced shooters, particularly when speed was a factor. By the time his mind stopped generating images and sleep started to tug at his consciousness, he believed there was evidence of what Danny had told him. Winning here was something that could be done as well. It was a three month competition, the longest one of his life, but Nathan Burdett was going to come out on top. Confidence flooded through him. No one could stop him now. The natural ability was his. Danny had confirmed it and all that was left was to learn to use it to the fullest. Conviction filled his sleep. He would make it. He was going to be a professional shooter.

As the weeks passed and the instructors did too, Nathan became more intense. He never let up. The class would train all day, but evening would invariably find him spending an hour dry firing in his room. On one occasion he signed out one of the rental cars and drove it to the range, using the headlights for illumination as he practiced late into the night. 'Just trying to iron out some wrinkles,' he had told George when the old hand had come out to investigate the gunshots. There was a price to be paid for the extra work and Nathan's hands paid it in blood. They became scraped and cut to the point where something had to be done. A file obtained from George helped. He used it to remove all the checkering from the grip of his gun, the checkering Bob had sweated to put there in the first place. He'd understand thought Nathan, and if he didn't it was too bad. Butchering the gun was a necessity, performing here and now was what counted, not how pretty your gun was. It wasn't enough. His hands still bled and he found it necessary to wear gloves until they healed. That took a week.

All six of the candidates improved steadily and began shooting faster and straighter than they ever had in their lives. As the weeks passed and the powder burned, it became obvious there was a ranking in abilities and Nathan and Aaron were on top. Whether man-on-man or conventional competition, it was always Nathan and Aaron who rose to the top. Everyone was improving but these two improved the fastest. The more they learned and the more they shot, the wider the gulf grew. The only time that one of them lost was when they screwed up and made a mistake. Nathan and Aaron sometimes beat themselves but toward the end no one ever beat them.

The other candidates accepted this ranking with little difficulty for they had all become friends in their time together.

However their competitive nature would not allow them do anything other than push their hardest and to be there to beat the two when they did make mistakes.

The separation between the abilities of Aaron and Nathan was a more difficult call. There was a consensus among the shooters themselves that Nathan was superior in terms of raw speed and was better at thinking his way through a course of fire whereas Aaron had a slight accuracy edge. No one wanted to have to live on the difference between the two.

Nathan was amazed that Aaron was able to keep up with him at all, especially considering his freakishly short reaction times. The jock was a good shot, no doubts there any more. Who knew how he did it, but he did. Regardless, Nathan was pleased to be at the top and happy to have his friend there with him, he knew that someone pushing, challenging and constantly nipping at his heels was a key to improving.

Christmas and New Years had come and gone. It was late January and the candidates' time at the ranch was coming to an end when Danny called an unexpected meeting one morning after breakfast. Danny, Kim and George sat at the front of the classroom in a manner that suggested a formal announcement was going to be issued. Their somber looks, however, quieted the six young men facing them and drove the usually light morning spirit from the room.

Danny spoke first. "I had planned, three months ago, to sit here in front of you and announce the winner of the big sponsorship that you have all been working so hard toward. Unfortunately I can't do that now. A change of plans by our sponsor is the reason. I received a fax this morning, and confirmed it with a phone call, that our corporate benefactor has had a change of heart. There has been a change of leadership at the top of the corporation that instituted this program and the new hierarchy has seen fit to kill this project."

Danny paused to let the reality of his proclamation penetrate. There were cries of disbelief and anger from around the room but it was Aaron who first questioned Danny. "They've spent one huge pile of money on this project. Now, they're just going to cancel the whole thing?"

The room quieted to hear the reply. "It looks that way. Remember what I said when we started here? This company is not in the shooting industry, which means they feel no compulsion to support the shooting sports. It's strictly a business decision to them. They looked at the balance sheet and didn't agree with the previous administration's figures. They saw red ink instead of black and now they're going to cancel and cut their losses."

"Cut and run . . . same old story," said Bruce to no one in particular.

"Anything we can do to change their minds?" asked Brian.

"Absolutely not," said Danny. "This was apparently a Board decision and for those of you who know how these big companies work, that's basically an edict from God. It's over guys. I'm sorry."

There was a sick feeling in the pit of Nathan's stomach. This couldn't be happening. He felt like he had just been disqualified on the last stage of a match he was about to win. DQ'd by a rookie Range Officer who had made a gross error in judgement. Three months of work, pain and sacrifice for nothing. He'd just been shafted.

Nathan pounded a fist on the table and half stood out of his chair. "Well we're sorry too, Danny! Where do these overpaid bean counters get off pulling us out of our lives for three months by waving a juicy carrot in front of us and then taking it away without even a chance to grab for it? We're all competitors and none of us are strangers to losing a competition but we get really upset if someone runs a match, we pay our entry fees, do our best and then they don't live up to their part of the bargain on awards and prizes!"

There were mutterings of agreement from the others, which subsided when Danny spoke again. "I don't need to remind you that there weren't any promises you would all be winners when you left here. The company has kept its bargain, you've all been receiving a steady pay cheque since you showed up. You've probably also received the best training and coaching of any six people in the history of IPSC shooting. Additionally, there's been a dramatic improvement in your shooting abilities.

"I feel as bad as you do that things didn't work out the way they'd been planned. And no one wanted it more than me." Jamming an index finger into his chest he looked each shooter in the eye. "This was my project!" he boomed. A long pause became awkward until he said defeatedly, "Some things are just beyond our control."

Nathan had buried his face in his hands but he lifted it upon catching the hurt in Danny's voice. "We're not blaming you Danny. You've been as straight with us as anyone could be. When I first met you, Bob Coombs told me you were legit and I've never seen anything to convince me otherwise." Danny looked uncomfortable, staring down at a pen he twirled in his hands. "But why don't you tell us who these jerks are so we can go find them and at least dish out a little attitude adjustment? It would make us *feel* better."

There were calls of concurrence from the other candidates but Danny shook his head. "I'm sorry I can't do that."

"Fine," said Nathan. "We promise not to hurt them but we sure would like to know so we can avoid ever buying their product in the future. How about it?" Danny shook his head. Nathan threw up his hands in resignation, "Like you said, some things are just beyond our control."

Emotions still simmered close to the boiling point but Nathan's comment set the tone for the conclusion of the meeting. He seemed to have accepted it and since it was obvious to the others that he would have won the contract and they a plane ticket home, they choked back their disgust. Every one of them made a point of coming to Nathan and telling him how sorry they were for this twist of fate which had robbed him of a dream.

No one spoke to Danny as he left the room delegating Kim to issue administrative instructions detailing gear and plane tickets home. They weren't wasting any time noted Nathan. This day would be spent on clean up and packing and tomorrow morning people would head home. Nathan, it turned out, was the last one George would ferry to the airport and that wouldn't be until evening. It looked like he wouldn't see Calgary until shortly before midnight.

Nathan had his bags packed and was sitting out on the veranda of his cabin watching the sun go down and waiting for the Suburban and George. He'd said his good-byes last night when they had all gone to Tucson for one last dinner together and then again today as the others left for the airport. Even Kim had come along for the dinner, at least for a little while, before making some excuse and leaving early. She was a strange one alright, thought Nathan.

He wondered if he could get his old job back. It was probably still there if he wanted it, but his feelings were telling him not to bother. A living had to be made one way or another and EMT was his best marketable skill at the moment. On the other hand if he was going to make a move, now was the time. The winters in Arizona sure beat those in Alberta, the last three months had taught him that. Maybe he should try and find an EMT job here, now that was a thought.

As the sky's color was converting to orange Nathan heard a coyote yipping in the distance. Another one answered the first and they carried on a brief conversation challenging each other's territory. Radar came out from around the buildings and looked off into the hills where the howling had come from, but then turned to look the other way once he heard the Suburban coming.

Nathan was expecting George, who was driving, but not Danny, who was occupying the passenger seat. George opened the back of the vehicle and Nathan heaved in his gear. Once he was loaded the closing thump of the rear door expressed the finality Nathan felt. As he climbed in himself, Danny silently passed back a plane ticket package without meeting his eyes.

"Get everyone else off okay?" asked Nathan.

"No problems," said George in his usual terse manner.

Nathan flipped open the ticket, there was just enough light left in the day to check times and gates. One more flight than needed appeared on the schedule. Was this a mistake or something else? He looked up at Danny and then at George but saw only the backs of their heads. If they'd expected a reaction from him they weren't looking for it. Maybe it *was* a mistake. Might as well find out, he thought.

"Danny, this ticket's all screwed up. It's got me going home but there's a return on here for two weeks from now. Didn't you check this when you picked it up?"

"Yeah, I checked it Nathan. There's no mistake," said Danny. "You're going home all right, just like all the others, but you don't have to stay there. You can come back if you want. For you, training isn't over. Sit back and relax, we have to talk."

* * * * *

85

Red's temper was short and fearsome these days, so Mack was careful about how he approached the subject. "Hey Red," he asked over the din of the bar's music. "When are we going to do something about the punk who shot up our hogs? It's been a couple of months and we still haven't evened the score. Isn't it about time we did something?"

The questions were broached in an appropriately respectful tone and his body language indicated that whatever Red said was okay with him. Mack was only asking out of curiosity – only asking, not demanding.

Red had been scary enough before the fire but now a monster had replaced him, a monster that was being slowly revealed as the bandages came off. The back and top of his head had been burned the worst. He'd been lucky about that, thought Mack, at least his face wasn't too bad. Still, the sight of him made a man's mouth go dry and you looked away when you saw him. But then you're eyes kept drifting back out of sick curiosity because you'd never seen anything like that before – you couldn't help yourself. Scarring had replaced the hair and only about half the right ear remained, that side of his head had been burned the worst. Maybe some of the scarring would fade over time.

Red exhaled another long plume of cigarette smoke to contribute to the bar's already thick carcinogenic atmosphere and wished Mack would just go back to his whore girlfriend and leave him alone. He was irritating and besides, he wasn't sure he liked being called 'Red' any more. The name had been attached to him since he was a boy, the label prompted by his flaming red hair. Teasing had come as a result of the hair but learning how to fight had been the result of the teasing. Eventually, though, he became proud of it and invariably wore the red mane long and well looked after. It was a head of hair that would have made any Irish maiden envious, thick, long and beautiful . . . at least it had been until the night their Harleys got shot up. Now 'Red' may as well have referred to the color of his scars. The hair was gone and red, blotchy, puckered scarring remained.

"We're still working on the guy Mack," said Red. "Nobody wants him more than me. He's dropped out of sight but we'll find him."

"Well if you need us you just say the word. We'll do anything to get this guy, you know that."

"Sure, I know that," said Red. "We've got some stuff in the works but if it doesn't pan out we'll need everyone's help. I'll let you know."

Mack left Red in the booth, nursing his pain. Pete came back in time to see him go. He put their drinks down on the table and slid onto the bench across from the president of the Satan's Riders.

"What'd Mack want?"

"The boys are getting anxious. They want action. They don't like waiting." Red took a long pull on his beer. The alcohol helped dull the pain.

"I can understand that. I don't like it much neither," said Pete.

"You read the report that private dick wrote up, right?"

"Yeah. Where'd our lawyer find such a loser?"

"Hey, he's supposed to be good," said Red.

"We don't need no private eye to tell us this Burdett guy has dropped off the face of the earth. We know that."

"Sure we know that Pete. But there's more in that report than what Burdett's address is right now and the fact that he's not there. It tells us who his best buddy is – that gunsmith down the road from his place. I'm willing to bet if we watch that small valley he'll show up eventually."

"It could take a while," said Pete.

"It could. But with his buddy and his mother both living in that valley it's guaranteed to happen. We should have done this over Christmas instead of pulling back and letting that private eye find him. But we'll find him, don't worry." Red pointed a thick finger at Pete. "We've got lots of time and twenty guys we can trust to do whatever it takes. It's time to do this ourselves."

Pete nodded his agreement.

Red looked at his watch and thought for a moment. "Go get the rest of the executive together for a meeting at the clubhouse, tomorrow night, ten o'clock."

Pete left to make some phone calls while Red pulled a bottle of pills from his jacket pocket and washed down four with beer, hoping they would get him through the night. It seemed like yesterday that he'd tried to pull the line of bikes apart to stop the chain reaction, but instead another gas tank had blown just as he started pushing one clear. Burning gasoline had rained down on him and shared its fire with everything it touched. His hair and beard had been fully engulfed in seconds. His clothes ignited too but the leathers he was wearing saved his torso from widespread damage. Sleep became a casualty as well, for now flames ruled his nightmares, the choking, suffocating flames that had changed his world into one of agony. The pain could be managed, especially with drugs, both legal and illegal – but he didn't want to see the flames again. Red didn't tell anyone else about the dreams. That would be a sign of weakness. He wouldn't let the others see the fear he had felt either, only the hate and there was plenty of that to see. The flames had destroyed his flesh but they'd created his hate and now they nurtured it every night.

CHAPTER SIX

George maneuvered the Suburban out onto the secondary road that ran by the front of the ranch while, seated behind him, Nathan finished the examination of his ticket. Leaning forward in his seat, Nathan's curiosity was completely aroused as he now listened intently to Danny.

"You see Nathan, I haven't been completely honest with you. What you've been told so far hasn't exactly been the truth," said Danny as he twisted in his seat and handed back a brown leather wallet. "Open it," he said. Nathan took it, flipped it open and read the lettering on the badge.

Sagging back into his seat he tossed the wallet back and took a deep breath to control a rising anger. "Okay, you're an FBI agent. What gives here Danny? You better have a good explanation for this."

"Yes, I'm FBI Nathan, not a consultant working for a company looking to sponsor professional pistol shooters. I'm a cop, over fifteen years in the outfit now. And George here isn't a ranch hand, he's a veteran of the Dept. of the Treasury. What's really going on here, as you put it, is a research project."

"Research into what?" asked Nathan coldly.

"Let me start by telling you a story." Danny readjusted his position in the seat, still facing the rear where Nathan sat. "Do you remember a hostage taking incident that occurred a couple of years ago in Boston? The one where a bunch of ex-military types, with a little inside help, tried to hold up an armored car depot? Our Hostage Rescue Team ended up assaulting the place and got all the bad guys but in the process we lost one of our own with two hostages wounded."

"Sure I do," said Nathan. "It was all over the media. Your guys were heroes. It could have turned out better in some ways but you got the job done."

"That about sums it up," said Danny. "Except I was leader of the entry team." The occasional lights from oncoming cars showed a harder look washing across his face. "We got the job done, as you put it, but obviously I wasn't happy with two critically wounded hostages and one dead friend. That, as you can imagine, was the worst part, losing a friend, someone close to me and everyone else on the team. The outcome, however, served to gel something I had been working through in my mind for some time. More than that though, it gave me the necessary profile and stature in the Bureau to push through this particular project.

"You see Nathan, assaulting a barricaded criminal or terrorist's position with an armed entry team is never a good option. The only reason it's ever carried out is because something has to be done and every other idea is worse. Sure, sometimes it works out perfectly but there's always a huge potential for disaster. My perspective on Boston is that although we accomplished our objective, it was a disaster because we lost one of my men.

"The best part of the whole operation was the way our snipers performed. They had two bad guys in view when the entry team breached the door," Danny drove his right fist into his left palm, "and took them out on cue. That evened the odds for us once we got in. They proved once again that highly trained, precision shooters can surgically eliminate a threat with no risk to themselves and minimal risk to hostages. Specially equipped snipers like ours are a staple of all SWAT teams, they're specialists who have proven their worth and have a unique and specific role to fill. I see that same kind of potential for a pistol shooter of your abilities."

Nathan interrupted. "Wait a minute, I think I see where this is going. But why recruit someone like me, when you could train one of your team members to shoot up to my level? Wouldn't that be simpler than going through this kind of charade?" He opened his arms to indicate everything around him.

"Good assumption, but you don't know much about SWAT teams or tactical history. All the people on these law enforcement teams are dedicated people but they aren't shooters in the sense that you and your kind are. We could train them for five years straight and still not bring them up to your skill level. They don't have the natural ability or the desire, that fire in the belly, that drives people like you to shoot a handgun faster and straighter than anyone else. Imagine taking an average weekend golfer and trying to train him to be the best golfer on the pro circuit, not just good but the very best in the world. Sure, his game would improve a lot, but to be the best in the world? It's not going to happen."

Danny paused to ask a question. "Ever heard of Carlos Hathcock?"

"Sure," said Nathan. "I read the book about his work in Viet Nam. Probably the best sniper in modern warfare."

"Do you remember his history prior to joining the military?"

"National Champion rifle shot at Camp Perry," said Nathan, letting the words out slowly. "Won the 1,000 yard Wimbledon Cup match." He was beginning to see the picture Danny was painting.

"He isn't the only one," said Danny. "Over the years, the very best snipers we or any other military has fielded have been accomplished rifle shots before they ever joined the military. A sniper needs two basic skills, marksmanship and fieldcraft. It's far easier to teach someone fieldcraft than it is that level of

91

marksmanship, and I emphasize the *high* level of marksmanship. It's easy to achieve a basic level or even an advanced level but to be cutting edge, absolute best in the world, you either have it or you don't and you're not going to learn it unless you're gifted.

"If there's a place for shooters with your kind of ability in law enforcement they need to have two basic skills, marksmanship and tactics. It's far easier to teach tactics than it is marksmanship, especially with handguns. You know as well as I do that competency with a handgun is far more difficult than with a rifle. The way a short gun magnifies all the operator's errors is unlike anything else. Even basic skill can be tough to learn and don't forget the level I'm looking for is 'best in the world'."

Nathan said nothing. He felt the same butterflies in his stomach that showed up there the day before a big match. The interior of the Suburban was quiet, the pale greenish lights from the dash accenting the age lines on Danny's face. Nathan realized he didn't have his seatbelt on and suddenly felt an odd compulsion that he should be wearing it, especially if he was riding with a couple of cops. He put it on as inconspicuously as possible. If either of them noticed, they didn't comment. For a minute the only sound was the unique symphony of road noise from the tires on the pavement, the rushing wind and the sound of the engine. A passing car broke Nathan out of his reverie.

"So why not just go recruit one of those guys who instructed us over the past few months? They *are* the best in the world, not wannabe's like us."

"Two reasons," said Danny, turning in his seat again. "The main reason is that they're too well known. I can't take a chance on them being recognized in some of the situations they'd find themselves. Secondly, I really believe what I told you on the first day you came to the ranch, that people like you will meet and exceed the level of performance those top shooters are producing now. In my opinion you're almost there now."

That made Nathan pause. He was still holding his ticket and now set it down on the seat beside him. "You're right about me not knowing anything about SWAT operations Danny. So fill me in on how a shooter like me could benefit one of your team's operations."

"Obviously, Nathan, you couldn't be used in every situation, any more than snipers or explosive experts are used in every operation. But someone like you would be a fabulous resource, meant to be used in appropriate circumstances. And not just SWAT operations, but other types of specialized work also."

"For instance?"

"For instance, if I could get someone like you into a room occupied by perps and hostages, it's my belief you have the ability to neutralize the situation faster than any other means at our disposal. You could do it with less risk to the hostages than a full-blown entry team with battering rams, tear gas and stun grenades. I see someone like you as a short range precision sniper who does his work at extreme speed.

"I see potential in protective operations, or what you maybe know as VIP security. Also in various high risk undercover operations and even in some arrests or warrant executions. There are times when all of these jobs could benefit from someone with your abilities. And those are the obvious ones, that's where we'd begin.

"The other thing you need to realize, Nathan, is that this isn't just an FBI project. The Federal Dept. of Justice is funding and coordinating the project and the Bureau is running it because the idea originated here. All Federal law enforcement agencies have a stake in what we're doing and most have contributed people or resources to the project. There is, of course, bound to be a trickle down effect to other enforcement agencies and maybe even the military. The international anti-terrorism community has shown an interest in what we're doing as well."

Nathan, however, was stuck back at Danny's first sentence. "Neutralize is cop talk for kill, isn't it Danny?"

Danny paused. "The official answer is no, but the real world answer is yes," he said. "Neutralize means to stop a person's current or intended actions, the less violent the means the better. But when we have to go in with guns, death becomes an acceptable and expected outcome."

The conversation in the Suburban yielded once again to the hum of the road noise as everyone seemed intent on watching George pull out and pass a slow-moving pickup. When he was safely back in his own lane ahead of the truck, Nathan spoke again. "How would you get someone like me into that sort of room or situation you just described, where I could act as a 'neutralizer'?"

"Obviously we couldn't pull it off all the time, but I've been involved in enough of these operations to know there are ways to do that kind of thing. Trust me, it can be done. Creative thinking is the key."

"So what do you want from me now, Danny?"

"Go home, take a couple of weeks off and think about where you want to go from here. If you want to continue in this project, use that return leg of your ticket and come back in two weeks. If it's not something you care to take further, then give me a call and just stay home. The project will continue without you and we'll move down to the next candidate in line. I'd like you to stay, but it's a personal decision and whatever you decide, I'll live with. Understand though that you can't talk about this with anyone. The project is classified Secret and you can't discuss the details with anyone. Is that understood?"

"Sure, I understand," said Nathan. He was quiet for a while, trying to decide if he really wanted to know the answer to a question that was running through his mind. He eventually decided he did. "Danny, does this project have one of those corny government code names like in the movies?"

Danny laughed at the question. "It sure does," he said. "Its official name is The B-Zone Project."

"B-Zone?" said Nathan "B-Zone? I understand the reference to the scoring zone but I don't get the link to this. Know what I mean?"

"Don't worry kid. If you come back, you'll get it," said George.

Nathan dropped the subject and said little else during the rest of the trip. His mind was reeling. He'd been working toward a sponsorship as a professional shooter and was close to having it nailed when the whole project got shut down. But it was all a scam anyway because now he had a new offer not imagined in his wildest dreams. He'd need the two weeks to figure *this* out.

At the airport George stopped in the drop-off area and opened the rear doors to allow Nathan to pull out his bags. The other question that had been nagging Nathan came to the surface then. "What about Kim, Danny? Will she still be at the ranch two weeks from now?"

Danny steadied the luggage cart while Nathan stacked the bags. "I expect she will."

"So she's a cop too. Well, what agency does she work for?" asked Nathan trying to sound disinterested.

"Israeli National Police."

Nathan stopped in mid-bag-toss. "Pardon me? You mean like the Jews? The Holy Land? The other side of the world?"

"Exactly," said Danny. "They're one of the agencies interested in this. They believe the project has potential and sent

95

her to us. Know of anybody with more terrorism experience than the Israeli's?"

"Danny, I don't know *anybody* who has experience with terrorism," said Nathan, wondering to himself if destroying a pack of Harleys from seven hundred yards with a high powered rifle qualified as terrorism.

"You're right, of course you don't. Believe *me* then, they know their stuff. Those people are knee deep in terrorists. I've been on tactical exchange workshops with them and always learned plenty, but occasionally we in North America have a good idea as well. That might be what they see here now."

Nathan threw the last bag onto the luggage cart and shook hands with the other two men. "You guys have more surprises than a box full of bad reloads. Thanks for keeping life interesting. I'll be in touch." With that he moved off into the terminal.

As they pulled away from the curb George turned to Danny. "Think he'll be back?"

Danny grunted. "Are Glocks plastic? He'll be back."

"Still think it'll work?"

"Yeah . . . Yeah George, I still think it'll work."

The trip back North was a time warp for Nathan. He arrived back in his old life, leaving the new one that had started to develop in Arizona behind him. From old to new and now back to old and then, maybe if he wanted to, back to the new again. It was confusing. His friends and family were here though, that was something that hadn't changed. There had been friends in Arizona but they'd all caught airplanes recently, just like him, and weren't there anymore. Danny, George and Kim would still be there but they weren't friends, at least not yet. He supposed they could be once he was an equal and no longer a 'candidate.' That was a new thought, it was something to consider.

If he was going to keep his word to Danny, there could be no discussion of this with anyone. That left him feeling cold and lonely even though he was home. Well not really home. Calgary was okay as far as big cities went, but it wasn't home.

From the airport Nathan went directly to his mother's new apartment. She'd been uncomfortable living alone in the country ever since her daughter's house had been Swiss cheesed by the Riders, and so the house had stood empty since Nathan's departure. Bob and Frankie were keeping an eye on it because Emily Burdett had yet to decide what course her life would take from here. She'd left her job with the Cochrane RCMP and a friend in the Calgary Police Service had pulled some strings, netting her a job in that department's property room.

Regular phone calls to and from Arizona had kept Nathan informed of the essential facts about family and friends and now with the clock well past midnight and the coffee pot emptying his mother filled in the details. Being the absent son coming home to visit was a new role, one he wasn't used to. As they talked, he came to the realization that if he went back to Arizona this would become the norm.

His eyes tracked around the apartment, recognizing almost everything as having been moved from home and therefore not belonging in this place. The furniture, the pictures on the wall, even the dishes on the table didn't belong here, they were supposed to be in a small country house northwest of here. It was as if they'd been stolen while he was gone, and he'd had no say in the matter. His mother wasn't there though, she was here. So was this home now? This apartment didn't feel like it, there was no past here, no memories.

His sister, Louise, and her husband were still in hiding, living with friends out on the coast. Todd had found work there

97

and it looked like they might never return. He wouldn't get to see them in the immediate future. That had changed too. He wondered what had changed in Bob and Frankie's lives, or his friend Paul's, maybe some things had remained constant.

"Mom, would you make out okay if I moved away and took a job elsewhere," asked Nathan.

Emily Burdett ran a tired hand through her hair and Nathan saw it had noticeably more gray now than four months ago. It hadn't been an easy time for her. "Of course I would dear. I've actually been thinking about that myself. I would sell the house and move into Cochrane or maybe even stay here in Calgary. Maybe buy a condo, something that doesn't take as much work to keep up. Don't worry about me Nathan. You have your own life to live and I have a good job here and lots of great friends. I can make out just fine on my own." She paused. "Is there something I should know?"

"Oh, probably Mom. The problem is I can't tell you. At least not yet. I have some decisions to make in the next couple of weeks. But I promise I'll tell you when I can. Okay?"

"Of course dear. Why don't you get some rest now? You've had a long day and it's very late. How about just staying here on the couch?"

"Thanks," said Nathan, "but I'll stick with my original plan and drive up to Cochrane tonight. I slept some on the plane. Is it still okay if I borrow your car?"

"Certainly. And make sure you go see Bob and Frankie tomorrow. I told them you were coming home and they're expecting you for lunch."

"Absolutely the first thing on my agenda Mom."

At the door his mother put her hand up to the side of his face. "I've missed you. It's been a long haul and I'm glad you're back." She gave him a quick hug and watched as he walked down the hallway, disappearing around the corner by the stairs. Then she listened to his footsteps, until they were gone too.

Nathan drove to what he still called home, but with no one there and much of the furniture gone the house in the country was lifeless and empty. It didn't feel right. At least his room was the way he'd left it. Emptying bags and putting clothes and gear away occupied him until weariness overtook to the point of driving him to bed.

When Nathan awoke the clock said 10:00 a.m. and the calendar said winter. The clock was right but the calendar was wrong. A Chinook wind had rolled in off the mountains while he slept and now the warm weather it brought was making a liar of the calendar. Taking advantage of the spring like conditions, Nathan walked the quarter mile to Bob's shop.

Growing up, it was a road he'd walked regularly, at least until acquiring a driver's license, then he drove. For a long time it had been important to drive everywhere, even when walking could have been done just as easily. Until he'd left for Arizona he still ran the road regularly during his training runs but never seemed to walk it. During the walk over he hoped to have time to think about what he was going to say to Bob. He was still uncertain about how much Bob knew, though he suspected it was everything. It wasn't as long a walk as he remembered.

Bob jumped up from his bench when Nathan entered, pumped his arm unmercifully and slapped him on the shoulder. "You look great Nathan, even a California tan!"

"Arizona tan," Nathan corrected him.

"Whatever. It's really good to see you. We've missed you around here."

Nathan allowed that he had missed Bob too and then chairs were pulled up and the talk began. Nathan had seriously considered giving Bob a blast for not telling him everything about Danny. As he sat with him now, he realized he couldn't do that. Whatever Bob hadn't told him had been for his own good. In their conversation Bob was avoiding the topic, obviously unaware that Danny had leveled with him and told him what and who he really was.

They had talked for almost an hour, Nathan telling about the instructors, George, the Amazon Queen, the work he'd done and the skills he'd learned when a lull occurred in their conversation. "Before I left Arizona, Danny told me who he really is," he said, watching for Bob's reaction.

Nathan had hoped for surprise but there was none to be seen, only visible embarrassment as Bob's face reddened. "Did he tell everyone, or just you?"

"As far as I know, just me," said Nathan.

"He offered you the job then?"

"Yeah."

"Well?"

Nathan didn't reply at first, thumbing mindlessly through an American Handgunner issue from the coffee table. He didn't look up and his voice was softer when he spoke. "I don't know Bob, I thought I was working toward something I wanted badly, a professional shooting sponsorship. It turns out I was on a different road the entire time and didn't even know it. I'm not happy about that and I honestly don't know what I'm going to do."

The rebuke wasn't lost on Bob. "Let me give you some background," he said. "What I've told you about knowing Danny for a long time is true. I got to know him before I retired from my 'other' job and we've stayed in touch. When he got his little project approved and started on his scouting I suggested he take a serious look at you. Over the last year of competition you managed to sell yourself without any help from me and, from what you tell me happened in Arizona, I guess I was right."

"Was the big charade really necessary though?" asked Nathan.

"I talked to Danny about that," said Bob. "I wasn't comfortable with it either but the people who approved the project had security concerns, valid ones. So I can see why it was done that way. Can you imagine the headlines? 'Federal Police Force Recruits Civilian Assassins.' We both know better than to expect the media to have an understanding of the technical and tactical issues surrounding something like this."

"I guess you're right there," admitted Nathan. "But I still don't know what I'm going to do."

When he initially walked in, Nathan had noticed a poster missing from the wall immediately opposite the shop door. It was one of the first things a customer saw when walking in from the outside. Bob changed the poster occasionally but this time it was completely gone. The most recent one had been of a pretty girl in western garb holding a Colt single action revolver, 'Real Cowgirls Shoot Colts' it had read. The poster's purpose was to cover a hole in the wall. There was a shelf in the hole and there should've been a pistol on the shelf but it was as gone as the poster.

This was Bob's idea of having an accessible but securely hidden gun handy. Gun shops being a favorite target of armed and violent criminals had prompted Bob to create this hideaway, placing a loaded .45 on the shelf and covering it with a poster. The idea being, if he ever needed a loaded gun in a hurry, the only thing necessary was to stuff a hand straight through the paper poster, grab the gun and come out shooting. He called it his ace-in-the-hole. Because Nathan couldn't tell Bob what his future held, the lull in the conversation became awkward and so Nathan asked about the missing gun in order to change the topic.

"Come on back here," said Bob, leading the way past the shop's lathe, mill and other machine tools to his workbench at the back of the shop, where a window overlooking the rear of the property provided the natural light needed at the bench for detailed hand work. "I've been working on it for about a week now and it's almost done. I'd appreciate your opinion."

Nathan followed Bob and accepted the heavily modified 1911 handed him. Attached to the front of the dust cover, he recognized a frame extension that ran to the very front of the slide and supported a one-eighth inch thick steel plate that projected up in front of the muzzle. It was profiled to match the slide contour but wasn't attached to it. A generous hole in the plate protecting the muzzle allowed a bullet to exit there. The whole thing looked like an over engineered front-end weight. Bob saw Nathan's puzzled look and explained.

"As you know Nathan, on the 1911 design, if the muzzle is pressed against something, even slightly, the disconnector will activate and the gun won't fire. In close quarters work, with a defensive pistol, it's a real possibility that the shooter will either deliberately or inadvertently stuff the muzzle up against a bad guy and pull the trigger. This device will keep the gun functioning in that kind of encounter. Go ahead," Bob encouraged, "try it."

Nathan rechecked the gun to be sure it was clear and holding it in a firing grip pressed the muzzle firmly against the bench top. The slide stayed completely in battery and when he pressed the trigger the hammer dropped. "Heh, that's great," he said. "This looks like an accessory rail you've machined on the bottom of the frame extension. I hope that's not for hanging a laser on?" He cast a questioning glance at Bob knowing this couldn't be the case because Bob had no more use for them than Nathan did.

"Now you know better than that," said Bob. "It's for a simple light hooked to a pressure switch in the grip that the middle finger can activate when needed. It eliminates the need to have a flashlight in the other hand to identify targets and tell friend from foe in bad light. All I have to do is buy the light some time."

Nathan nodded, running his eyes in detail over the rest of the gun. "Still too cheap to buy night sights, eh?" He looked further. "What are these small curved plates you have welded to the rear of the slide on either side of the hammer?"

"That's for close quarters work again. At hand to hand distance if somebody grabs your gun they can block the hammer fall, maybe not intentionally but it'll happen nonetheless. Those side shields will help prevent it, while still allowing you to manually cock the gun by bringing your thumb onto the hammer directly from the rear."

"You didn't go all out with a high-capacity frame?"

"I suppose if cost was no object I might do that. But cost is always a factor and this old single-stack Colt has always been my ace-in-the-hole. I just thought I'd rework it a little during my slow season. And don't get the perception these are all my ideas, most of this has been gleaned over the years from a lot of other people.

"Here's something else." Bob handed Nathan an empty magazine he'd picked up off the bench. "Slide this in."

Nathan obliged. "Okay. Looks like a standard Wilson ten round mag."

"You see how it sticks out of the bottom of the frame about an inch? I plan to machine a stainless steel sleeve that is open only on one end, where the portion of the magazine that extends out of the frame will fit into it. The other end will be closed with rounded corners and the top edge will be a close fit to the bottom of the grip frame."

"That's a lot of work for a fancy magazine bumper pad," said Nathan.

"Not just a bumper pad, Nathan. Remember, this gun's for close work. I've repaired a lot of cop's guns that have been used as impact weapons because that was what they had in their hands at the time they needed to smack someone. Guns don't stand up to that kind of abuse. This pad will be long enough, heavy enough, properly shaped and sturdy enough to be used as an impact point if necessary."

"And because of the close fit to the bottom of the grip frame that's the portion that will take the brunt of the impact rather than the magazine catch," said Nathan, beginning to understand. "Can you get the right balance between having enough clearance so that the mag locks in reliably and still have the frame take the impact from a clubbing rather than the mag catch?"

"I think I can," said Bob. "It goes without saying that each mag will have to be fitted to one individual gun because the clearances will be pretty tight. Too tight for it to work on any kind of a general purpose duty gun because of the crud and dirt they get subjected to. Probably only good for this kind of a special purpose gun."

"Yeah, I see what you mean Bob. A special purpose gun . . .very specialized . . . the kind a pro-shooter might use?" He raised his eyes from the gun and looked at Bob. Bob shrugged his shoulders and smiled. Nathan laughed aloud, shaking his head. They talked about the gun for another half-hour. Nathan contributing thoughts and comments from a shooter's perspective and Bob analyzing them from the technical side.

Bob eventually terminated the conversation and suggested that Nathan go into the house and see Frankie. He would be in himself shortly and they could all have lunch together. As he wound his way back through the machine tools, past the sitting area, and toward the house door Nathan noticed a flyer taped to the exterior door, advertising something called 'The Icebreaker Pistol Match.'

"I see the boys are running The Icebreaker over at the city range again," he said. "I'd forgotten all about that."

"It's that time of year," replied Bob. "Paul dropped that off a couple of weeks ago when a patrol took him out this way. While he was here he put the touch on me to contribute a $250 gift certificate for gunsmithing work as well. He sure is good at arm twisting." Nathan was busy reading the details and didn't respond. "Maybe you should go on over," said Bob. "It would be a good way to check in with some people who have been concerned about you and your family. A lot of the guys have been stopping by here over the last few months. They all assume that Frankie and I know everything that goes on in your family's life and they usually try and pump us for information. Personally I just play dumb. That's easy for me but Frankie has to work at it."

"Maybe I'll just do that," said Nathan. "I've been practicing all winter, might be time to see if I learned anything." Bob handed him one of the notices from a small pile he had under the counter and Nathan slipped it in his pocket as the door closed behind him.

Frankie's bright eyes and warm smile were as welcome a sight as ever and of course she gave him a hug. It felt good to sit at her kitchen table and enjoy her company and conversation again. He told her about the past few months and summarized the conversation he'd had with Bob in the shop, but when she pressed for details about the future, Nathan tried to change the subject. Sometimes, however, she didn't let things go and this was one of those times. It wasn't because she was nosy but rather because she realized the special role she played in Nathan's life.

"I'm sorry Nathan, I know it's your future but you can't put me off like that. You said you have decisions to make. To make wise decisions you need advice and counsel, and who are you going to talk to if not Bob and me?"

"I know, Frankie," he said. "I know. But can you tell me what I should do? Should I stay here and help out my family, work my job and pursue my shooting as a hobby or should I hook up with Danny and see where that takes me? Am I shirking my responsibilities if I give in to the exciting and adventuresome things Danny is talking about? There are real hazards in what he's suggesting as well, what about those? I can't help anyone if I'm dead." Nathan shrugged his shoulders. "I thought I was working towards my goal of being a pro-shooter, but that rug got pulled out from under me. Now I don't know which way to go."

"Nathan," said Frankie. "You said you told Bob you were at a fork in the road and you had to decide which one to travel down. That's a good analogy and that means you've been giving it some real thought already. The fact that you haven't made such an important decision on the spur of the moment means you have a good chance of making the right one. Make sure you apply all the wisdom you can muster to this decision."

She got up to check something on the stove and continued speaking as she stirred. "Remember that you don't know what the future holds, no one does, you only know what you can reasonably anticipate down each road. There are advantages and disadvantages to each path, foreseeable things that affect not only you but others as well. Why don't you tell me what you see down each of them and we'll talk about them."

It was all the prompting that Nathan needed as he began to unload his hopes, dreams and fears in Frankie's kitchen. She sat listening to them all, as she always had in the past, providing her own thoughts and insights. By the time Nathan was talked out he had made no new decisions and Frankie had not recommended any particular course of action but he did have some new perspectives on his choices.

"You still have time Nathan," said Frankie. "Use it wisely. The next time I talk to Danny I'll have to compliment him on giving you enough time to make such an important decision."

Nathan's face broke into a smile. "So how much time has *he* spent in your kitchen Frankie?"

She patted Nathan on the arm, smiling mysteriously, as if keeping a secret. "We've had some good talks. Now go down the hall and tell Bob that lunch is ready."

"Yes ma'am."

Next Saturday Nathan drove into Calgary, found a place to park and made the short walk to Gunsport Ranges. The facility consisted of two twenty-five yard indoor pistol ranges and a forty yard archery range attached to a gunsmithing and retail business. It was a relatively small facility but the two owners aggressively promoted the action pistol sports and carried a stock of the shooting related items which were the sport's lifeblood. That and the fact the weather was always good indoors made it a popular place for area shooters to practice, compete and socialize.

Nathan had been there many times and as he walked in, carrying his shooting bag, his first thought was that nothing had changed. He'd been gone three months but it seemed like a lifetime. Here, however, the same merchandise was still on the racks – a display of western gear and clothing for the cowboy action shooters, a grouping of more modern gear for the IPSC competitors and in the middle, reloading supplies and equipment, a necessity for everyone. The same people were present as well, with twenty or so gathered at the end of the counter where worn stools stood on the floor and a coffee pot rested on the counter.

Dale, one of the owners, was busy behind the counter taking registrations for the match and didn't notice Nathan walk in. Several other people did though and that was when Nathan realized things had indeed changed. Those who noticed him stopped in mid conversation, or if not speaking, touched or nudged their neighbor in the way that communicates something significant is happening here. The noise in the room dropped into a well of silence and it seemed to take an eternity for Nathan to walk the distance from the front door to the counter. Dale looked up through the hush and in his outgoing manner reached down into that well first and pulled out the remains of the noise that had been in the room.

"Nathan! Man, you are a sight for sore eyes! Good to see you. Get over here and tell us how you're doing."

Others picked it up.

"Hi Nathan."

"You're looking good."

"Looks like you came to shoot."

For a short while Nathan thought that perhaps the awkward silence had been an anomaly. He and his family's encounters with the Satan's Riders had nothing to do with this. He'd been gone quite a while and probably just surprised these people. However, by the time he had paid his registration fee the realization had come that this wasn't the case. A feeling of isolation had taken over and he didn't like it.

He had encountered this once before. A few years ago tragedy had struck Kevin Hammil, one of the men that used to compete here. Kevin's wife was raped and murdered in the underground parking garage of the building she worked in. Whenever he had come back into the range after that Nathan had found it awkward. What do you say to someone in that situation? Surely you can't act normally and pretend nothing happened. Not knowing what to say, Nathan had taken the same route as many of the other shooters. They avoided Kevin and kept their contact with him at a comfortable level until the healing effects of time dulled that edge of conscious anxiety.

By the time Nathan had registered himself at the front counter and carried on through the store to the lounge area behind the indoor ranges he had chatted with almost everyone in the building. As he worked at getting organized and putting his gear on, he started mentally categorizing their reactions to him. There were those who just uttered some sort of greeting, a socially acceptable pleasantry, and left it at that, they were obviously most comfortable leaving him alone. There were those who actually showed some degree of concern for what had happened to his family and who spoke words of encouragement. The sincerity level fluctuated widely but he found himself appreciating the effort these people were making. The only people that bothered him were the ones who came to him muttering offers of help to either 'settle the score' or 'join the war' or 'dust some bikers.' The ones doing that were the same people he had watched come in on the fringes of competitive shooting because they were attracted by the macho image of the gun on the hip. They talked more than they shot and their stories were better than their scores. They were the kind of people who never impressed anyone but themselves.

Any kind of shooting related news or gossip would get headline priority at the Saturday morning coffee pot in this place, so everyone here had heard about someone shooting up the Riders' Harleys and most of them probably suspected he had done it. As far as Nathan was concerned, he was finished with the Riders. He had done his piece and it was over.

Through one of the two soundproof glass windows that allowed a view from the waiting area into the two ranges Nathan had seen Paul working at last minute adjustments to props. He was adjusting a moveable section of wall that the day's competitors would have to shoot around to engage a group of targets at the far end of the range. There was a low 'window' cut into the wall and it was this shooting port that seemed to be giving him the most trouble. From where he stood Nathan couldn't tell if it was a safety concern or some other difficulty that necessitated the adjustment. When Paul finally came out the range door, a broad smile broke across his face as he saw Nathan and strode across the room to greet him.

"I didn't know you were coming!" he said, grabbing Nathan's hand and shaking it firmly.

"Well, it sort of worked out that way."

"That's great! But listen we need to talk. Can we go to that pizza joint across the street after the match? I'm match director here today and there is no way I can talk to you now. Everybody wants me for everything and I don't have time for any of it. What do you say? Have you got time later?"

"Sure I do. But only if you let me buy."

"You're on. I see you've got your gear ready. So get in there, join a squad and let's get this thing going."

Once inside the ranges everyone settled into a familiar routine; shoot, score, patch the target and collect the brass. The range officers kept everyone hustling to get the work done and insure things ran smoothly. Nathan was thankful that in the ranges the need to wear ear muffs, the shooting, and the drone of the ventilation fans precluded the possibility of idle conversation. Talking to people seemed too much of a chore at the moment and besides, he wanted to concentrate on shooting.

On the range which Nathan's squad occupied, three short and separate stages were arrayed in such a fashion that when all three had been completed individually, they would be combined into one larger field course. The other range was set up similarly.

B-ZONE

The first stage was a simple one requiring the shooter to begin seated at a desk and from there engage four paper targets with the usual two rounds each, as well as knock down two steel pepper poppers. Nathan's position near the end of the squad allowed him to watch the other shooters and analyze their technique using his new skills. He watched intently and saw mistakes and perfection, as usual more of the former than the latter. The difference he detected now was that his skills at observing, and hopefully correcting, those mistakes were greatly improved, his training having made him a better coach as well as a better shooter.

When his turn came, Nathan's mind slipped into a preparation groove he had deliberately constructed to ready himself for competition. It was like putting a boxcar on a downhill railroad track and letting it go. His mind followed the groove that had been engraved there over countless repetitions, ticking through the loading and preparation ritual and then focusing on the shooting task at hand. When he declared himself ready and the timer sounded its hollow buzz, the start of motion was a conditioned reflex.

After the start, conscious action took over as the electronic sight's red dot sought the steel targets first and he triggered one shot at each of them. The clang of bullets on steel was almost lost in the concussion of the next four shots as his dot tracked to two exposed paper targets. There was no discernible pause in his rate of fire as he moved between targets. His mind was racing ahead of his body, pushing for it to catch up. The two paper targets that remained had both been obscured by the poppers, neither of which had yet fallen far enough to clear the center of the targets. Nathan realized he couldn't afford to wait so he shifted to the head's A-Zones and hammered two fast double taps there.

He scanned the targets to check the hits as the ringing sound of steel hitting the floor confirmed the poppers were down. After clearing and holstering his gun he turned to see the RO standing behind him with his timer in his hand and his lips forming a silent 'WOW.'

"Great run!" said the RO. "Time 2.14 seconds," he called to the scorer. "That's the one to beat today," he said to no one in particular as he finished calling out the scoring. The shots had all been A's. Even the head shots. Nathan signed his score card and walked back to the rear of the range where the shooter who had been picking brass handed the empties to him.

"Looks like you're dialed in," he said.

"Thanks," said Nathan. "Everything felt pretty good there." He was starting to realize how much his skills had improved over the winter. Shooting now on a familiar range, with shooters he had competed against for years, was giving him a benchmark from his past that was a meaningful reference. He was light years ahead of where he had been last summer.

The next two stages were short ones also and Nathan blazed through them at warp speed with only one shot a C and the remainder A's.

Stage four, the field course, was next and by the time Nathan came up to shoot he had an audience. When the buzzer sounded, Nathan's gun began to bark and each time it spoke an empty case kicked out of the ejection port. To those watching it seemed clear that the entire magazine was expended before the first of the flowing brass stream hit the floor. Reloads were a barely discernible hesitation and where a pause should have occurred as he moved from one vantage point to another, there was none. Nathan shot the entire course moving constantly down the target line. He scored two C's and the rest A's.

Nathan was half done the match and even without checking the score sheets knew he was far ahead of his nearest competitor. The squad shooting on the other range wasn't finished yet so he took a break in the waiting area. He had his hearing protection off and was cleaning his safety glasses when Paul came by, looking busy and harried. They spoke briefly and Paul had time to express amazement at how Nathan's shooting had improved. He left quickly though and Nathan was getting ready to go back in and shoot the other half of the match when Dale appeared.

"Hey, hoser," he yelled, pointing his index finger at Nathan. "Telephone for you."

"What? Who is it?" Nathan had never received a call here.

"I don't know, you moron," Dale joked. "I'm not your secretary. Come get the phone." Dale waved him down the hallway and Nathan followed. "Get off the line as quick as you can," he teased. "This is a business I'm trying to run here, not an answering service."

When Nathan answered the phone, it was Danny Forbes' voice at the other end. There was mild static on the line and Nathan guessed Danny was on a cell phone. He looked around to see if anyone was within earshot but saw only one customer wandering around the store looking at merchandise and drinking coffee. Dale tried to strike up a conversation with him but the man obviously wanted to be left alone.

"How in the world did you know I was here Danny? What's going on?" asked Nathan quietly.

Danny ignored his questions. "I hear there's a match going on," he said.

Nathan answered in the affirmative. "It's a 'come out of hibernation' kind of thing. What's up?"

"How are you doing?"

"What? You mean in the match?"

"Yes."

113

"Well, really good actually. Looks like all that training paid off. Why?"

"Is the match over yet?" There was an edge to Danny's voice now, one Nathan hadn't heard before. The easy going familiarity had disappeared and it was business being done now, unpleasant business.

"No. It's only about half over. Why? What's going on Danny? Why the third degree here?"

Except for the static there was only silence on the line for what seemed like a long time. When Danny spoke again the edge was even sharper. "Nathan, we don't want you winning any matches. If you're going to work for us, we need you to be anonymous. A well known hot shot is no good to us. Do what you want but don't win! Do you understand?"

Now it was Nathan's turn to be silent. "Sure Danny," he eventually said. "I hadn't thought of that. I understand." There was another awkward pause. Nathan watched the customer drinking coffee and looking at pistols in the display case. "Anything else Danny?"

"No," said Danny. "Nothing else."

Nathan hung up the phone gently, without saying goodbye and walked back to the ranges feeling depressed. Life was getting too complicated.

They teach him how to shoot, even convince him he can be the best shot in the world and then don't let him shoot. This was crazy. Shoot to win and forget the opportunity Danny had offered him or throw the match. Is that what it came down to, he asked himself? A born competitor, he didn't like the idea of throwing anything. Like most of the people here his competitive spirit was fierce. As long as he could remember a fire had burned within him that drove him to match his skills against others. He didn't even like playing team sports because he believed it provided no real measure of his own skills. You could have a bad day and someone else would pick up the slack, or if you were hot it often only served to make up for someone else's failings. Win or lose, Nathan wanted to be accountable for how he performed. He strove to succeed at everything he did. Never content to be second, he'd been one of the first to buy a T-shirt that said '*Second is only first place Loser.*' Now Danny Forbes wanted him to throw the match! Well, he could stuff his job. And besides that, someone had phoned and told Danny he was shooting in this competition. That probably meant Bob or Frankie. He would deal with them when he got home.

Nathan retrieved his ear muffs and safety glasses, donned them both and strode into the ranges. His squad was now in Range 1 and when his turn came up for stage five, he shot all A's at what his friends referred to as 'light speed.' Stages six and seven were two more short stages and if anything he was faster. By now the other top shooters present were there just to see who could get second and they knew it. Nathan was unbeatable.

Nathan was waiting for his turn at stage eight, the second field course and the last stage of the match for him. Like the previous field course it was made up of components of the last three short stages. Nathan found himself standing with his back to the large window that allowed people in the waiting area to see into this range. Al, another shooter whom he knew casually, was standing in front of him talking reloading technique and waved briefly to someone on the other side of the glass. Nathan turned to see who it was and saw a pretty blonde girl waving back. He smiled and nodded to her as he turned back to Al. In so doing his eyes swept across a man standing next to the girl. It was the coffee drinking customer he'd seen in the storefront during Danny's phone call, he was also watching the shooting. The man had his arms crossed while he watched and as a result his yellow jacket sleeve was pulled back somewhat, revealing the edge of a heavily tattooed stretch of forearm.

Nathan felt a chill run through him. The man was all of six feet tall with broad shoulders and large strong looking hands. Like Nathan he had blue eyes. Eyes that showed an interest in the shooter before him but revealed no emotion whatsoever. It was that coldness in the face that had caused the chill. Could he be a Rider? If so, were they watching him or even after him? Was he being paranoid? He tried to sound casual. "Who's the girl?" he asked Al.

"She's my daughter," came the reply.

"Who's the big guy beside her?" asked Nathan not turning around himself.

Al looked off over Nathan's shoulder and shrugged his own. "I have no idea. Never seen the guy. So what do you think is a good practice drill for . . ." But Nathan had turned and walked away.

He found Paul in the adjoining range, Number 2, and pulled him aside, away from the squad of shooters he was with. "Paul," he said, holding his friend by the shoulder and bending closer to get his mouth next to Paul's left ear muff. He didn't want to talk any louder than he absolutely had to. "There's a guy in the gallery of the other range watching my squad shooting. I don't know for sure but I think he might be a Rider. He looks clean cut enough but at the same time he has a hard kind of look. I'm sure he was watching me. I saw his jacket sleeve ride up when he crossed his arms, and he's spent some serious money at a tattoo parlor. You must know some of these bikers. Would you go give him the once over and tell me what you think?"

Paul's eyes were already wandering to this range's gallery window but there was no one there. Those in the gallery had gathered at Number 1's window hoping to see Nathan shoot. Nathan was somewhat surprised that Paul didn't chide him for being paranoid but rather asked for a description and told Nathan to stay in the ranges. He set off to see if he could find the man. Nathan followed Paul out into the other range, staying there as Paul carried on through and out into the public area. Nathan glanced at the gallery but as far as he could see, the man was no longer there.

Nathan moved off into the back corner of the range. The window was now six feet to his right and he leaned against the wall there. Where he stood he couldn't be seen from the gallery window and so he waited for Paul to return.

After fifteen minutes Paul still had not come back. He was thinking of going to look for him when the RO caught his eye and beckoned at him to come up.

"Hey Nathan, you're up!" he yelled. "Let's go."

Nathan detached himself from the wall slowly and scanned the window again as he walked to the stages' start point. There were more people at the window now but not the man he was looking for. He tried to shake the complication. It was time to shoot.

He was distracted. There was no doubt about it. Mentally he wasn't ready to compete. Time to focus. He resolved to try a technique learned in Arizona and began to visualize a big bubble around himself, one that kept all the confusion out. The bubble was distraction proof; they couldn't get through and they couldn't get at him. They tried, but only bounced off. It was actually funny watching the distractions bounce off. They made a funny kind of boinging sound when they hit the bubble. A noise like in a cartoon when someone gets whacked on the head with a pipe.

He tried to visualize himself calm and serene at the core of the bubble. There was immunity here and he could focus on his shooting. It was working; his mind was starting to clear. His thoughts began to crystallize as he focused on what needed to be done. He began to think his way through the stage, visualizing the targets, the tan colored paper and the lead smeared steel. He visualized the reloads, when and where they'd be executed. In his mind's eye he saw his movements, from position to position with no wasted motion. A crouch to shoot through a low port and then a hard lean to the left to shoot around a corner. Move through a short straight stretch shooting on the move. Reload. A full stop would be necessary to engage a bank of seven targets on the left side of a wall, then on with more targets waiting on the right side including a distant steel B-Zone. Lots of no-shoot targets, but they were easy enough to avoid, the angles weren't that tough.

As his mind worked its way through the stage, he began to understand it. The distractions were staying outside the bubble. They weren't influencing him here. He owned the stage now. It was his. Everything had become much clearer. He knew exactly what to do.

Nathan wasn't sure how many times the Range Officer had called his name. It wasn't until he waved his hand in front of Nathan's face that he finally broke through the 'bubble'.

"Sorry," said Nathan. "I got distracted."

"Sure," said the RO, sounding a little annoyed. Then in his official voice, "Do you understand the course of fire?"

"Yes," replied Nathan.

"Load and make ready," came the command.

Nathan performed his loading drill and moved his hands to the start position.

"Are you ready?"

Nathan nodded ever so slightly.

"Standby!"

Nathan felt himself tense.

The timer beeped, the range erupted in gunfire and between Nathan's third and fourth shots the pictures came.

He was expecting them. His concentration and focus had been complete and therefore he knew they would come. It happened when his body began operating faster than normal thought patterns could instruct it. This time it was somewhere between the third and fourth shots. Words left his consciousness and pictures replaced them. He saw images in his head, that was all. There were no words and no thoughts. To form a thought required stringing words into a recognizable order and mentally verbalizing them. For the pace at which he was now performing complicated functions, thoughts were too slow, they couldn't keep up with his movement. Only images existed – each flashing across his mind for a nanosecond; evaluating, analyzing, deciding and then showing him the way. Information was still being processed, only the method was different.

He had encountered it first in Arizona, on the night he had used the car headlights to get in extra shooting time. At first he thought it was an illusion, brought on by poor lighting and the pulsing muzzle flashes, but two days later it happened again, in broad daylight. Within a week he had learned what it meant but even now he couldn't do it on demand. One thing was certain, he was only nibbling at the fringes of the capability it suggested.

It was the Range Officer's job to watch the shooter more than the targets, that was where his responsibility lay. Being curious, however, and there normally being plenty of time, he commonly watched downrange to see how the shooter was scoring. This run, however, wasn't normal. He felt like he had to sprint to keep up with Nathan. Sprint and watch for foot faults . . . sprint and insure his finger was out of the trigger guard when required . . . sprint and keep an eye on muzzle direction. As Nathan blazed through stage eight the RO was aware of the clang of lead on steel and peripherally saw some of it dropping but he had no opportunity to see the paper hits. Except for the fact that Nathan's time was incredibly fast, he had no idea how his shooter had scored. When he had finished clearing him, the RO relaxed and for the first time took a look at the targets, at the same time becoming conscious of the gasps coming from the rest of the squad.

To confirm what he thought he was seeing the RO walked back along the line of targets. All the steel targets were down and there were two hits on each of the paper targets, including all the no-shoots. As a matter of fact, those were the only good hits. Each no-shoot was neatly centered by a pair of holes fully justified in being described as 'snake-eyes.' The targets that were supposed to have good hits had hits all right, but they were all out at the edges, virtually all D's, nothing better than a C.

The RO stared at the targets and all of his professional neutrality disappeared as he blurted, "Nathan! What happened to you? This is awful. You crashed man. You crashed and burned!"

Nathan scanned the targets from where he stood. He could see most of them as well as the RO. Shrugging his shoulders he said, "Yeah that's pretty bad isn't it." He shook his head. "I guess I got distracted."

Nathan signed his scorecard without waiting for it to be filled in. Without speaking to anyone he left the range to find Paul. The RO was sure he saw Nathan smiling as he walked out.

CHAPTER SEVEN

Nathan found Paul in the storefront, leaning on the counter, talking to Dale. As he walked up he caught the last of their conversation, it was about the man whose presence had spooked Nathan. He stayed back a polite two steps and eavesdropped. Dale remembered the man but couldn't recall having seen him in the store before, nor did he recall having seen him leave the shop. But then the place had been busy this afternoon with lots of people coming and going because of the match. Paul thanked Dale and walked off, dragging Nathan with him as he went. They stopped in the hallway by the bulletin board.

"No luck Nathan," said Paul, looking deep in thought. "He seems to be gone."

"Okay. Well, maybe I'm being a bit jumpy. It was probably some guy who just wandered in to look around." He waited for Paul to nod his agreement. It seemed the appropriate thing for Paul to do.

Instead, Paul slowly shook his head, a look of indecision on his face. "I don't know Nathan." He took off his cap and scratched his head, looking up and down the hallway before putting the hat back on and turning to Nathan. "I heard from Jim this week. Remember Jim – the guy who works the outlaw biker squad? He says the word on the street is that the Riders figure it was you who did in their Harleys and they've been looking for you."

Nathan didn't say anything. He just avoided Paul's eyes.

"Oh relax," said Paul, exasperation in his voice. "Every cop in this part of the country knows it was you who sent the Riders' Harleys to hell. They're all just sorry none of the owners

121

were on them at the time. This business with the bikers is what I wanted to talk with you about after the match. Are we still on?"

"Sure. We're still on," said Nathan. "I'm getting hungry."

"Good. Things are winding down and we should be able to get out of here in about an hour. After I present Match Winner to you and the rest of the awards to everyone else, we'll get lost."

Nathan looked down at the worn linoleum floor, intent on scuffing it with his toe. "The only award I'll be getting is the one for Turkeys. I crashed and burned on the last stage."

"Really?" said Paul. "That's too bad." Then he laughed out loud and walked away shaking his head.

An hour and a half later Paul and Nathan were ready to leave the range. As they donned their jackets and picked up their range bags Nathan noted that Paul had his department issue 5946 attached to his right hip in a high ride concealment rig. He didn't usually carry it off duty, thought Nathan, but he chose not to comment or ask about it now.

Paul's duties as Match Director meant that by definition he was ultimately responsible for everything about the competition and therefore couldn't leave until everything was done. Consequently, they emerged from the Gunsport Ranges complex among the last match participants to leave. A large modern clock tower formed the focal point of the nearby college and dominated the view at the north end of the street as they walked in its direction. The influence of the Chinook was still holding, making for a pleasant day considering the time of year. A late afternoon sun added its warmth to the few people still on the street, the last of the Saturday shoppers heading home. Like most of the other shooters, Paul and Nathan had parked in a lot owned by the college and reserved for its students. But it was Saturday and so parking at the lot was open to the public.

As they walked, Paul commented on the Match Winner's scores. "Alex did pretty well for an old guy, didn't he?"

"Goes to show you that consistency is what wins in this game."

"Yeah," said Paul chuckling. "A good reminder that old age and consistency beats youth and blinding speed every time."

Nathan swung his shooting bag, aiming it at Paul's stomach but Paul dodged it easily. "Heh, I wasn't referring to you," he said.

"Yeah, right," replied Nathan sarcastically.

At the corner they stopped and faced west, waiting for the light to change. On the other side of the street was the pizza joint where they planned to eat, while beyond that was the parking lot holding their vehicles. Neither man said anything as they waited for the light.

As they crossed the street Nathan tried to see through the dark tinted windows of the restaurant ahead. This was often the place to go for food after a day of shooting and he wondered who had gathered there now. He didn't really want to sit with a crowd. A chance to talk to Paul alone and without distractions was what he needed, so his efforts were focused on trying to spot an empty booth or table.

They were almost to the opposite curb when Nathan, about to give up trying to see through the dark glass, shifted his focus to a movement in the glass itself. The tinted glass, acting like a mirror, clearly showed the form of someone purposefully striding up behind them. He was the man Nathan had seen at the range, halfway across the street and moving rapidly toward them. His right hand was thrust deep into the pocket of his yellow ski jacket while his left swung free.

Nathan's head swiveled around to confirm what he was seeing in the mirrored window. At the turn, the man's stride hesitated but then he surged forward, his eyes locked on Nathan. His right hand came out of the pocket and a large black pistol came with it.

He was a predator; an urban one, but a predator nonetheless. He'd been watching the entrance to Gunsport and eventually his prey had emerged, totally oblivious to his presence. They were always like that, never knowing you were there till it was too late. Once identity was confirmed he had followed about twenty paces behind, stopping only long enough to look south and rub his nose. His driver flashed back a similar signal confirming all was clear. Normally he wouldn't have considered attacking outside of a place frequented by shooters, but this was Canada. He loved working in Canada and had done two previous jobs in Quebec during the biker wars there. The only people carrying guns in this country were predators like him and the cops. Here there were no worries about armed civilians making life complicated for him while he plied his trade. Even shooters like these guys were all carrying their guns unloaded and behind double locks, just as the law said they had to. If he wanted to he could kill at least three with a knife before anyone could stop him. With a gun it would be like killing a staked out lamb.

Nathan felt his world go into slow motion. In the time it took him to realize a gun was coming out of the pocket, he found he also recognized the open-top slide of the Beretta 92, either that or the Taurus copy of the same design. He couldn't really tell which. By now the gun had cleared the pocket and Nathan's vocal chords were responding to the message his brain had sent them.

"Paul! Behind you!"

Nathan turned completely then, as did Paul. Paul had seen nothing, but the tone in Nathan's voice needed no explanation. He dropped his shooting bag and as he turned, his right hand knifed aside his open coat, reaching for the grip of the stainless Smith & Wesson 9mm. By the time he was turned completely his hand was locked onto the gun and his eyes onto the threat.

The man's gun was up now, his arm fully extended toward Nathan who had a securely locked gun in his bag as well as half a dozen empty magazines. A gun in hand but unarmed. Nathan started to step aside, away from Paul, looking for someplace to run but seeing only barren concrete and pavement. The man, he noted, was aiming one handed; hopefully a sign he didn't know what he was doing . . . add a little distance and he may not be able to hit me.

The Beretta roared and Nathan wasn't sure if he'd been hit or not. Then he became aware of tinkling glass behind him and realized the shooter had missed.

Paul finished his draw stroke as the first shot rang out and it appeared as if the would-be-murderer recognized in his peripheral vision the distinctive motion of drawing a pistol. He probably hadn't expected this, thought Nathan. Everyone's guns were supposed to be locked up and empty in their clearly visible range bags. The gunman's attention switched to Paul, his pistol tracking across the open space that separated the two as he started to pull the trigger rapidly before the muzzle even centered its new target.

Paul, locked into a firing stance by now, triggered a double-tap as his view of the killer's muzzle became much too clear for his liking. His first shot missed completely. The second impacted the edge of his opponent's forearm. The bullet turned inward there and shattered the bone, it staggered the

125

shooter and caused the now useless hand to release the gun which clattered onto the pavement.

The killer barely missed a beat, reaching down he scooped up the gun with his good hand even as Paul fired twice more. Nathan saw the fabric in the chest area of the man's jacket tap inward and from his angle saw the rear fabric balloon out slightly as the bullets exited. 'Good hits,' thought Nathan. 'It's over.'

The killer, however, didn't even slow down. As he brought the gun up from the pavement he began firing as rapidly as the trigger could be pulled. With fifteen rounds in the Beretta magazine Nathan knew he had a fair amount of shooting left to do. Paul too was shooting but it wasn't double-taps any more, now he poured a continuous stream of accurate fire into the man's chest. Suddenly the killer went down, his legs buckled and the body dropped, followed by a loud thud as the back of his skull struck the pavement. He didn't move.

When the first shot was fired Nathan had heard the fragile sound of breaking glass behind him. Now a huge crash accompanied by a tidal wave of glass came from the restaurant window. A table bounced off the sidewalk between Nathan and Paul. Nathan's head turned at the sound and he looked past the table to see Paul too, lying on the street. He was on his back with his gun in his right hand and his arm extended. The muzzle was wavering as it continued to point at the still body of the killer. His finger was on the trigger, head up, trying to see if he should shoot again.

Nathan ran to him, vaulting the table that teetered on the edge of the sidewalk's curb. Movement through the remains of the glass window caught his attention as he saw a single file group of men launching themselves through the newly created hole. Each of them held a pistol high and ready to fight. Rage was stamped on their faces.

Nathan reached Paul first and snatched the pistol from his trembling hand. He looked up as the platoon of armed men descended on them forming a circle around the two friends. The circle, however, was protective. These were the other competitors, who had stopped in the restaurant and they, like all the patrons, dove to the floor when that first bullet punched through window glass. However, as *they* dove to the floor their hands clawed open gun cases and they came up from the carpet not as helpless sheep but as angry lions. Now they stood with their backs to Paul and Nathan, their guns pointing outward; every last man and the one woman who stood there, begging God silently for a target.

The closest thing they got was a dark green late model Jeep Cherokee half a block away. Tires squealed in protest as the driver cranked a hard U-turn and accelerated away from the scene at the corner. Its windows were blacked out and the occupants never seen.

The wail of distant sirens reached Nathan's ears as under the protection of the armed circle he examined Paul. A growing pool of blood under the left leg suggested that might be the place to look first. Four inches below Paul's knee an ugly wound was oozing blood and bits of bone, Nathan confirmed this was the only injury and worked to stop the bleeding. With a combination of skill and luck Paul had survived, thanks in no small part to the assassin's sloppy shooting.

One of Nathan and Paul's protectors pointed out that when the approaching sirens finally materialized into police cars it would no doubt be a wise move to disarm. The others agreed and as flashing lights appeared around the corner they carefully laid their guns on the pavement in front of them. They maintained the circle however, while one of them walked forward to meet the first officers on the scene to explain what had happened.

Once the officers had satisfied themselves as to the security of the area, the crime scene control and investigation procedures that are the reflex action of any efficient law enforcement agency took over. Like well rehearsed dancers, the officers knew their roles and no one missed a step. At first the pace was one of frantic action but then it began to slow as the tension eased and the rhythms eventually became slow and methodical. Nathan understood the change in pace, it wasn't much different from his response at an ambulance call. What he didn't understand was all of the choreography, but then it wasn't his field and he didn't get to stay around long anyway before being whisked away in the back of a police car.

Several hours later Nathan left the police station. Having called his family to assure them he was all right, he headed directly for the hospital to see Paul. It was well past visiting hours but he didn't anticipate having any problems getting in to see his friend. He was right of course, the Emergency Ward staff knew him, but it didn't help. Paul was being prepped for an operation to repair the bullet's damage and Nathan knew better than to try and push it further. He resigned himself to returning tomorrow.

Driving toward home helped him wind down from the day's events, for the first time giving him an opportunity to think about what had happened and what he was going to do about it. He found himself checking his rear view mirror, but it was fully dark now and all he could see behind him was an anonymous line of headlights. If he watched closely maybe he could keep track of which ones were turning off to their respective destinations and which ones weren't.

The killer had been after him, not Paul, of that there was no doubt. There was also no doubt in Nathan's mind that he was one of the Satan's Riders. That meant they had figured out who did in their bikes and they were out to shed some blood over it, preferably his. There was nothing he could do about it now except be ready for them if they came again. His family hadn't been bothered so hopefully it was just him they were after. Either the bikers weren't interested in them or because his mother and sister were still in hiding, the Riders hadn't found them yet. It looked like they should stay hidden.

Nathan had been watching a vehicle behind him for some time. At the next opportunity he made a right turn and watched in his rear-view mirror as it turned right also. Two blocks further, he turned left. The other vehicle didn't make that turn but continued straight through the intersection. Nathan made his way back to the through street that was taking him out of the city and resumed his thoughts.

He was glad he'd purposely blown the last stage of today's match. The decision made this afternoon had been the right one. With his family in hiding he would now work for Danny. That would get him out of town long enough that the Riders would hopefully cool down and forget about him. He could survive this, things had worked out so that he could. And, he realized now, not because of anything he had done right. So far he'd been lucky, but luck only took you so far.

Nathan didn't go home. He drove past his house and pulled into Bob's yard parking at the back of the house and thus hiding his vehicle behind Bob's shop. Bob's dog, Sandy, didn't bark, he never did at Nathan's truck. The rear light came on and Bob opened the deck doors and stepped out. Bob's right arm was extended downward and his hand was tucked in behind his leg. Nathan saw him visibly relax when he recognized who it was and at the same time caught a glimpse of blued steel in that hidden hand.

From above him on the deck Bob spoke first. "I saw the six o'clock news and since you're parking back here I guess it's safe to say you had something to do with that little altercation outside of Gunsport's?"

"Yeah," said Nathan wearily. "Did you figure that out all by yourself or did someone paint you a picture?"

"Come on in smart guy. You look beat and hungry. We'll find some dinner for you." Nathan walked up the steps and in through the open door as Bob put a friendly hand on his shoulder. "Glad you're okay Nathan."

"Thanks," said Nathan. "That's due mainly to Paul. He didn't make out as well as I did though." There was a quaver in his voice.

Frankie had a hug for Nathan. "Come in and tell us about it Nathan, maybe we can help."

The smell of cooking and the warmth of Bob and Frankie's presence drew Nathan into their home once again. He felt secure and safe here and as a result spoke freely about what had happened. The chronological details were easily related but it was Frankie who dug deeper to see what his emotional reaction was. She wasn't surprised when she saw the anger was back, just like after the bikers had shot up his sister's house.

Like Bob, she too suspected that Nathan was responsible for destroying the biker's Harleys, but by the time he'd returned from Arizona it was old news, things had died down and she hadn't brought up the topic. Now she wished she had, she'd have told him that had been a mistake and would have dire consequences. If she had done that, she could at least give him an 'I told you so' lecture tonight. There was no point in trying that now. Well, maybe he'd learned something about revenge on his own.

When the discussion turned to Danny's job offer, Nathan steered the conversation toward the phone call he'd received at the range. "Did one of you phone Danny and let him know I was going to this match?" he asked.

B-ZONE

Bob and Frankie exchanged glances and both shook their heads. "Not us," said Bob turning back to Nathan.

"Well somebody did," answered Nathan, an edge in his voice. "It seems I can't so much as burp without him finding out about it. I'll find who it was . . . don't worry, I'll find out."

The next morning Nathan walked into Paul's hospital room and found the answer. Paul was lying in bed with a heavily bandaged leg. Morning sunlight streamed in through the east facing window making the room seem brighter and cheerier than hospital rooms had any right to be. Driving into Calgary, Nathan had resolved to be that way himself, for Paul's sake. He had no idea what the prognosis was but he wanted to be as positive and encouraging as possible. As Nathan took in the room, his plans disintegrated like a lead bullet against a steel target. Sitting in a chair next to Paul's bed was Danny Forbes.

Danny stood up and walked over to Nathan, extending his hand. "Hi Nathan. Good to see you again."

Nathan took the offered hand and turned to Paul. "So, I take it I don't have to introduce this guy to you?"

"No, you don't," said Paul.

Danny returned to his seat. "I met Paul two weeks before I made you your job offer," said Danny. "I was doing background checks and thought it would be useful to get a street cop's perspective on how you might handle yourself in a shooting situation. He knows about the project."

Nathan shook his head in resignation. "You know something Danny? You really are a manipulator of the first magnitude." Turning to Paul, he said accusingly, "And you, you're not much better, are you? He called me at the range because *you* tipped him off!"

Paul seemed to think this was funny. He wore a goofy grin and giggled as the painkillers overcame his normal reserve.

131

Nathan gave up. "Oh never mind. I'll kill both of you later." Danny slid him the room's other chair and he sat down as well. "How's the leg, man? The last time we talked I was trying to plug a hole in it to keep you from bleeding all over the street." Paul was trying unsuccessfully to control his giggling. "It's pretty good. It only hurts when I laugh or somebody threatens me. The Doc said it's broken and there is some other miscellaneous damage but it should heal up okay. Because of the stainless steel pins they put in last night I won't be able to walk through an airport metal detector without setting it off but that should be the only permanent effect. It's going to be a long time, but I'll get back normal use of it, lots of time and therapy she says."

"That's good to hear," said Nathan, his tone becoming serious. "I was afraid there might be something permanent."

"No. Nothing that won't heal," said Paul.

Nathan looked over at Danny. "So how come you're here?" he asked.

"Paul called to give me the news that you had deliberately blown your last stage. Frankly, that was welcome information. Within two hours I heard about this little incident so I caught the night flight out here to see what's going on for myself." Danny looked intently at Nathan. "So what's the word? Does the fact that you blew your last stage mean you're coming back to the ranch?"

"No," said Nathan. "At that point all I wanted to do was keep my options open. I was pretty ticked off when you told me you didn't want me to win any matches, but some common sense filtered through at the last minute. At that point I realized getting myself locked into one particular course of action would not be smart. But now Paul has this hole in his leg and as far as I'm concerned, *that* means I'm coming back to Arizona with you. I think it would be best to get lost for a while."

"Sounds good," said Danny thoughtfully, as he got up to leave. "And consider this an apology for not telling you ahead of time that you weren't to burn up the ranges with your skills. It was an oversight on my part. I didn't anticipate you getting into a major match. Again, I apologize."

"Wait a minute," said Nathan. "Aren't you worried about the publicity that could come my way as a result of this shootout? If you don't want me winning pistol matches you surely don't want the publicity from this gunfight on 43rd Street."

Danny stopped at the door. "You're right Nathan. We'd prefer as little publicity be brought your way as possible. In this case the witness' statements indicate no one saw the first shot being fired specifically at you, all they saw was the short gunfight between Paul and the biker. An off duty police officer engaged in a simple righteous shooting is all this is. Paul will attract some publicity but you're just another witness. The accused is dead so there will be no trial although there will have to be some form of inquest or inquiry. That's all. My RCMP liaison officer tells me the Chief here in Calgary and Paul's boss will both be receiving suggestions later this week on how this matter should be handled. I don't anticipate any problems."

When the echo of Danny's footsteps had faded down the hallway, a puzzled look came across Nathan's face. He looked around the room in mock bewilderment. "Do you hear it Paul?" he asked.

"Hear it? Hear what?"

"It sounds like . . . no, it couldn't be."

"What are you talking about? I don't hear anything."

"It's gone now, but just as he left I was sure I heard the theme music from X-Files."

Paul was quick to laugh and just as quickly winced in pain and grabbed his leg. "Cut it out," he said. "That hurts."

CHAPTER EIGHT

Nathan Burdett devoted the remainder of that week to living carefully. He paid close attention to where he went, what he did and whom he was with. When in public, his right hand spent a good deal of time in the large right pocket of his jacket, clutching a Glock model 23 he had won at a match in Spokane four years ago.

At the earliest opportunity he'd gone to the local RCMP Firearms Officer, and asked about obtaining a permit to carry the Glock lawfully. Nathan knew these permits were almost never granted and was pleasantly surprised to find a sympathetic and understanding ear. After listening to Nathan's strategically told story he conceded that yes, on the face of it these were the sort of circumstances under which a permit might be issued. If Nathan wished to apply for one an investigation would commence and if justification was found he would indeed recommend the issuance of the carrying permit. This could all be done in a couple of weeks, barring any unavoidable delays in the necessary paperwork of course.

Delays? Nathan thought getting killed was a delay, and getting shot wasn't necessary and surely was avoidable. He planned to be in Arizona in a week, though he couldn't tell the Firearms Officer that. A carry permit in two weeks did him no good whatsoever, so he politely told him to forget it and quietly kept the Glock in his pocket.

Nathan had a firm direction now and as a result he worked like a person with a plan. There was a destination to arrive at and things that had to be done in order to get there. He helped his mother make arrangements to sell the house and property and helped her look for something more permanent than the apartment she was living in. Storage, moving and sale of all their other goods, as well as the sale of his truck, were all necessary. Nathan was also going to sell most of his guns until Bob talked him out of that, agreeing to store them for him instead. He'd been on a leave of absence from work but now a formal resignation was submitted.

And therefore on the following Monday, eight days after the attempt on his life, he was once again pushing a luggage cart out of the Tucson terminal. The drive back to the ranch was made with George, who was no more talkative than usual. And the ranch, when they arrived, was as quiet as George. No people were seen moving about the facility and only three vehicles were parked in front of the main buildings. When Nathan got out of the Suburban, he heard gunfire coming from the direction of the ranges and asked George about the shooting.

"You didn't think we'd hold this place empty, just waiting for you, did you?" George gruffed, "We got a job to do here besides training you kids."

"Hey. Now that we're not keeping secrets any more, what is this place really?" said Nathan. "I never thought to ask about what this place really does."

George opened the back doors of the Suburban and let one of Nathan's bags fall onto the ground without making any effort to stop it. "We put the sign back up after you all left," said George. He pointed toward the ranch's office, where the rock garden around the flag pole now had a large heavy wooden sign planted in the middle of it. The weathered log sign, carved with a chainsaw, looked like it had been there forever, in large block letters it read LOST GLOVE RANCH.

"Okay," said Nathan. "So you actually have a name for this place. But that doesn't tell me what you do here George? George?" He turned to look for George and saw him limping off to the ranges. "Thanks for the help George!" he yelled after him as sarcastically as he could manage. Hauling out the remainder of his bags and piling them in one spot on the hard packed Arizona dirt took a few minutes and then he set off toward the ranch office to find his assigned accommodation.

Nathan was again given one half of a cabin. It wasn't the same one as last time but you couldn't tell that from the inside. On the desk in the room was a faxed message from Danny telling him to get comfortable, unpack and that Danny would be around to see him after breakfast tomorrow. With nothing else planned, Nathan did just that. This place was home now, like it or not. There was a familiarity here but that was all. He wondered how long he'd have to live here before it became home but then realized just as quickly that the cabin would have little to do with it. How the people here treated him now would make the difference, and George hadn't been a good start.

With the unpacking finished Nathan was faced with killing some time so he picked up the novel he'd started on the airplane. After collecting a cold drink from the vending machine by the ranch office he settled into a wooden chair on the cabin's veranda. Putting his feet up on the railing that ran across the front of the porch he returned to the unfinished paperback, a western. It occurred to Nathan that this was an appropriate place to read it; in the Arizona desert, on the veranda of a ranch building, with his chair tilted back against the wall squinting across what could pass for a dusty street. Maybe he was born a hundred and twenty years too late. Nathan Burdett could have lived in the old west quite comfortably, he thought. Well, perhaps, but only if life really was anything like that depicted in the 'duster' novels or movies that provided him an enjoyable distraction. Oh well, that probably wasn't the case he thought, most likely it was a boring place. He stopped his daydreaming and turned back to the book.

Nathan had been absorbed in his book for twenty minutes and his now lukewarm drink was almost gone when the sound of someone stepping onto the veranda to his left made him look up. It was Kim. He dog eared one of the book's pages and closed it as she walked over.

"Hi Nathan," she said. "Welcome back." She remained standing and leaned against the railing looking down at him.

"Hi Kim. Nice to see you again." Nathan motioned to the other chair on the porch. "Sit down." Nathan took his feet down from the railing so she could walk by him and get the chair.

She pulled it over, closer to Nathan and settled into it with a sigh. "Hot today."

"Yeah."

"Have a good flight?"

"Yeah."

"What are you reading?"

"A book."

Kim was quiet for a few moments. "Okay," she finally said, her brown eyes fixing on Nathan's face, "I apologize for the deception. I was part of it. I knew all along what was going on. You do understand that it was necessary?"

It was Nathan's turn to be quiet. He drained the last of his drink. "Sure, I guess I can understand that. And I've accepted everybody else's apology so I'll accept yours too. Well everybody's but George's. He hasn't apologized yet, but then I don't expect he will."

Kim laughed. "Oh, you're probably right about that."

"I guess from here on I won't be shooting at targets?" said Nathan.

"Oh there will still be targets," said Kim. "It's just that these could be shooting back. Think you can handle it?"

137

Nathan turned to look at her. She had said that like someone who had been there and had the T-shirt. Kim continued to stare out over the ranch yard as Nathan studied her intently, seeing nothing on the face to indicate one way or the other. "If the training they're going to give me now is as good as what they gave me for the first three months, then, yeah, I think I can handle it." There was a pause in the conversation as they watched a dust devil dance across the yard. Nathan spoke first, quietly, still gazing out over the railing. "About a week ago I had a little taste of what it might be like."

Kim raised her eyebrows and turned to face Nathan. "Really? What happened?" she questioned.

Nathan then for the first time, told Kim most of what had been happening with the Satan's Riders, from the accident with Todd, to the attempted murder of him on the streets of Calgary and how Paul had saved his life. "You really didn't know did you?" he finally said.

"No, I didn't," said Kim. "Danny's like that. He won't reveal a lot of personal details about a candidate's background. Well," she corrected herself, "I guess you're not really a candidate any more. Now you're a team member."

That gave Nathan reason to pause; a team member . . . maybe things would change now. But it brought up another question. "And what's *your* role in this team?" he asked. "Still more PT?"

Kim smiled. "Lots more PT," she said, with what sounded like sadistic joy. "But I'll be assisting with all other aspects of your training as well and when you go operational I'll sometimes travel with you and help out on some of the projects." She steered the subject back to the bikers then. "So how come this guy was trying to shoot you? You never told me that."

Nathan had deliberately omitted his role in shooting up the Harleys but now he told her about that portion of it as well.

He cautioned her not to mention any of that to Danny. "He knows," said Nathan, "but he hasn't brought it up and I'd just as soon leave it that way."

"That was a remarkably dumb stunt," said Kim. "I thought you were smarter than that."

That stung. "What can I say," said Nathan, shrugging. "It seemed like a good idea at the time. I guess I was pretty mad. You would be too if it happened to you."

"I suppose I would," replied Kim. "I suppose I would. I sincerely hope you've seen the last of those guys Nathan. A lifetime of looking over your shoulder doesn't sound like a lot of fun."

"You're right. That's part of the reason I'm here. I'm hoping to get good and lost for a long time and have everyone forget the whole thing. I want nothing more to do with them."

"I hope it works out that way," she said. During their conversation gunfire had started at one of the ranges. Nathan's feet had made their way back up on the rail and now Kim jumped up and kicked them off with glee. "Come on," she said. "Let's go for a walk. I bet I know who's wasting all that ammo. I'll introduce him to you."

They moved out from the shade of the veranda into the yellow heat of the day and started walking toward the ranges. There was still shooting going on, the sound consistent with a single shooter practicing. As they walked, Radar appeared and trotted along beside them.

They found a shooter on the first range plinking away at a bank of steel plates with a handgun, a portable table holding his ammo and magazines stood beside him. He saw them walk up while reloading and Kim gave him a small wave. He returned it before loading another magazine in his pistol and turning back to the standing steel. The shooter was in his fifties and relatively small and thin. Heavy prescription glasses were perched on his nose and he sported a short, neatly trimmed goatee. The gun appeared to be a fairly stock 1911 and his accuracy was entirely credible. He didn't display any great speed, in fact he was quite slow, but then it didn't look as if he was trying for speed either.

They watched from the back of the range as the shooter fired three more magazines after which he turned and walked back to where Nathan and Kim were leaning against one of the trailers. Kim waited till he removed his hearing protection.

"Nathan, this is Dr. Miles Papin."

They politely shook hands and Nathan spoke first. "I've heard that name before. Are you the same Dr. Papin who's done the research on mental aspects of armed encounters?"

The doctor smiled. "Yes, that'll be me. Have you read some of my research?"

"No, not really," confessed Nathan. "I've heard of it second hand. You get mentioned in some of the popular gun magazines occasionally. That's really all I know about your work."

The Doctor nodded knowingly. "Yes. Yes. That's how most people have heard of my work. But you must allow me to say that it really is much more scholarly than what is often portrayed in those newsstand gun magazines. They do little more than summarize some of the highlights. If they get it right at all," he added, emphasizing the 'if'.

Sensing a lecture coming on, Kim interrupted. "Dr. Papin is going to be your first instructor in this portion of your training Nathan, and you have your first session with him tomorrow, right after breakfast."

"That's great," said Nathan. "I've got some medical background because of my EMT training but not much in the way of psychology so I'm sure I'll find it interesting."

The doctor nodded and Nathan saw there were dancing blue eyes behind the thick glasses. "I'm sure we can have a good and a profitable time together, Nathan. However, the name is Miles. Please feel free to drop the Doctor title entirely."

"Whatever you say," said Nathan.

Kim jumped in, "Who wants to go to town for something to eat?"

"I'm in," said Miles.

"Me too," added Nathan and the negotiations for where to go began.

The next morning after breakfast in the ranch's small cafeteria the same threesome made the short walk to the classroom where they found Danny waiting. As they conferred with him, Nathan noticed something different about Danny. The clothes were not what he was used to seeing him in; instead of the suit and tie or the casual businessman's clothing that had been his standard apparel, today he wore part of a tactical uniform. His dark blue combat trousers were bloused at the top of black jump boots and he wore a black T-shirt with an H-K logo and the silhouette of an MP5 on the right breast. It was more than the clothes though. The businessman and government administrator he had come to know had been replaced by someone else. There was no bureaucrat here. He didn't make suggestions like he once had; now he gave orders. Politeness was still there but the firmness had increased, the edges hard. Nathan suspected this was the Danny Forbes who led men into harm's way, and not from the rear either.

Danny outlined the program for the days to come. "For the next month, the schedule will be pretty much the same every day. Physical training every morning at 0600 hrs. with Kim. Breakfast at 0730 hrs. Classroom session at 0800 hrs. Dr. Papin here, will be your instructor for the first week and others will come in on rotation. Lunch at noon and then tactics with me each afternoon in either the classroom or on the range, or maybe both. Remember I told you the last time you were here that I can't teach you anything about how to shoot. That's still true. I'll teach you tactics. Tactics I know, that's my job. After dinner you are expected to keep working on your shooting skills by practicing on your own. Weekends are off.

"Understand too, Nathan," said Danny, "That while Kim will be your PT instructor, we will also use her as an operational partner when required. She will train with you as an assistant and will be used in a logistical and tactical support role. Any questions?"

Nathan responded with a "No sir." He hadn't intended to add the 'sir,' never having used one before when talking to Danny. It just seemed to fit now.

As Miles Papin taught, Nathan learned and in so doing slowly began to see the fascination in this field of study. He learned about the physical and psychological responses that can occur in body and mind when a person enters a potentially deadly struggle.

Nathan was even able to identify some of the phenomena the doctor talked about in his own survival of the murder attempt on him outside Gunsport Ranges. His recollection of how he had been able to identify the make of the pistol the gunman had pulled from his pocket did not surprise the doctor in the least. This was explained to him as tachypsychia. Nathan hadn't realized there was a clinical name for things appearing to occur in slow motion and it took several tries to get the pronunciation right. He wasn't sure he would ever be able to spell it.

In the days that followed he also learned about auditory exclusion. How the ears seem to shut down and shouts, noises even gunfire, cannot be heard or are barely discernible. When he pointed out that in the same situation quite the opposite had happened to him, he had clearly heard the glass breaking, the doctor conceded that in some people he had indeed found the opposite to occur; that is, enhanced hearing. There was no explanation for why it occurred in some but not in others but it was a documented fact.

Nathan reviewed case histories, read statements from both witnesses and participants in armed confrontations and watched videotaped interviews and reenactments. There were similarities, he saw, between a competitor like himself walking up to the line at a match and having to deliver then and there and the person who finds himself in a life or death struggle on a dark street. Much of the resemblance, he concluded, was because of the adrenaline dump that occurs within the body in a high stress situation, the epinephrine that causes trembling hands, a pallid face, loss of fine motor skills, massive increases in strength and who knew what else. He'd seen competitors, first timers especially, so nervous they puked their guts out before a match, their hands shaking so badly the RO made them take a 'time out.' For Nathan, controlling that sort of thing at a pistol match was an achievable task, but he remembered holding a long range rifle on a moon bathed hillside and losing that mastery over his body. The memory made him wonder what he would have to do in order to maintain it in his new role.

Danny's training time complimented what the doctor was teaching and Nathan came to the realization that tactics did not exist in isolation from what Miles Papin taught. It all fit together. One morning Miles explained tunnel vision, a phenomenon in which a person loses their peripheral vision and becomes unaware of what is happening outside of a narrow cone of interest. In the afternoon Danny demonstrated how to overcome it and they did drills that forced Nathan to evaluate and deal with indistinct threats at ninety degree angles to a primary target.

"Just because you see only one person trying to kill you," he explained, "be aware that there may be others that aren't obvious. Look around. Don't assume anything. Be alert."

Nathan noticed he never took a classroom session alone. One of the other three, Kim, George or Danny was always present. He wasn't sure if they just didn't want him to feel lonely or if they were monitoring his interaction with the instructor.

One of the more interesting phenomena was precognition; explained by the doctor, as the ability to accurately predict an individual's actions. When Nathan began humming the theme to The Twilight Zone, Kim jabbed him in the ribs.

Miles, overhearing, said, "No, no. This is not ESP or seeing the future or any of that mumbo jumbo. When this phenomenon manifests itself, what occurs, as best we can determine, is that the subconscious mind observes and records behavior clues that a potential assailant gives out. The mind correlates these clues and filters them through its training and experience which, if adequate, can be enough to accurately predict what the threat will do next."

"Like telegraphing a draw?" suggested Nathan.

"Exactly. Think about the physical motions required to draw a pistol from a holster or even from a pocket. The first physical action that most people take will not be moving their hand, they invariably move their feet to achieve a better balance. But even before that, they shift their weight to one foot so that they can move the other. An experienced officer sees that weight shifting, maybe not even consciously, and his alarm bells go off. It's called precognition."

"Sounds like that can be used against someone too," added Nathan.

"Definitely," agreed Miles. "And that's something to remember about all the phenomena we've discussed. You'll be subject to some or all of them but so will your adversaries. Your advantage comes from the fact that you know about them while your adversary doesn't." He pointed at Nathan, "That is a significant edge."

In the afternoons, with Danny as primary instructor, they spent time unlearning what Nathan had acquired as poor tactical habits. The habits were good ones from a competitive perspective but competition, he already knew, does not entirely simulate reality. Chief among these sins, as Danny referred to them, was the poor or ineffective use of cover. He detailed the difference between cover and concealment; the former will protect while the latter will only hide he explained, as he showed Nathan how to use both properly. Using the props that were available on the ranges Danny showed him how to obtain meaningful cover while shooting over, under or around objects. Sometimes speed was sacrificed but Danny demonstrated how to determine when speed was primary and when it was secondary.

"Aggressive speed or defensive cover is one of the toughest choices you'll have to make," he said. "And you won't have more than a fraction of a second to make the decision. If you choose wisely you'll be able to explain your choice at the after-action debriefing. If you make the wrong decision . . . the relative details will come out at your inquest."

By the second week Kim had started to pick up the pace of the morning workouts. The runs, sit-ups and pushups that were the staple of her physical training when all six of the candidates had been at the ranch were now a fond memory. Kim had brought free weights into one of the empty cabins and she began using them with what Nathan was sure was too much enthusiasm. Lung busting runs and intense workouts formed every morning's ritual and Nathan predicted Kim would make him stronger and fitter than he had ever been.

The Drill Sergeant – Amazon Lady persona that was Kim's had all but disappeared and was replaced by The Coach. The Coach was still firm but she was kinder and even allowed a small degree of friendliness. It was demonstrated in their runs. Previously all the candidates had run behind Kim but now Nathan ran beside her. Radar's position, of course, did not change – he trotted in front of everyone. The three of them were on a five mile run into the desert when Nathan determined to see how different The Coach really was.

"How come you don't have an Israeli accent Kim?" he asked shortly after they started out.

"You mean a Hebrew accent," Kim corrected. "I learned to speak English long before I did Hebrew. I was born here."

"Really?"

"Really. Chicago. One of the suburbs. My parents moved our family to Israel when I was eleven. I knew some Hebrew before we emigrated but actually learned it there. And English is very much present in Israel so I had no problem maintaining it." Her words were spaced and rhythmic, as if keeping time with the soft thud of her feet on the old road leading into the hills.

"So this is like coming home for you."

"More like visiting an old family friend. Israel is my home, not by birth but by choice. You see Nathan, Israel is largely a land of immigrants. Don't forget that it didn't exist as a modern country until after the Second World War."

"I knew that," said Nathan, "but I've never really thought of it as being a country of immigrants. I guess that makes sense considering its history." Neither spoke as they labored up a short hill. Dust puffed up from their shoes as they planted them methodically into the ground gaining elevation each time, with Radar waiting patiently at the top. Nathan continued down the other side. "So I take it you have no desire, like the rest of the world, to move to the good old USA?"

"Not me. I'm where I belong."

Nathan tried shifting topics. "You seem to know a lot about physical training. Do you have some education in this stuff?"

"Very perceptive," said Kim. "I have a degree in physical education from Tel Aviv University. That and my good English is probably why they sent me here."

"That and your police experience?" prompted Nathan.

"That too," she said.

"You join up right out of University?"

"No I didn't. I served two years in the IDF first."

"IDF?"

"Sorry," said Kim. "Israeli Defense Forces."

"Oh," replied Nathan. "Military and then police?" They were both sweating profusely and the words came harder as the breath to form them became scarcer.

"Yeah," said Kim. "That's pretty much it."

"So what's police work like over there?"

"Probably not much different from North America. Thieves, drugs, booze, assaults, all the usual stuff."

"What about all the terrorists."

"There are special units that handle those."

"Ever work with any of them?" He was pushing it now and he knew it.

"Yes." She said it tersely, with no elaboration. They ran on in silence for a few minutes. Then she slowed the pace slightly. It could have been part of the interval training but Nathan had the feeling she wanted to have enough breath to be able to make something clear to him. "You've got to understand Nathan, our country is surrounded by enemies whose sworn goal is to destroy us as a people and a nation. These enemies are

147

inside our country as well as outside and they'll stop at nothing to achieve that goal. To me and a lot of others that means we have to pursue and eradicate them with the same vigor. If we don't we will lose and we will die. I'll do whatever is necessary to prevent that from happening."

Nathan tried to see her face to read what he could beyond the words. But the bouncing hair and beads of sweat masked whatever was there, if anything. "I can't relate to that," he said.

"No, of course not," said Kim. She picked up the pace again and Nathan took that to mean the topic was closed. He concentrated on his breathing.

It was during the second week that another doctor, an expert in wound ballistics, arrived and Nathan began to study the morbid details of what bullets do to human flesh. Here Nathan, with his medical training, had some grasp of the technical language. As the doctor came to realize this, he easily slipped into a more technical medical idiom and Nathan delighted in replying in kind and watching whoever had been assigned to sit in the class with him get lost in the jargon.

Danny was there for one morning session that the doctor had entitled 'Instant Incapacitation' and took the floor before the doctor did. "This is a key one," he said. "The good doctor here, is going to tell you where to shoot someone so that they immediately cease whatever action it is that's threatening you or someone else. The emphasis is on 'immediately.' Often there are likely to be people around who are innocents. Therefore stray shots from the bad guys, spasmodic jerking of the trigger finger, even reflex twitching that might cause their gun to go off and send a bullet labeled 'to whom it may concern' will have to be avoided as much as possible."

Danny then turned the floor over to the doctor who immediately slid an X-ray onto the overhead projector and asked

Nathan if he recognized it. Somewhat surprised, Nathan conceded that he did not. This, the doctor pointed out, was the torso of the man who had tried to kill Nathan. A series of red dots indicated the strikes of Paul Simmons' bullets. Reading portions of three witness statements dealing with Paul's final burst of gunfire at the killer he pointed out that Paul's shots into the man's chest had no apparent effect until suddenly the man collapsed and fell to the street. He then read an excerpt from the medical examiner's report which detailed six bullet strikes in the central chest region, all of which penetrated to either heart or lungs and all of which would have eventually been fatal. He emphasized 'eventually.' The autopsy report listed one other bullet as having reached the spinal column, severing it and causing immediate collapse.

"It would be hard to imagine a better example," said the Doctor, "of the importance of bullet placement in achieving instant incapacitation. Forget everything you have seen in the movies or on TV about this topic, virtually none of it is true. To achieve immediate incapacitation you must disrupt your adversary's central nervous system, either by severing the spinal column, as happened here, or by a direct shot to the brain. Since the spinal column is a very narrow target with a lot of mass protecting it from the front and the brain is much larger and more vulnerable, the brain shot is the only effective shot that you can take."

"Additionally, it's the only place you can be assured of no body armor," added Danny from behind Nathan.

"B-zone," said Nathan to no one in particular. Then he swiveled in his seat to face Danny. "That's why you called it The B-Zone Project isn't it?"

"That's right Nathan. The accepted gospel in virtually all firearms' combat training is always aim for center of mass, that means torso or chest. It's absolutely correct too, and the reason it's right is that under combat conditions most people are not capable of the kind of accuracy needed for a central nervous system shot. About the only exceptions are snipers and that's only because of the solid rest they can usually take as well as the specialized equipment and training they get. But remember that's what I said you are, a high speed, short range sniper. The bottom line is this, if you are going to fulfill your mission you will have to do close range head shots with a handgun at warp speed."

The room was quiet. Danny sensed the stadium lights had just come on and reality was making its entrance onto the playing field. What had started out as a game or a contest was now in the second half and had turned into a deadly confrontation in which people would die. Danny saw the growing realization in Nathan's eyes that a time would come when, standing alone with only his courage and his skills he would face an opponent on that field – waiting for the scoreboard to record the outcome. And whatever the score was, it would be final for one of them.

"Let me remind you," Danny said, "of the fact that you are likely the best pistol shot on the planet. The only reason I believe this will work is because of your abilities. I cannot make it work, there isn't a cop or a soldier anywhere that can make this work. The only reason it's possible is because of who you are and what you can do; translated that means the courage I believe lies within you and the skills I know you have. Your abilities are, in effect, allowing us to rewrite the rule book about how this is done."

The doctor carried on then, showing slides, discussing medical theory and also running news crew video clips of various and assorted people being shot by police. Nathan learned the significance of the medulla; an egg sized portion of the brain at the very top of the spinal column. This, the doctor explained, is where all involuntary motion originates and is theoretically the most precise location to direct an instantly incapacitating shot. Practically speaking though, he taught that the damage generated by any shot from a powerful firearm into the region around the medulla will have the same effect as a direct hit. The result simply being an instant lights out with no twitching or spasmodic movements, just a sudden drop to the floor.

The session was almost over and they were starting to think about lunch when a thought that had been working its way through Nathan's mind came to the surface.

"What if I don't need to kill someone? Perhaps it can be avoided and all that's necessary is to disable them? Where do I shoot them then?"

The doctor was at a momentary loss for words but Danny spoke up. "You will never be deployed if the death of the perpetrator is not a morally or legally acceptable outcome. A request to 'only disable' someone will not be entertained because the risk is too great. If the circumstances warrant that you shoot, then you have to be prepared to shoot to kill. I suppose the doctor could give us anatomical locations where a surgically placed bullet could disable someone, at least in theory, but the consequences of not being able to pull it off are too serious to consider."

"Wait a minute," said Nathan. "Earlier this morning you said I had such high abilities that we were rewriting the rule book. Now you're saying I'm not good enough to pull off a disabling shot as opposed to a killing one. I think maybe you're wrong." He turned back to the doctor standing at the front of the classroom. "Where do I aim for a disabling shot Doc?"

"I've never been asked that question before," came the answer. "I suppose . . ."

Danny cut him off. "Don't bother Doc, this is a non-starter. Nobody here is going to be shooting guns out of people's hands *a la* Roy Rogers. This is one thing we're going to do the way we've always done it. Shoot to kill. If they survive, that's fine, but no fancy stuff. We've already set a higher standard for you, Nathan, by suggesting that your most frequent target will be the medulla. That's tough enough, going beyond that is absolutely unrealistic.

"Class is dismissed," said Danny. "Meet you after lunch at the range."

Class was finished but Nathan's mind wasn't through with the topic. Continuing to think about it, he sifted through the medical knowledge his EMT training and experience had conferred upon him. He wondered if Danny was right.

Eventually, one of the sessions with the wound ballistics expert led to a discussion of what caliber and bullet type would best serve Nathan's purposes. The doctor's opinion was that the .45 ACP with a heavy expanding bullet design was the best choice. It was his belief that to get through the heavy facial bones as large a caliber as possible and as heavy a bullet as possible was necessary to provide a straight wound track to the target area. Danny agreed and spelled out his agency's experience with the .45 to Nathan, especially in the hands of the Hostage Rescue Team. It had all been positive. Danny followed up by presenting him with a custom 1911 of the same configuration as currently being issued to their HRT.

"This is just a start," he explained. "You'll have more than a dozen pistols issued to you before this portion of your training is over, concealable guns, large guns, compensated guns, guns with flashlights attached and guns with electronic sights, the best guns for the job, built and tuned any way you want, plus spares. Shoot this one for a couple of days and then start making out a wish list. I have an agreement from the firm who makes these. They'll fast track any orders I call in, so it won't take long. From now on I'd like you retire your .38 Super. It's a great competition caliber, but it's not for the real world."

"My times are going to go up with a stock gun like this," said Nathan.

"Compared to your Super, yes," agreed Danny. "But feel free to order a .45 tricked out in whatever way will increase your speed. Don't be shy on this. I know it's always the shooter who makes the difference but part of the reason we have better shooters than we've ever had is the quality and type of equipment available now. You will have the best and you will have what works for you."

To balance out the issued stock gun, Nathan immediately ordered two new .45's, a fully equipped match gun and a compact carry gun. When five thousand rounds had churned through each of those he ordered more. He shot those guns and ordered more and then shot them and ordered still more. Guilty feelings about the money he was spending occasionally rose to the surface but vanished as quickly as a puff of gunsmoke, largely because of the sore muscles inflicted during Kim's workouts. Additionally, the tactical training was becoming more physical as the scale of realism increased. Bruises, scrapes and cuts were now the reward for showing up for one of Danny's afternoon sessions. The daily pain soothed Nathan's conscience about the expensive guns he kept ordering.

More instructors circulated through the ranch, sharing their knowledge with Nathan in an effort to prepare him for his role. He began to learn the behind the scenes basics of SWAT operations as specialists in communications, surveillance technology and negotiations visited the ranch. Explosive experts lectured about their skills and conducted minor demonstrations. A tour of an aircraft, a Boeing 737, was arranged so that Danny could explain the process a rescue team might use to defuse a hostage situation on an airliner. To discuss legal issues, two law instructors from the Bureau's Academy arrived one morning, both had law degrees and held full agent status as well. They took turns leading a discussion about when shooting another human being was justified and when it was not.

After breakfast on a cool and cloudy Monday Nathan reported to the classroom to find the week's schedule listed the morning instructor as G. Markatz. The name meant nothing to him and there was no indication what the topic was, so he massaged sore muscles, wondered and waited. He was still wondering when George stepped into the classroom.

"Morning George," said Kim, who was sitting in with Nathan this day.

George as usual, didn't respond but he did capture Nathan's interest when he closed the door and, with a loud clack, threw the deadbolt into its locked position. The interest level moved up another notch as George, without a word, walked to the front of the classroom and began peeling off his clothes. Nathan looked over at Kim and the two shared an agreeing glance to the effect that the old boy had finally lost it.

This was embarrassing for the old guy thought Nathan, he was about to get up and gently herd him out of the room when Kim, reading his face, shook her head in objection. George continued disrobing, not uttering a word until all of his clothes, except for his boxers, which he thankfully still wore, were neatly piled on a chair. By the time he was done he didn't need to say anything, the clearly visible scars on his body said it all.

"The topic this morning," said George, "is survival. At least that's what I'm supposed to teach you. I figure I'm no expert but not everyone agrees with me and so I'm here. We're going to talk about getting hit by bullets and finding the will to survive while those around you are dying. Any questions?"

Both Nathan and Kim listened in rapt attention as the old man told them story after story about shooting incidents. Initially the stories were personal ones, linked to a scar on his body that showed where a bullet's passage had left its mark. George's voice cracked when he talked of missing friends and it became obvious that the bullets besides marking his body had also marked his mind and emotions. At other times when he spoke of those who had tried to kill him and failed, his voice was hard and cold. Then he moved on to personal stories that had no physical scars linked to them. There was a black humor present in all the stories and Nathan recognized it as a coping mechanism developed by people who frequently encounter violence. Finding humor in violent death was something he had used himself as an EMT. It helped keep you sane.

Eventually George progressed to tales in which he was not personally involved. He was most comfortable with these, observed Nathan, there was distance to these stories that provided security. Like the others there was a lesson to be extracted from each one. The message was obvious and usually about never giving up, about striving till you won, but George bluntly pointed it out anyway.

When he was done Nathan and Kim plied him with questions. George answered them succinctly but contrary to his normal behavior, with care and patience. When the clothes were put back on, it was a sign the session was over and once he'd left, Nathan and Kim went to the cafeteria for lunch. Danny was there already and he waved them over when they had picked up their trays.

"You guys are quiet today," commented Danny, when no one at the table had spoken for five minutes.

"Just thinking I guess," said Kim, glancing at Nathan, who was spending an inordinate amount of time chewing on a mouthful of salad.

"What did you think of George's stories?" asked Danny. "It's incredible that one person could have run into so many gunfights," replied Nathan, speaking at last. "Yeah. It is if you don't know all the details," said Danny. "George doesn't tell you the details about the work he was doing at the time, and although I know most of them, I'm not going to tell you either in deference to his wishes. They did call him a human bullet magnet in his day though."

"I can see why," agreed Kim.

"Another thing he probably didn't tell you, is that he lives in constant pain from that leg wound of his. Personally, I think that's why he's grouchy at times. You need to know that to understand him. Don't be too hard on George."

"No fear of that now," said Nathan.

After lunch they walked to the ranges with Danny and saw some unusual equipment set up on the short range. There were six identical and highly complex steel targets positioned about three-quarters of the way to the earthen backstop. As they examined them, Danny explained.

"This is one of the final phases of your tactical training. With this equipment, over the next few weeks, we are going to learn what your capabilities really are. Each of these steel contraptions has a B-Zone head target dimensioned to accurately reflect the brain shot you've been practicing. Connected to it, in the torso area, is an air powered paintball gun that fires a conventional dye filled marking ball. Mounted on the gun is a video camera and manipulating the gun is a remote control system that allows an operator behind the firing line to aim and fire it. A proper B-Zone shot will activate a sensor which will in turn deactivate the gun and prevent you from being shot, just like with a real adversary. So, tell me – what do you think?"

"This is incredible," said Nathan, walking around the device and examining the back side. "I've never even heard of anything like this. These things really work?"

"They certainly do," said Danny. "It's a relatively new product put out by a company in Florida. We've played with them in Quantico a little but only enough to know there's real potential here. I've contracted with the firm for six targets and one technician for as long as we need them. We're going to give them a good shakedown here and if they perform, this outfit is going to get a sizeable government contract."

"These paintball guns hurt," whined Nathan as he examined the gun and its magazine full of red balls.

"Just like real bullets," agreed Danny. "That's the idea. You'll get goggles to protect your eyes and face but that's it, if you don't want welts shoot fast, accurately and use cover wisely. Come back into the trailer, you can check out the remote units and I'll introduce you to Colin."

In the trailer, they found George sitting with a young overweight man, at a bank of joysticks, each of which was paired with a small monitor. Danny introduced him as Colin, the representative from the company marketing the shoot-back target system. Danny directed Nathan's attention to one of the monitors. It displayed a view from one of the targets' guns.

"The target body itself doesn't move," said Colin adjusting his glasses. "At least not on this model, although we are working on one where the torso will rotate. In this case only the gun/camera combination moves." He tracked the gun across some other targets to demonstrate and fired a shot at one. They saw the gun fire on the monitor but heard the pop of its report out the open door. The operator fired again and immediately tracked to another target firing at it.

"That's impressive," said Nathan. "George, why don't you go stand outside there and I'll see if I can hit you?"

"I don't think so," said George, not looking up.

Nathan turned to the technician, "That gun seems to respond quickly enough to your controls Colin, but can it move as fast as a real person with a gun."

"It's close," came the reply. "We're using state of the art high speed robotics with this unit and we've set it up to closely simulate the speed and precision with which the human arm can move."

"What happens if a bullet hits the camera?"

Colin shook his head. "You'll do a first class job of destroying it, that's what. They're shielded against lead splatter from strikes to the steel body but they can't withstand a direct hit. Besides, Danny told me you're pretty good and I don't have to worry about cameras being shot. Isn't that right Danny?"

"That's right Colin," said Danny. "If any cameras do get shot, we'll know it was deliberate. Right?" He fixed the sternest look he could muster on Nathan.

"Accidents can happen," said Nathan, shrugging his shoulders and looking innocent. "This looks like fun Colin, can I try it."

The technician explained the controls of the remote units and let Nathan play with them for a while. Danny eventually interrupted. "Okay pinball wizard, you're not going to be at this end of the system, you're going to be at the receiving end. I just wanted you to be familiar with what you're up against. Get your gear on and lets see you face down these steel monsters. It's high noon Mister and you have an appointment with six paintball gunslingers on a hot piece of the Arizona desert."

It was indeed a hot afternoon. The morning clouds and coolness had given way to a sun that extracted beads of sweat from Nathan's face wherever it was covered by the protective face mask. He stood in front of the robotic gunslingers as Danny explained the drill. "Nathan you're up. Stand five yards in front of this target. Then . . ."

"That's Jesse," interrupted Nathan.

"Who?"

"That's Jesse," said Nathan again.

"What are you talking about?" asked Danny, impatience beginning to show.

"I named the targets while I was getting ready," replied Nathan. "That one in front of us is Jesse . . ."

"Like in Jesse James?" interrupted Danny.

"Right," continued Nathan. "And that one's Ike, and Cole, Billy is the ugly one, and that's Frank and the one that looks like you is Sam."

"Okay. Okay. I guess I started it with that High Noon comment," conceded Danny, holding up his hands in mock surrender. "This one's Jesse. Can we get back to work now?"

Nathan nodded, barely able to contain his smile.

"You will stand five yards in front of . . . Jesse here . . . and when you're ready, draw and neutralize the target." Nathan moved up to the firing position that Danny indicated. "Colin will have the gun pointed two feet to your side and your objective, Nathan, will be to neutralize the target before he can react to your movement, index onto you and fire. By the way, after you've loaded initially under my command you can consider this to be a hot range. It's your responsibility to be loaded and ready at all times." Nathan nodded. "Load and make ready." Danny stepped out of what he expected to be the paint ball kill zone. "There is no start signal. Begin whenever you're ready."

Nathan stood and contemplated the target for a few moments. This should be easy enough he thought. Action beats reaction every time and I should be faster than this guy on the remote control. He took a deep breath and let a third of it out.

His mind said 'now,' not loudly or vigorously or even with much emotion, just quietly and with calm determination.

In the trailer, it appeared to Colin that he had missed something. His mind must have been wandering or perhaps he had looked away from the monitor. A gun had appeared in Nathan's hand and he had missed seeing how it got there. He didn't recall letting his mind wander and he had tried to concentrate but somehow he'd missed the whole thing. The shooter had beat him cleanly, the reduced B-Zone had been knocked over and the relay switch behind it deactivated the paintball gun before Colin could even think about reacting. He spoke into the microphone of the headset he wore. "Danny can we repeat? I wasn't ready."

Out on the range Danny smiled as he heard Colin's comment in his headphones and replied into his own microphone while resetting the target. "Sure. Stand by, here we go. Same drill again Nathan. On your time."

Nathan turned to face Jesse again. He paused briefly, thinking about how much that paintball would sting at five yards with nothing more than a T-shirt covering his chest. He focused on the B-Zone, drew and fired again.

This time Colin knew he'd been watching, there had been no distraction and his mind had remained focused. But he hadn't seen much more than the last time, a flicker of movement on the monitor and Nathan's gun had fired, deactivating his unit. During product development he'd beaten lots of shooters at this game, and they had always had huge center of mass target zones to shoot at, not these dinky little B-Zones that had been specified here. Danny had warned him this guy was good, but he hadn't been prepared for *this*.

They repeated the exercise three more times with the same results, Nathan won them all. Danny called a halt and spoke into his mike. "Next level of difficulty Colin. Index your gun directly onto Nathan's chest and when you see him draw, shoot him."

"Normally, I would say that's not very sporting," said Colin. "But in his case I'll make an exception." The note of glee in his voice suggested he was going to enjoy inflicting some pain. Colin was keyed up. He'd lost this round but was anticipating the next contest. This was like the interactive computer games he loved to play – strategy, movement and shooting were the key to winning. None of it was real of course. Actually running yourself was too much like work and with real guns someone could get seriously hurt, but in the make-believe world that appeared on a computer monitor there was action without risk or effort. No one ever did well in computer games until they learned about their adversaries. Well he'd learned a few things about this guy. Now it was time to put that knowledge to use.

Nathan had been confident about being able to beat the technician when Colin was required to move his gun in order to shoot him. Now Nathan seemed to be looking directly down the cavernous muzzle of that paintball gun and he wasn't nearly as self-assured. He had to draw his gun, align the sights and fire an accurate shot before Colin could press the remote trigger, on which his finger already rested. It didn't seem fair, but fair wasn't something Nathan was likely to find in a gunfight. He knew that, so he took a deep breath, let out a third and snatched his gun from its holster.

Colin cursed. He'd been beat! The guy had beaten him! This was incredible. No one could shoot like that. It was his turn to take a deep calming breath. "I'm ready Danny. Let's try again," he said. There was determination in his voice.

Colin tried focusing on Nathan's gun hand. If he could see it start to move perhaps that would give him the edge he needed. He watched Nathan wipe his hand on his T-shirt before moving it back toward the side of his body where he'd been letting it hang for a moment before drawing.

Nathan wiped his gun hand on his T-shirt as if it were sweaty, it wasn't. His hand moved down toward its usual start position and on its way brushed by the holstered gun, abruptly reversing direction as it jerked the .45 clear and fired, dropping the B-Zone plate.

Colin slammed a fist on the counter as he realized he had not only been beaten but suckered as well. He watched as Danny passed in front of the camera and out of sight on the monitor. The green light on Colin's remote showed he had reset the target.

"Three more reps," said Danny over the headset.

"Ready," Colin muttered. I don't flipping believe this, he thought.

On the third round Nathan waited. He waited until he was sure Danny would be losing patience and was about to say something to him. Then he drew and fired, a part of him cringing in anticipation of the incoming red ball. Once again the paint gun was silent.

On the fourth round Nathan risked stepping left as he drew and fired. The paintball that sailed past his right shoulder told him the unexpected move had outweighed the delay involved in making it.

Danny issued the 'Ready' command for the last round and Nathan drew and fired while the sound of the last syllable was still hanging in the air. He holstered his gun in relief as no paint stains appeared on his shirt and then wiped his now sweaty palms. Nathan pulled off his protective headgear as he turned around to talk with Danny but a sudden dread coursed through him as he heard the hum of the target systems' robotics activate, tracking the gun. He dove to the ground, pulling his own gun and twisting as he went down, bringing it to bear on Jesse, just in time to see it fire a burst of three paintballs into the torso of another target. Jesse was shooting Billy. Nathan picked himself up, looking embarrassed and perplexed at the same time.

Danny pointed to his headphone. "He says it's a systems check." Then he covered the microphone with his hand. "I think we have one frustrated technician back there."

Danny gave Nathan a high five as he passed him on his way back to the trailer. There was a smile on his face that couldn't have been wiped off with a bull whip. "Take a break," he said. "Get something to drink."

Three pulls from a water bottle later, Danny entered the trailer too. "Now let's try it with multiple targets," he announced.

Nathan groaned.

Jesse and Ike were set up while Kim readied the second remote. Danny gave her and Colin specific directions as to the state of readiness they were to employ. They first ran the two targets with guns relaxed and pointed away from the shooter, then with guns indexed on Nathan and totally ready for the slightest twitch. Combinations on both themes were tried as well. By the time his last empty .45 case had spun to the ground Nathan had a good idea how well he could do against two armed opponents, especially if he could get a reading on their state of readiness. He walked away nursing two welts that would serve as reminders for several days.

Danny was pleased. "That's good Nathan. You did well. Remember that Colin is sitting back there one hundred per cent ready and waiting so that he can pop you. But," he held up his hand, "in the real world no one will be that totally focused and prepared when you make your move and if someone is, you're better off to pass. If you can't pass, you've seen here what your odds are of winning."

After another water break they moved up to three targets, with George operating the third remote. Nathan longed for a stack of cowboy hats, one hat for each target. Now that would be fun. As Jesse, Ike and now Frank all fell repeatedly to his gun he was surprised to learn that with the operators in a relatively low state of readiness he could consistently neutralize all three targets and walk away unscathed. Six months ago he would have said this was impossible, for anyone, let alone himself. Now here he was doing it, repeatedly.

That day was the beginning of two weeks of intense work with the shoot-back targets. Nathan's afternoons became devoted to avoiding paintball hits. The previous lessons about cover and movement were relearned and George's drilling about continuing to fight even after taking hits took on practical meaning . . . too often for his liking. Mostly, he faced the shoot-back targets alone, but sometimes Kim or Danny would join in, taking their share of hits when they did. To allow him to see through the eyes of an opponent, Nathan sat at the controls and watched videotaped replays of his own runs, worst and best, learning from everything. He drew from holsters, concealed and exposed, and he practiced snatching guns from table tops, desk drawers, under counters and from all manner of containers. To simulate potential scenarios in protective or undercover operations they switched roles and let Colin initiate the hostilities. It was significantly more difficult that way but he learned through it all and as the days passed Danny observed his confidence growing.

Nathan began to develop a strong sense of how many adversaries he could successfully face and what elements had to be evaluated before the decision to engage could be made. To survive any encounter an evaluation of the alertness of his opponent was necessary, as was the distance, lighting and location of the target. What kind of tool did he have at hand? A match gun with a dot sight . . . that was the best, or a compact hideout piece . . . tougher to shoot one of those well. Where was the gun? In his hand, in a holster or in some other container?

It all made a difference. And, he thought, who got to start? Even the guy with the fastest reaction time in the world is still reacting to someone else's start – which means *beginning* in second place and playing catch up. But he had learned it could be done and now he knew when and how.

There was a confidence growing in Danny too. For all the speeches about pushing the limits and going beyond what was believed to be possible, there had originally been surprise when a doubting Nathan pulled off something Danny insisted he could do. Confidence in the young shooter's ability to learn, perform and then to learn again had taken up residence in Danny. That led to a measure of pride in his creation. Nathan could tell as much one Monday morning when the usual workout was canceled and, after breakfast, he, Kim and Danny gathered in the classroom.

"There will be no lecture or theory instruction this morning," said Danny from his favored perch atop the front table. He sat on the edge, his legs swinging, arms splayed out on the table top, elbows locked. "We're going straight out to the range which you will, no doubt, find a little crowded. This is my time to show you off to my peers and at the same time further your training.

"I've brought in one of our Hostage Rescue Teams to work with you for a couple of days so that we can put everything together and see if it works. Like individual components are assembled into a functioning round of ammunition, you're going to see how snipers, assault teams, technical teams, negotiators and yourself combine to make a successful unit. You'll get to watch them first and then we're going to throw you into the mix. With a shooter like yourself involved this will be different for everybody, but it's a learning process and believe me these guys are always willing to try something new.

"Those people out there on the ranges right now are a tight knit bunch of operators. You're the intruder," he pointed at Nathan, "and some of them may find you threatening because of the skills you have. I can guarantee, however, that there won't be any major problems from anyone. The type who can't handle advice or outside expertise don't make it this far. Be warned that you may be treated coolly, it will be professional but it'll probably be cool.

"You also need to know that at the end of the week the suits are flying in." Danny pulled a sheet of paper from a portfolio on the table beside him and Nathan could see on it a list of names. Danny stared at it as he carried on. "We've been spending a lot of their money and they want to see where its gone. The B-Zone Project worries them, not only because of the money but because this has never been done before. New and innovative are not welcome concepts in a bureaucracy, I've been around long enough to learn that. Getting this project approved initially was tough," Danny waved the list in Nathan's direction, "but now you still have to win the approval of these same people before you can be deployed.

"This project has evolved in scope. While it wasn't international when I first conceived it, some of the more visionary people in our organization saw further than I did. When Kim, and then you Nathan, came on board we went irrevocably international. The world's law enforcement and antiterrorist community will be closely watching what happens here Friday.

Danny put the list back into his portfolio and zipped it closed in a manner that suggested he was getting ready to leave. "We've broken new ground by bringing the best of modern action pistol competition into the law enforcement arena and whatever happens this week you've exceeded my expectations,

Nathan. You're the best there is and you're working for the right people. Any questions?"

There were none, so they made the familiar walk to the ranges together.

Danny had been right about the crowded range. People were everywhere. Two large cube vans and half a dozen Suburbans were parked along the road and around Colin's target video arcade. Every prop wall stacked at the end of the range was now part of a two room scenario employing all of the shoot-back targets. The place was a swirl of activity. Everyone seemed to have a job and was busy doing it.

Danny led Kim and Nathan to the back of one of the cube vans. "This is a mobile command post for the team," he explained. "A flexible center that can be changed to suit the situation and the available resources." A man stood up from a stool at a fold down desk, came to the rear of the van and rather than using the fold-up stairs jumped to the ground. He held a silver aluminum clipboard tucked under his arm as Danny introduced him. "This is Terry. He's our Training Officer today. He'll brief you on the first scenario."

Terry shook hands with Nathan and Kim, saying he had heard about the project and was looking forward to working with them. Then he launched into an explanation of what was about to happen.

"Like Danny said, I'm Training Officer today, that means I write the scenarios, set them up and act as referee to make sure everything happens realistically and safely. I also help out in the debriefings whenever we finish an exercise. Right now we're just doing assaults on this specific range mock-up so we don't have to involve negotiators, electronic experts and all our other resources.

"Danny says do a number of scenarios, each one twice. Once using the team and the way we've always done it and then trying it with you Nathan. It should be interesting." Terry walked to the other side of the van gesturing for Nathan and Kim to follow. He pointed out three large white boards mounted on the side of the vehicle, each contained scenario details and Terry explained how they were utilized as Nathan and Kim tried to keep up with his description. As they watched, he pulled a typewritten sheet from his clipboard and gave it to one of the men hovering near the boards, then turned and strode rapidly away, taking his two students with him.

"What I've just done," he explained, "is give the team leader an update telling him the Operations Commander has approved the assault plan he submitted half an hour ago. Within fifteen minutes he has to execute. Let's get out of here and move over to where we can watch our range mock up."

Terry led them as they climbed one of the ranges' side berms, staying well back from the firing line but positioning themselves so as to have a view inside the walls. They saw the shoot back targets arrayed in a seemingly random pattern throughout the first room and three life size department store mannequins propped up in one corner. Nathan asked Terry about them.

"Rubber hostages," he explained. "That's who's got to be rescued. After the team neutralizes all the perps, they have to drag them to safety. You'll see how it works."

They watched as the team members gathered at what Terry explained was their staging point, from which they moved as a unit to a position near the door and then at some signal, neither heard nor seen by the observers, they struck.

Nathan thought it looked like a well rehearsed dance. The kind his mother used to drag him to as a grade-schooler when his sister still took tap-dance lessons. Louise and her fellow students had always known their roles and performed them acceptably but in those early years everything was stiff, clumsy and awkward. That's how the team members looked to Nathan, stiff, clumsy and awkward. Of course, Nathan conceded, he could only imagine how much the body armor, ballistic shields, fireproof jump suits and other assorted equipment they carried or wore must weigh. He doubted anyone could be graceful with all that gear on.

Terry had warned him about the stun grenades but their detonation still elicited a start. The smattering of gunfire that followed gave Nathan the distinct impression of discipline and tight control. Then commands were shouted and men started dragging mannequins out of the building and depositing them in what appeared to be a predetermined area. It was a deadly serious exercise but the spectacle of solemn men with sub-machine guns dragging mannequins made Nathan smile.

Terry continued providing a step by step explanation until he was satisfied the exercise had gone as far as was profitable. He then shouted a command into a Motorola radio clipped to his belt. Relaxation spread visibly through the men below as the exercise ended and those left in the roofless building filed out. The three watchers immediately saw the paint smears. One team member had taken a hit in the head and another in the chest. They didn't look happy. Terry shook his head but didn't say anything.

"Have they worked with shoot back targets before?" asked Kim.

"No," said Terry. "It does look like they're getting an education from them though."

"Yeah, I have a doctorate in bruising from them," nodded Nathan.

"Debriefing time people," said Terry. "Come with me please."

They followed Terry to the white board side of the cube van and stood behind the knot of black clad men.

Team members stripped off the most uncomfortable parts of their gear and sat on the ground in a semicircle as the man, who Terry had identified as their team leader, led them through a debriefing of their entry into and engagement within the rooms. Most of the seated men drank from water bottles as they listened and some added their ideas. Terry tossed in thoughts as well.

When it was over Danny stepped up to summarize the B-Zone Project and introduce Nathan and Kim. When none of the faces looked surprised Nathan knew they all had some knowledge of the project. Terry handed Danny a sheet from his clipboard and he held it up to the team without reading it.

"Once more from the top," he said. "This time there will be a two-person news crew in the room when you go in." There were some good natured collective groans from the men seated on the ground. "The news crew will be our people," explained Danny, "Kim and Nathan. A mock up of a TV camera that conceals a pistol will go in with them. This is a routine they've practiced before and are good at. Nathan will pull the gun from hiding, neutralizing as many targets as possible while you will be waiting in an assault position outside the door. When you hear shooting that's your cue to do the entry and finish the rescue."

He turned to Nathan. "Your role in this is to draw your pistol when the time is right, whack as many targets as you can and then drop to the floor. Kim should already be there. No movement. No looking for targets. Draw, shoot, then find a hole and crawl into it till these guys are finished. Got it?"

Nathan nodded.

"Just like we've done in practice," said Kim, nudging Nathan.

Danny relayed the sheet of paper in his hand to the team leader and stepped aside as he barked orders at his men.

"Get your gear ready," Danny said quietly to Nathan and Kim. "And don't forget your vests."

B-ZONE

Half an hour later Nathan and Kim were gathered at the staging area with the assault team. The news crew moved forward to the doorway and went in as directed by Terry, who positioned them in the room while explaining where to set up a TV interview so the location would be most beneficial to the entry team.

They played their roles, interviewing Ike for the benefit of the cameras recording their actions. Once sufficient time had elapsed for the entry team to move into position, Nathan feigned camera difficulties. Kim, the interviewer, stepped up to help and as they popped the top cover off the large camera Nathan's hand found his pistol and brought it into action. Kim dove to the floor and rolled hard against the wall. Nathan had previously noted the robotic gun arms and the direction each pointed was his clue to the state of readiness specific targets were simulating. He took the most dangerous ones first, then moved to secondaries and eventually thirds. In a heartbeat he was done and hugging the floor as well.

It was only seconds but they lasted an eternity and then the assault team came through the door. Shouts of "Clear!" followed a surge of activity after which the 'dead' hostile targets were guarded and the mannequins rudely dragged out again. Nathan and Kim were also hustled out by team members and shortly after, saw the men with them relax in indication that Terry had terminated the exercise.

The debriefing followed a format identical to the previous one. The defining comment came from the first man in the entry team to hit the room.

"There wasn't much left for us to do," he said. "Personally, I had no idea shooting that fast and hitting anything was humanly possible. I don't know how he did it but I sure would like to learn."

Danny answered the man, speaking to everyone as he did so. "I'm sure you could all learn to be better shots if we put you through the same program as Nathan, but you still wouldn't be his equal. I believe Nathan is the best in the world. He has a combination of natural ability, personal desire and good training that has made his skill level possible. It cannot be easily duplicated. I can assure you that you'll see Nathan do even more amazing things over the next few days and that you too will become believers in the resource someone like him can be."

Danny was right. After three more scenarios all heads were shaking in disbelief at how fast Nathan could shoot and still maintain a practical level of accuracy. Before breaking for lunch, the best shot on the team was prodded into taking on Nathan in a contest. Danny ordered the set-up of two banks of steel plates, one for each shooter, with overlapping poppers as stop plates. He allowed the HRT member an MP5 but restricted Nathan to his stock pistol.

"Let it all hang out," he whispered to his student as he left the pair alone on the range.

Their skill levels were so drastically different that the contest became a non-event. Nathan showed no mercy, destroying his opponent and with him the last lingering doubts that might have been present in the assembled tactical minds.

On Friday the people that Danny had referred to as 'the suits' arrived to see the product their resources and risk taking, at least in a bureaucratic sense, had netted. Nathan counted fourteen people assembled to watch the demonstrations and he was introduced to all of them. He saw two American military uniforms and an assortment of well dressed men, of which a few stood out.

One was a man Kim spent a lot of time talking to, in what he presumed was Hebrew. In his forties, a scar running through the left sideburn and lining up with a notch in the nearby ear gave him an 'experienced' look. He inserted only one earplug when shooting started and Nathan supposed there was no ear drum on that left side. The left eye wasn't quite right either. It must have hurt . . . whatever *it* was.

Danny spent most of his time with a man introduced to Nathan as Mr. Kent. A distinguished looking man with a horseshoe of gray hair that encircled a bald skull and a modest mustache of precisely the same color, he wore a navy blue pin stripe banker's suit set off by a blazing red tie. Nathan wondered if he knew the Arizona desert dust had crept up the fancy suit's pant legs making him look like a kid whose Sunday suit had been soiled by playing in the sandbox. A strong British accent rolled from his lips, while his eyes, like Nathan's, were blue but several shades paler. As he shook hands, Nathan was struck by the sensation that there was a massive intellect behind those eyes, an ability to reason and understand that was unusual. He'd had the same feeling two years ago in California when a fellow shooter, a employee of Sea World, had allowed him to interact with a dolphin . . . a recognition of surprising intelligence. It was here too. Two other people accompanied Mr. Kent but they didn't look like bureaucrats. Either bodyguards or consultants, guessed Nathan. They looked like young versions of Kim's Israeli friend.

In the end, the American and Canadian authorities gave their permission for Nathan to operate within their countries while under the direction and supervision of the appropriate domestic authorities. The Israelis hinted that their approval would be forthcoming shortly and the other countries present remained interested but uncommitted.

Nathan pulled his first assignment on Monday.

CHAPTER NINE

The darkness prevented Nathan from seeing much as he looked out across the runway. The Corvette in which he sat was a convertible though, and now with the top down he could at least look up at the stars. What a gorgeous night, he thought. Judging from the glow in the sky, Portland had to be off to his right and, according to the breeze, the ocean straight ahead. So maybe he wasn't completely lost. He'd been lost most of the night as they drove all over the greater Portland area, following directions phoned in by their targets. Now it looked like they were finally going to make the connection.

Nathan was the passenger in the car and his liaison officer, Chimo, was driving. A third obvious presence in the car was Nathan's gun, partly because of its nature, it was a full blown race gun, and partly because of the way he wore it, a cross-draw appendix position in a minimal holster. The semi-reclining position of the Corvette's seats made the .45 stick up like a second gearshift and while not exactly discreet at the moment it was the right gun being worn the right way for the job at hand. He wore a long, loose, duster coat to cover it prudently when needed, but now the coat was open and would stay that way until it was time to go to work.

This was actually his second job. The first time out Danny had traveled to Denver with him to assist the authorities there with a botched bank robbery and resultant hostage taking. But the negotiator had done his job and talked the lone gunman out, convincing him to surrender in exchange for a cup of coffee.

Now Nathan was in Portland working with a west coast drug enforcement group. Danny had explained that this particular group was one of the usual combinations of various agencies teamed together to target whatever people needed attention in their part of the country. Nathan would have liked Kim along but Danny said she wasn't needed and he had other things for her to do. Even he had not come.

Nathan had found this unit headquartered in rented space in one of the numerous nondescript office buildings on the fringes of downtown. In this case, there was no great effort being made to conceal who they were or what they did. The tenants' listing next to the elevator gave only the initials of the unit but without knowing what they stood for it was just alphabet soup to the casual observer. A secure underground garage with their own entrance and their own elevator kept the agents sufficiently out of the eyes of the public to maintain a workable anonymity.

Nathan had joined this group of men and women to assist them in their efforts to capture two individuals who were making the rip off of drug dealers a specialty. At least that was what his liaison officer had said when he picked Nathan up at the airport, introducing himself as Chimo. He looked about Nathan's age but shorter and slightly built. His dark hair and complexion suggested he might be of Mexican extraction. Nathan wasn't really sure though, he hadn't met many Mexicans and Chimo didn't volunteer any information about his ancestry, so Nathan didn't ask.

About the only thing Nathan was sure of was that Chimo wasn't his real name. When they first met at the airport Chimo had made a comment about Nathan being 'the shooter' that was coming to help them out. He never varied from that initial assessment and introduced him as 'the shooter' to everyone in the unit they encountered.

"Spike, this is the shooter. Shooter, say hello to Spike here."

"Hi. My name's Nathan Burdett. Nice to meet you." Nathan and Spike shook hands.

"Glad you could come by to help out Shooter. See you around," Spike said, as he hurried off with a handful of papers. Chimo guided Nathan over to an older woman working at a computer monitor. "Blondie, this is the shooter we heard about," said Chimo. "Blondie here runs this office. If you need to know anything administrative just see her."

"Hi. My name's Nathan. Nathan Burdett."

"Welcome aboard Shooter. If you need anything from a cell phone to expense money come see me."

"Yeah. Sure," said Nathan. "I'll remember that."

Finally, after being introduced to Buzz, Slim, Bongo and Flip, Nathan began to get the idea that no one here used anything resembling a real name. He gave up giving his and resigned himself to being Shooter. He didn't like it but it appeared he had no choice.

"Lights coming in from the south end of the runway Shooter. You see 'em," asked Chimo.

"I see them."

"You got that space gun of yours ready man?"

"Yeah. It's ready." Nathan bent his head down and confirmed the C-More sight was turned on. It was probably the hundredth time he had checked this night but Chimo didn't know that and he didn't tell him.

The lights stopped four or five hundred yards down the runway and Chimo turned on the Corvette's headlights in response. There was no movement from either vehicle, but then there wasn't supposed to be for at least five minutes.

According to the briefing, there should be two men in that vehicle, both of them on their way to becoming quite wealthy and both multiple killers. The unit had been working

176

these guys for several weeks, building their confidence in Chimo's undercover character and setting up the drug buy that was going to happen in the next few minutes on this runway. In a briefcase in the trunk, Nathan and Chimo had an even one hundred thousand dollars in cash, intended to buy a considerable quantity of heroin from that distant car. Only there was no heroin in that car. The bad guys knew they had none and the drug unit knew they had none. But as long as the bad guys didn't realize that the good guys knew and as long as he shot straight and fast, if necessary, then Nathan thought they might get out of this alive. To Nathan it sounded too complicated to work.

One of the men waiting out there even considered himself a talented gunman. At least that's what his ex-girlfriend was telling the undercover female cop who had befriended her and become her confidant as they exchanged men-are-rotten-creeps stories. That was how the unit had initially picked up on these two. The jilted girlfriend, too afraid to go to the cops but needing to talk to somebody, was ripe for the plucking when a good operator stepped in. Her story was that she'd been told of five dealers they'd ripped off, each time killing two people.

From the details given him, Nathan acknowledged that it might even be easy if you were any good with a gun and willing to do the necessary killing. The two rip-off artists would make contact with a mid-level dealer, progressively supply him with small but increasing amounts of product and once they had him hooked, offered a large amount of merchandise at a very attractive price. Then, when it came time to consummate the big transaction and on the pretence of being cautious and somewhat spooked, they would send their victim on a vehicular version of musical chairs. Which would inevitably lead them on short notice to an open desolate spot, such as this airstrip for private planes, where the deal could be done in security and anonymity.

To keep things fair, they always agreed that each party would have two people present, one deal maker and one bodyguard. Normally, Chimo told Nathan, there was nothing unusual about that. But these two had either more guts or talent, or maybe both, than most of the people in this game; for when the deal maker had confirmed the presence of the money a signal would pass between the two, they killed the would-be buyers, disposed of the bodies and the evidence, and pocketed the money. It would only work a couple of times in any given part of the country but it was a big country and these two seemed to have figured that out as well. They were cold, calculating, and remorseless about killing.

Nathan sat, speculating about his counterpart in that other vehicle. What was his background? What had caused him to start killing for money? Was he, as Chimo had suggested, a user of the drugs he was pretending to sell? Nathan doubted it. He didn't know much about drugs or users but from what he did know, he doubted if the guy could be pulling this off, especially as well as he was, and be hooked on some brain frying powder. The shooter in that other car had faced down at least ten men on five separate occasions and killed them all. He was either really good, had a gimmick, or maybe both. Either way he'd done this a lot more than Nathan, which gave him good reason to worry.

"Why do you think they're making us wait out here like this?" asked Nathan.

"Night scope is my guess," replied Chimo. "That's what I'd do, take a night scope and check out the area around us, real careful like. It's why they picked this place, flat and open enough that you couldn't hide a pussy cat out here, let alone some kind of back-up or rip-off crew."

"The way they've kept us driving around town we wouldn't have had time to set that up anyway," said Nathan.

"You're learning Shooter. You're learning. These guys are smart and careful. I hope you're as good as I've heard, 'cause they're starting to worry me."

"I hope so too."

"That's it," said Chimo. "Times up. He just flashed his lights."

Clipped to the visor was what looked like a garage door opener. Chimo pushed one of the buttons sending a signal to a back-up unit five miles distant. A miniature video camera concealed in a radar detector on the dash activated and began sending out its signal. "Okay. Just like we planned it," he said putting the car in gear. "I do the talking. You do the shooting."

Nathan didn't reply. He was too busy talking to himself, trying to get his heart to stop racing and his mind to focus on the job and off of the possible negative outcomes. Just another stage, he told himself. Two hostile targets. Distance unknown but probably short. Start signal unknown. There won't be any no-shoots unless Chimo gets in the way and definitely no walk-throughs or reshoots. Just another stage. And if I blow it we all die. He took a deep breath. Just another stage. Yeah, right!

Both cars rolled slowly forward to the center of the runway, their headlights forcing back the reluctant darkness which steadily regained its domain behind them as the vehicles moved forward seeking new blackness to penetrate. A picnic table came into view at the leading edge of the light. It was supposed to be there but was nonetheless a surprise, probably because it looked so out of place. A weathered table made of two-by-six lumber with side benches and splayed out legs, it sat on the runway's centerline, looking as if it had dropped from the sky.

Chimo hung back and watched the other car stop twenty yards away from the table, illuminating it with its lights. Then he drove up to the table also, stopping an equal distance away on the other side. No one exited the Corvette until they saw two men leave the other vehicle.

"Chimo!" yelled one of them, too far away and too dazzled by the lights to be able to recognize anyone. "Is that you man?"

"And you were expecting the Feds maybe, you ugly gringo. Of course it's me."

That started everyone drifting toward the table.

"Are you ready to do business?" called the same man. Nathan couldn't make out what he looked like yet.

"I was ready long ago my friend, but we've been driving all over this stinking city for the entire night while you play your games with us."

A laugh sounded from the silhouette, close enough now that he no longer needed to yell. "My apologies for the inconvenience Chimo, but I'm sure you can understand that I'm the one who must be careful. After all, I have the drugs. All you have is a suitcase full of money. The cops have been known to try and buy drugs but they don't usually sell them, do they?"

"Okay," said Chimo, in full role-playing mode and expressing as much righteous irritation as he dared. "Careful is good but now that we're here let's get on with it."

"I haven't met your friend before," said the man pointing toward Nathan. They were standing on opposite sides of the table, close enough for the breeze to bring Nathan the distinctive smell of stale cigars.

"He works for me," said Chimo, briefly putting a hand on Nathan's shoulder. "He doesn't say much and does what I tell him."

"Then why don't you tell him to fetch the money and I'll have my man get the drugs and we can all go home and call it a night?"

"Get it," said Chimo, while across the table a hand waved, sending Nathan and his counterpart back to their respective cars. Nathan came back carrying a black briefcase in his left hand and the other man a nylon gym bag in his right. There was something heavy in the gym bag.

Nathan kept his long coat unbuttoned but closed enough that it covered the pistol on his left front at belt level. His right hand never straying far from the coat's opening as he walked back, taking the opportunity to examine the other side's shooter.

At a little over six feet he was three or four inches taller than Nathan and probably fifty pounds heavier. None of it looked like fat. Not bad for a man who must be close to forty, he thought. He doesn't look like a burned out druggie. What he looks like is a hard professional. Maybe even ex-military thought Nathan, the buzzed hair cut and square jaw adding to the impression. A short leather bomber jacket, half zipped, kept the chill off. There won't be any speed draws coming out from under that jacket. No indication of a gun.

"Let's look at the money," said the dealer.

Chimo took the case from Nathan, being careful not to cross in front of him. Putting the briefcase on the table, he popped the latches and lifted the lid. Then he spun it around to let the dealer view the contents and stepped back.

Had a Range Officer been present, the 'standby' command would now be issued, thought Nathan. Once he's confirmed the money's there he gives the signal and whatever happens, begins. Nathan stepped away from Chimo, intent on putting some distance between the two of them. No use bunching up and making it easy for them, he thought.

That got a reaction from the big guy. Nathan watched him tense and shift his eyes from one to the other as he readjusted his position to keep the left side leading. Trying to keep us both in his field of fire and probably right handed, he guessed. But his right hand still held the gym bag and he can't do anything till he drops the bag? Talk about telegraphing a draw!

The dealer pulled the briefcase toward himself and was extracting stacks of bills and fanning them to apparently check the quantity and condition of the money. Nathan focused his attention on the shooter, trying to figure out where the gun was. Where else but the gym bag? It was the only place he could get at it quickly. But it was securely zipped up and the man had a firm grasp on all three handles. Three handles?

Just then the briefcase tipped off the edge of the table spilling its contents to the pavement. The wrap on a cash bundle had broken and the breeze caught the bills immediately, sending them fluttering across the runway as the headlights created dancing paper shadows.

Chimo tried to catch the falling briefcase and was just realizing his mistake as the man holding the gym bag released two of the handles. He pulled up sharply on the third. Nathan had stayed disciplined. His eyes hadn't left the other shooter and as he watched, the gym bag fell away and a Calico M960A, attached to the third handle, came up out of the bag – Nathan's gun had already cleared leather, his dot tracking to the target.

Nathan was surprised at how easy it was. He had the man cold and for a fleeting moment he even thought the shooter might realize it and back off. Whether momentum or grim determination kept him going, Nathan couldn't tell. He was looking down the bore of Nathan's .45 when his left hand hit the submachine gun's vertical foregrip, activating a laser sighting device. Time's up thought Nathan . . . and he dropped the hammer. Twice. Just to be sure, he told himself.

Nathan's sight hunted for the dealer. Knocking the briefcase off the table had been a ruse all right. No effort was being wasted trying to recover the blowing bills. Instead his right hand was deep into his jacket, under the left armpit. Things were happening in slow motion and Nathan could see him starting to pull it out. He couldn't tell what was in there but he'd bet his gun hand it wasn't a cell phone.

The trigger pull of Nathan's handgun was set at four pounds. He applied 4.1 pounds. Twice. Just to be sure, he told himself.

He'd seen the first man start to go down while traversing to the second but he hadn't waited to see him fall. No time. The dot had looked good and you had to have confidence in your sight picture. He tracked back to him now as the second man started to fall, confirmed the shooter was down and came back to the dealer in time to see him collapse. Movement to the right caught his attention and he looked to see Chimo just clearing his own gun from it's behind-the-hip holster.

Chimo's mind was desperately trying to catch up with two seconds worth of events. The briefcase had fallen off the table and the money he personally was responsible for started blowing all over the runway. Then shots shattered the stillness and he'd instinctively gone for his gun. Now there were bodies. A wave of relief coursed through him as he realized his own body was still upright. They'd won, but how? Looking to his left he saw Nathan sidestepping away, his gun still covering the writhing bodies and the car these two had come in.

Another gunshot boomed across the runway and Chimo saw the two headlights on the killer's car wink out as his ears picked up the sound of falling glass. Nathan had shot out the lights glaring in their eyes – but how could he get two headlights with one shot. Or had it been a pair of shots? Things were happening too fast.

"Cover what's left of these two," yelled Nathan, "I'll clear the car."

Nathan melted into the darkness and Chimo tried to stay focused on what lay on the ground before him. There was still movement from the downed men and he couldn't go help Nathan until he was sure they no longer posed a threat. Some kind of submachine gun lay on the pavement a few feet from the bodyguard and as Chimo's mind and training started to catch up he shuffled over and kicked the gun as far away as he could. Over his gunsights he saw the man lift his head and look up at him, an ugly mixture of pain and hatred visible on the face. He tried to get up but collapsed in a moan. Ten feet away the dealer seemed to pick up the cue and began screaming in pain. Chimo stepped back five paces, keeping both covered while trying to ignore their screams.

An eternity later Nathan emerged from the darkness and declared the car clear. Then, working as a team, they checked both of the screaming men for weapons and eventually with Chimo covering him, Nathan started first aid.

No call for back-up and no notification of the operation's results had been issued. They didn't need to. The miniature camera in the Vette transmitted everything to the cover team and now the distant thumping of an approaching helicopter indicated their approach.

As he watched Nathan's makeshift first aid Chimo came to a startling realization that began as disbelief but which quickly progressed to anger. Both men were very much alive. As he watched, Nathan pulled a Lightfoot folder from his pocket and thumbed open the blade. He sliced one leg of the shooter's jeans into strips and fashioned four tourniquets. There were no chest wounds on either victim, no abdominal wounds with the characteristic protruding intestines, not even the common thigh hits of an inexperienced marksman jerking the trigger. Nathan had shot each man through the elbow, once in the right and once in the left. Four shots, four shattered elbows.

It was all Chimo could do to contain himself until the helicopter's EMT's took over first aid and he was able to pull Nathan back from the scene. He had regained his composure by then but still gripped Nathan hard by the arm.

"You shot those guys through the elbows!" The tone demanded an explanation.

"There was no need to kill them," said Nathan. "I had them cold. Taking out both arms was necessary though." He grimaced and looked back to where the men lay. "A man can still shoot you with only one arm. I had to be sure."

"You had *them* cold? *You* had to be sure!" Chimo put his hands over his face, losing his regained composure. "They had *us* cold! Are you crazy?" He flung his arms up and paced in a tight circle in front of Nathan. When he stopped his index finger was an inch from Nathan's nose. "Those guys were going to cut us in half with that little sub-gun and piss on our graves! You don't play nice guy and take stupid chances with hard cases like that!"

Nathan tried to explain, but Chimo was crossing himself and muttering something in Spanish that sounded obscene, so when his angry partner latched onto the arriving unit supervisor Nathan took the opportunity to catch a ride out in the chopper. Debriefing happened in one hour and he suspected it might not go well for him.

Danny showed up the next day, much cooler and detached, but Nathan knew he wasn't happy.

"I thought we agreed there wouldn't be any trick shooting," said Danny as they met for lunch.

"I didn't agree to that," said Nathan quietly.

"Okay then. I thought I *told* you there was to be no trick shooting."

Nathan shrugged. He twirled his water glass, eventually taking a sip but not looking at Danny till he spoke. "Danny, when the timer beeped out there on that runway and this thing went down I was so far ahead of those two I couldn't believe it. I fully intended to B-Zone both right up until the moment I picked up the sight's dot. With a full-blown race gun and a C-More sight in my hands I knew those bullets would go anywhere I wanted. The only thing I had to do was will it. I could kill them or let them live. It wasn't necessary to kill them, so I didn't." He drained the rest of his water. "The choice seemed logical at the time.

"I won't kid you Danny and tell you that I haven't thought about where to shoot someone in order to disable them. I have. Maybe too much thought. For the last five years my work's been saving lives and maybe that's a hard mindset to break." He shook his head. "I'm not sure it should be broken."

Danny looked out the window, avoiding Nathan's gaze. Outside, purposefully striding people filled the noon sidewalk as office workers escaped their cubicles. Danny, saw none of it. He saw a dimly lit hallway illuminated by muzzle flashes that blinded his eyes, hurt his ears and generated the odor of burnt gunpowder. As his ears and eyes cleared he heard screams and saw smoke and dust swirling in the light cast by a naked incandescent bulb. At first he thought the screams were from the dying robbery suspect in the doorway to his front – then he looked behind him . . .

He didn't acknowledge the waitress when she put his order down but it did serve to bring him back to Nathan, from wherever he had been. "That's very noble of you Nathan. But in our business nobility gets people killed. There's too much chance of something going wrong with stunts like this. I won't allow you to take that chance. If just your life was at stake I

186

would say fine, but its not. Most of the time there will be others, that's why you'll be there. Last night there were no hostages but there was your partner, this Chimo guy. You put him at risk." Danny allowed the beginnings of a smile to play across his face. "I understand he was pretty upset."

"Yeah, he was," said Nathan, recalling the animated image of his partner. "If I knew any Spanish at all I could've learned some new words." But then he turned the topic serious again. "He doesn't understand what I can do though. You should."

"What I'm coming to understand is that you might have a problem killing someone. There's a big difference between paper targets and live ones. Are you sure you're able to make the transition?"

So that was it, thought Nathan. A large bite from his sandwich gave him time to think before replying. Besides underestimating his abilities, Danny suspected that perhaps he had some mental block against killing. "I can't say positively," said Nathan, "but I don't think that's the case. That two man rip-off crew is alive simply because I didn't have to kill them."

He chose not to mention the rifle scope image of the burning biker still regularly seen at night. Lately in those dreams, he always pulled the trigger. Mercifully, the recoil would jolt him awake. Nathan figured the bullet made it to the two hundred yard mark, still climbing upward in its flight, before he fully woke up. So far he'd always been spared having to watch the hit.

"I hope there is no problem Nathan. I'm going to take you at your word and we're going to carry on. We've come too far together to stop now. Remember that I represent two people, I'm your friend and your boss. Both of us are concerned about this, though probably for different reasons. Can you understand that?"

"Sure I can Danny. But there's no need for the concern, really there's not."

"Okay. Let's leave it and we'll talk about the rest of what happened out there."

They stayed at the restaurant for another hour after that. To Nathan it was like detail stripping a gun and cleaning and examining every single part. Checking everything for possible flaws and then reassembling it back into a complete entity. They stripped the event into individual occurrences and analyzed every one. Then they discussed the event as a whole and finished by playing 'what if . . . '.

CHAPTER   TEN

When Nathan returned to the ranch he found Kim on the range, practicing a single round, draw and fire routine on the steel plates with her Sig. Nathan leaned against a barricade post at the back of the range and watched. Kim was a good solid marksman. Each time she fired a plate dropped. There was a fluid grace in those movements he liked. That grace, he suspected, concealed a strength lying beneath the surface. A strength that was more than the obvious physical one she possessed. There was a mental toughness there that had not shown itself yet. Maybe someday he thought. She was unaware of Nathan's presence until she turned around.

"Hi Nathan, you're back." Kim peeled off her muffs and shooting glasses as she walked over to where he stood. "Glad to see you're okay. I hear you were needed?"

He nodded in reply.

"I've heard the basics," said Kim. "But I don't know the details." She motioned to the lawn chairs sitting in the trailer's shade. "Sit down and tell me about it. I'll get us something cold out of the fridge."

They talked at length there in the shade, Nathan sharing with Kim what he had experienced and Kim asking questions similar to those Danny had.

"I shot a drug dealer once," she said abruptly.

Nathan's head snapped up, his eyes seeking hers. "Oh." If she wanted to talk about it the opportunity was there.

"I was on a team raiding a suspected dealer's house. It was early in my career, pretty much just out of training, so I was assigned to watch the back door." She rearranged two rocks with the toe of her left Nike. "When the rest of my team went in the

189

front, the dealer came running out the back. There was a small courtyard in the back with only one way out and I was blocking it." She paused, "So he started shooting."

"I take it he missed and you didn't."

"That's about it. I'd been taught well and had a good barricade position around the corner of the brick wall. He was foolish to try and shoot me under the circumstances." She looked directly at Nathan, "And I didn't try any elbow shots."

Nathan took her comment in stride. "It worked. Maybe you should try it sometime?"

Kim shook her head. "Not a chance. I haven't got the skill and you know it. Everything would have to be so right. I still can't believe you did it." She shook her head again. It was disbelief this time. "Danny's not happy about it."

Nathan ignored the comment about Danny. "Do you think I did the right thing? Was it reckless? Did I put other peoples lives needlessly in danger?"

"Probably! You took needless risks," said Kim. "I don't understand what you did for two reasons. First, because I have difficulty comprehending your abilities and the confidence that gives you in being able to make shots like that and secondly because I don't value the lives of people like that as much as you evidently do."

"Thanks," said Nathan sincerely.

"I didn't say I agreed with you Nathan," corrected Kim repositioning her chair, a touch of anger in her voice.

"No, I meant thanks for being honest with me," he explained.

Kim said nothing. She wiped at the condensation on the outside of her soft drink can. "Give Danny some time," she said. "I'm not sure he has a good grasp of what you can do in a real situation. But then do any of us? Do you? Like we've heard several times, 'this has never been done before'."

"Yeah, I hear you. Sometimes I get the idea that life is just one big experiment."

Kim chuckled. "Exactly. You know something? My mother says food cures all pain – that's probably why she's two hundred pounds – but I'm hungry. What kind of gastronomic experimentation should we try tonight?"

Kim's pager buzzed in the middle of a mouthful of burger and ten seconds later Nathan's echoed hers. Kim had looked down at her number display by then. "Danny?" she mumbled through a mouthful of gastronomic experimentation. Nathan nodded. "I'll get it," she said rising from the table. Chewing as quickly as possible, she made her way to a pay phone near the entrance.

The neighborhood pub in which they sat was situated at the corner of two major roads, a ten minute drive from the ranch. The food was good here and most importantly it was quiet. A place where people could talk undisturbed. It was five minutes before Kim returned from the phone call. Nathan was gone.

"Hey, redhead," said a familiar voice behind her. She pivoted and saw Nathan motioning her over to the end of the bar where a small TV flickered. Nathan was intent on watching its screen while the waitress behind the bar seemed intent on watching him. Nathan was oblivious to it. He was looking at an aerial shot of a prison. Black smoke rolled from one of the buildings in the compound and the caption at the bottom of the screen read 'Riot and Hostage Taking - Attica Correctional Facility.'

Nathan shot an inquiring look at Kim who nodded discreetly. "Would you turn that up please?" she asked. The waitress obliged and watched with them while a talking head announced a prison riot and a hostage taking near Buffalo.

191

A segment from a news conference given by the prison Superintendent added nothing. When the coverage turned to interviews consisting of 'How do you *feel*' questions, it was obvious the media had run out of facts and Kim and Nathan went back to their meals.

"We going to New York?" asked Nathan when he was sure the waitress was out of earshot.

"Yeah, both of us. A chopper at the ranch in half an hour and a private jet in Tucson."

"Somebody wants us there in a hurry."

"Danny told me about a riot there in the seventies in which thirty-nine people were killed. I guess it was a watershed point in prison history and made the place notorious. This appears to be a much smaller affair but they're throwing every resource available at it – and that includes us."

"Before my time," said Nathan shrugging his shoulders.

They ate the rest of their meals rapidly and quietly, tossed sufficient money on the table and left talking about which guns to take.

It wasn't the black hole of Calcutta but it wasn't the place to spend your next vacation either, that much was evident from their position in one of the Attica towers. The two aged brick and concrete buildings that had been the focal point of the prisoners' rampage were still standing, but the tops of the empty windows were highlighted by black smears where the fire had left its mark. They could only imagine the destruction inside the buildings, however it was easy to believe you could taste hatred in the air. As if to fit the mood, the sky was overcast with low leaden clouds that heightened the feeling of depression. The morning breeze shifted into their faces and brought with it the smell of tear gas, making Nathan sneeze.

"What's the matter," asked the FBI agent who had brought them in, "Allergic to riots?"

"No," came the reply. "Just prisons I think."

"I know what you mean," the agent nodded. "I'm glad that I'm only liaison here. I couldn't make myself work here permanently." He began talking about the riot. "This one started like most. It wasn't a planned event as far as we can tell, just a combination of bored and angry prisoners, a mistake on a guard's part and some bad luck." He motioned to them. "Come on we'll go inside."

By now the riot was over. It had been quelled with a combination of CS gas, cold water and brute force. The fires were out too, at least those visible fires that had consumed the physical structures. The invisible fires of hatred that burned in the minds of most inmates were largely exhausted as well, at least for now. In the minds of three of the inmates, however, the fires still burned fiercely.

Further inside the prison Nathan and Kim looked at the three pictures posted on the status board of the prison Command Center. It was more than a 'board' really, like most status boards it had grown to cover one complete wall and was moving slowly onto another, creeping like a living organism – which was exactly what it was. For this was where the information needed to play the game was visibly shared with everyone. It changed and flowed and adapted to whatever situation developed and those who made life or death decisions, based them on what was on the board.

"Those guys are even homelier than you," teased Kim.

"That's only because they're not as photogenic as I am," replied Nathan, checking the weapons list. He saw two AR-15's there. Probably grabbed from overpowered guards he speculated.

The activity in the command center had settled down to one of routine now that the hostage taking had passed the twenty-four hour point. The original frantic pace generated by any new incident had subsided to become the usual 'let's contain them and negotiate' action plan that was the standard solution. Standard because it worked.

The liaison agent led Nathan and Kim to their own preparation and standby area down the hall from the command center. It was an obscure administrative office that had served some routine purpose when the prison was running on a more even keel. The name plate on the desk said 'William Burke' but there was no indication of what he did there as they cleaned off the desk and countertop, piling everything in one corner. Then they dragged in their gear bags. Across the hall and closer to the command center was the Correction's Emergency Response Team's ready room. Nathan got some bored looks from the men in there and Kim got the kind an attractive female does in a male environment, but nothing more. That means they don't know who we are yet, thought Nathan. Fine, they'll leave us alone and we'll do likewise. At least until the preliminaries are taken care of.

With their gear laid out, Kim and Nathan were ready and made it back to the command center just in time for the morning briefing. At one end of the large room, ten men sat around a rectangular table, their faces revealed the adrenaline rush of this situation was long over and a creeping fatigue was taking its place. At the head of the table sat the Situation Commander to whom they'd already been introduced. He told them to stand near the briefing table and waved at a portion of wall.

A tall man with seriously graying brown hair, he looked as though he belonged in something more formal than the jeans and golf shirt he wore. A prison system logo on the pocket of the shirt appeared to be a nod to that formality. Obviously a senior official, thought Nathan, who spends most of his time out on a golf course. It was an opinion that began to change however, as he watched him work the room and prepare for the briefing. By the time the briefing was to begin, Nathan was willing to bet he'd done this more than once. He took a patriarch's position at the head of the table and there was no need to call for order as he began to address the group.

"Technical report Tom," he said, looking at the man to his right wearing a discreet wireless headset.

"Just one thing new overnight," the technician said, speaking to the entire group. "We finally got a camera into the first room and have a live video feed. Still no luck on the second room – sound only there. Indications are that all four hostages are still in that second room. Come by our corner of the world and take a look at the feed when you have a minute. As usual, anything significant we learn from monitoring will be up on the status board."

"Negotiations," said the Situation Commander.

The next man at the table spoke up. "The bad news is we're not having much luck establishing a rapport with these guys. We're working on it but it's getting more and more frustrating. I'm not sure if they're smart enough to realize what we're trying to do with them or if it's because they're so crazy. All three are lifers, so they know the routines well enough, but there isn't a hint of co-operation. I'm starting to worry."

"How about the hostages? How are they holding out?" asked the Commander.

"Good, as far as we know," said the Negotiator. "They let me talk briefly to Priller, the senior guard, and I got the usual stiff upper lip routine. What about Technical?" He looked across the table. "Tom, what do you hear on the wires?"

"Got a bunch of threats, ranting and raving and a bit of roughing up and slapping. Not too unusual, but," he cautioned, "it hasn't let up."

"Hmm . . . I agree that is unusual, they should be finished venting by now."

"Any Stockholm Syndrome?" someone asked.

"We haven't seen or heard indications of any."

"Neither have we," concurred the Negotiator.

"Assault report." The Situation Commander nodded to the next man in line.

An older version of Danny, in black combat fatigues with a Smith & Wesson on his left hip, opened a folder in front of him. "Just some fine tuning to the plans already posted on the main board," he said. "If we have to do it, it won't be pretty. The only window into the main room is boarded up with a table, eliminating our snipers completely. If we have to go in, the hostages will be in for a rough time because of the stun grenades. And we'd have to use lots.

"The AR-15's worry me, but then accurate firepower in the perps' hands always worries me. The other problem is that they know where we have to enter, namely the main door. Sometimes, I wish we didn't build prisons so securely. It's only the processing wing but when it's built to keep them in it keeps us out too."

"You have some new resources, Luke," said the Commander pointing at Kim and Nathan. "Those two people standing by the wall are Feds who have some . . . uh . . . advanced technical skills that may be of help to you. The Attorney General's office and his state equivalent called to tell me they have their highest recommendation and we are to use them wherever possible."

Every eyebrow in the room lifted. Those with their backs to the pair shifted in their chairs to study them.

"That's like a recommendation from God," said Tom leaning forward. "Just what is it you two do anyway?"

Kim folded her arms and looked expectantly at Nathan, who took the hint. "It's a long story," he said. "Before we get into it I think we should meet with Luke here and see if there's some way we can help first."

"Sounds like a plan," said the Commander moving on to the next report.

After the briefing, Nathan and Kim met with the C.E.R.T. leader, Luke, and two key people from his team. They briefly explained Nathan's skill and purpose – to skeptical and incredulous looks – and then went into detail about what he could or could not do. Kim produced the videotape taken on the Portland runway and they watched it together, first in real time, then slower with Nathan doing a play by play. He shut the tape off at a point shortly after the lights went out on the opposition's car. Kim dropped some names and handed Luke half a dozen business cards that were a who's who of the law enforcement tactical community. While Luke excused himself to go to the bathroom – everyone knew he was really making phone calls – Nathan showed some of his gear to the other two team members.

Luke eventually returned from his 'bathroom break.' "I've been thinking about it and I think we should put a plan together that includes you," he said. "Carl," he pointed at the younger of his two men, "you're with me. Let's do a show and tell to explain to Nathan and Kim exactly what we have here and then we'll draft up a few options that include them. Dave, you look after things while I'm gone."

And so it went. It took another full hour to get a physical tour, see drawings and review the status board. Another hour after that and by the midday briefing they had several plans worked out that utilized Nathan.

"Technical report," said the Situation Commander, signaling the beginning of the briefing.

"Good news, bad news and worse news," said Tom.

Nathan wondered if he ever took that headset off. Probably showered with it on.

"The good news is we wormed a camera into the second room and it's working fine. The bad news is they're shooting up in there. The worse news is we don't know what they've got but it seems to be making them more violent and aggressive."

Groans erupted from around the table.

"I'm working with Tom on this," said the Negotiator. "As is one of our prison doctors. He's seen it all, working in here but we're still trying to figure out what they're putting into their veins. In the meantime, Tom's right. They're becoming more violent and paranoid. I'm not getting anywhere with them and I don't like it. I recommend we increase our assault readiness a level."

The Situation Commander looked expectantly at his C.E.R.T. leader. "We have several plans ready," said Luke taking the cue. "Using our two new friends I think we can do it without stun grenades. The trick will be getting Nathan in the door, if we can do that our chances are good."

"I can probably set that up," said the Negotiator. "But just what is it he's going to do once he gets in there?"

"Well . . . he . . . it's . . .," Luke was having trouble finding the right words.

"He's a gunfighter," said the Commander.

Nathan winced. Kim's mouth dropped open and her eyes widened in surprise. Just as quickly she looked down at the floor to hide a growing smile.

No one at the table spoke. They looked at the Commander. They looked at Nathan and Kim. And they looked at each other.

"Pardon me?" questioned the Negotiator.

"You heard me. The kid's a gunfighter. I imagine they don't like that term," he said, scanning the two people leaning against the wall. "But that's what he does. Sorry you two but I don't have time to be diplomatic." He pointed at Nathan, who was wishing he could slink out of the room. "He can draw a gun and kill you so fast you can't see it happen. Word is, he's the best in the world. Personally I thought the last one died when Wyatt Earp kicked off, but I guess I was wrong. I don't know how he learned this particular trade or where he's from. But they're here and they're ours, so we'll use them. That gentlemen, is what they do."

Luke looked at Nathan and Kim and shrugged apologetically. He carried on speaking to the Negotiator. "We have some ideas for getting Nathan in. I know that normally it's not what's done because of the danger but this is different."

"*Different?* Now there's an understatement," said the Negotiator rolling his eyes and throwing up his hands. Adding in resignation, "Sit down with me after the briefing for a couple of minutes and if you want in with a bunch of drugged up violent cons with AR-15's I'll get you in. Personally I think you'd have to be crazier than them to want in there."

Tom held up his hand and leaned forward onto the table stopping all conversation. "You want crazy?" he said, his head cocked to one side, intent on a message coming in through his headset. "I've got crazy for you. They've cut off one of Priller's fingers."

The briefing was over.

"Luke," yelled the Commander. "Get ready to put your gunslinger into that room now! If we can't get Priller out of there, we're going in after him." He turned to the Negotiator. "Get one of those scumbags on the line and find out what's going on." He held up a cautionary hand. "And remember if he doesn't tell us what they've done to Priller then we don't know. Be careful what you reveal."

Luke, Nathan and Kim ambushed the Negotiator before he made it to his telephone. "Can you get Nathan in to do a food delivery?" Luke asked him.

"Are you out of you're mind Luke, you can't send someone in there?"

"I don't have time to argue," came Luke's terse reply. "Set it up!"

"I'll be okay," contributed Nathan trying to soothe the concerns. It worked, a sigh of resignation was his response. "Kim will work with you on what we need to tell them. I'll get my hardware ready."

"And I'll get my team into full standby position," said Luke. "If we have to go before we can do the food delivery then we'll do it with stun grenades."

Nathan stood twenty feet down the hall from the entry door holding the food tray of lasagna and salad. A large dome shaped metal cover with a handle on top was keeping the lasagna warm, its odor seeping out from under the lid. He liked lasagna and hadn't eaten for six hours, but he wasn't the least bit hungry. He was cold. It wasn't that the hallway was particularly cold, at least for a fully clothed person. But for someone totally naked, like himself, it was freezing. He was making the planned food delivery but they hadn't anticipated the con's specifying that the kitchen boy be naked. He hoped their demand was because they were nervous about someone sneaking in a gun. He'd heard stories about prisons. Well, if it was the only way to get in, that's how you did it.

He was on camera already. Even outside the door, there was a video signal piped into the command center. Normally he wouldn't have cared, but Kim was back there and that made him self-conscious. He allowed himself to think about it a little and found he wasn't sure if it was just because she was a female or if there was something else there, some other feeling. A mental slap refocused him – stay detached, stay professional. To take his mind off Kim he looked down to his left at the C.E.R.T. members lined up along the wall; each man crouched down and tucked in tight behind the one in front, carbines in hand. They looked like a coiled black spring, a deadly one. They were his lifeline – if he survived long enough to be thrown one. He had checked the weapons list on the status board one last time before coming down to the inner perimeter. The list had been modified to read two AR-15's and one knife. Nathan was fighting to control his mind, his heart rate and his breathing. He had to remain calm at the center, even though he was scared spitless. He tried to visualize an IPSC stage like this one. *Shooter will begin standing erect, facing targets, naked and holding a pan of lasagna. On start signal . . .* It was wildly funny but the laughs wouldn't come.

Luke stood behind Nathan. "Green light," he said, clapping him on the shoulder, and Nathan walked to the door.

"Food delivery," he yelled. The effort he had put into keeping his voice from cracking failed. The door didn't budge and he was opening his mouth to yell again when it swung open. He saw no one. That was to be expected.

"Step through nice and easy," came a voice from around the corner.

"This is insane," said the Situation Commander. "How did I ever get talked into this?" On the monitor he could see

Nathan inside the room, one con on either side. Both covering him with AR-15's.

"I can picture better arrangements," agreed Kim. "He'll want them both on the same side before he does anything." She checked the monitor showing the second room, the third con was still in there guarding the hostages. "On the bright side, if he can get one of them to move, and then go two-on-one, they're both dead."

The Commander looked at Kim, fully expecting to see the false bravado or facetiousness so common in people facing tense situations. To his surprise there was none of either.

When the door slammed shut behind Nathan the smell was overpowering. It was the worst locker room imaginable, multiplied a thousand times, with a malfunctioning chemical toilet thrown in. He fought the temptation to gag and tried to breathe through his mouth instead of his nose. A kitchen staffer would be nervous and scared and he tried to adopt the look, it took little effort. The room was trashed. Garbage and human waste littered the floor, while the walls were covered with graffiti and slime. Anything that wasn't broken was defaced. The con to his left started to move and stopped directly in front of him. He wore no shirt and Nathan could see he was sweating profusely. His pupils were dilated.

"What you got for us?" he asked.

"Lasagna," said Nathan.

He balanced his AR-15 with one hand, keeping it pointed in Nathan's general direction. Then abruptly reached out with the other and snatched the stainless steel lid off the pan. "Well lookie that! There *is* lasagna in there. Not even any tricks. Very good, boy." He shouted over his shoulder into the other room. "Hey Lou! We got us some food!" Then he slammed the lid back down on the lasagna and stepped back.

The con behind and to the right of Nathan now began shuffling around to his front as well. As he moved, Nathan watched them begin to relax. The eyes drifted away from him occasionally and their muzzles wandered off of his body. He stood naked and helpless in front of them and they were in complete and utter control.

The con who hadn't spoken yet was studying him, a puzzled look on his face. He sat down on the edge of a desk and rested the AR-15's butt on his thigh, muzzle pointing up. He shared the dilated pupils and wild eyed look of his partner and a steady stream of mucus ran from his nose as he stared at Nathan.

"Jimmy, there's something wrong with this here picture," he said deliberately, wiping his nose with the back of a hand. His head cocked to one side as he examined Nathan.

"Huh?" said the other con looking at his partner.

"Now!" said Kim. She saw it was perfect. Nathan had them. But Nathan didn't move. They heard the voice of the other con coming over the speaker, tinny and far away.

"I don't see nothin' wrong. What's wrong?"

The con on the desk hung his head and shook it slowly. "You don't see nothin' wrong because you're a moron Jimmy." He looked up. "Hey Lou, get in here and tell this moron what's wrong here. And bring one of the guards in – the one with nine fingers."

"What are they doing?" asked the Commander to no one in particular.

"What's Nathan doing?" asked Kim, also to no one in particular. "He should have taken them."

"Nathan going into the room has been a major event in an existence that hasn't changed in two days," said the Negotiator. "They're going to get some entertainment value out of it just like we predicted. But I can't figure out what he sees as being wrong. Any ideas?"

The monitor showed Lou stepping into the room pulling the guard Priller in with him. Those watching could see the hand more clearly through this camera, unbandaged and dripping blood. The other hostages were still handcuffed to standpipes in the second room.

"So what's wrong," said Lou, as he held Priller. "What gives?"

"You see," said the smart one, speaking to Nathan who was still standing there holding the tray. "You see the kind of morons I have to live with. Look at him guys. Look at him!" All he got back in reply were shrugs. "You ever see kitchen help with a body like that? Well, have you man? This puke is cut. He's no kitchen slob. He's a ringer."

The Commander swore. Kim echoed it. The con was right. Nathan was fitter than he had ever been and he looked it, especially with no clothes on. They hadn't even thought of it but one of the cons had seen it right away.

"That's it. He has to do something now," said Kim.

"Diversion time?" asked the Commander.

"Definitely. He'll need all the edge we can give him."

At the Commander's nod a C.E.R.T. member beside him spoke softly into his microphone. "Diversion is keyed . . . the lady's on the button . . . standby." He looked at Kim. "Your call ma'am. On your mark."

Kim's face was inches from the monitor now, her hands sweaty around the remote control. She glanced at another monitor showing the entry team coiled and waiting at the front door. There was so much energy built up there, they looked ready to burst out of whatever was containing them at any second. Then she looked back to Nathan's monitor and waited with her thumb on the button.

Nathan could see the light come on in two dim brains. Make that three, he thought. He could include himself. At the moment he didn't feel any smarter than the dumbest of these thugs. They had been adamant about no cops – kitchen staff only. He had to admit it, while he wasn't big and muscular, when he took his shirt off these days he didn't look like a potato peeler. At least they didn't feel threatened yet. They were still the big boys with the bad guns and they were still in control.

The con holding Priller scratched at the stubble on his jaw with his shiv, a prison yard special, fabricated from a piece of scrap metal with white bandage tape wrapped around one end to form the handle. "Whada ya say we make *him* a nine-finger and see what he tells us about what they're planning? How 'bout it?"

Nathan sucked in a deep breath and let out a third. The cons took it as a sign of fear. They were half right, Nathan was also anticipating the start signal. The knife just made you number three, he thought. The snot faucet sitting on the desk to the right is two, and Jimmy here in front is number one.

Kim saw it the same way, and pushed the button.

Outside the boarded up window a cat started to meow. Not loudly, just soft gentle meows. A plea to come in – as if his owner had left him out too long. It was, after all, another miserable and dreary day and cats don't like to be outside on days like that. The sound was so innocent and at the same time so out of place that the people in the room could only have one immediate reaction. They looked toward the source and did so with no body alarm reaction occurring. They all looked except Nathan. Nathan let go of the tray.

Gravity hadn't yet started to drop the tray earthward when his left hand seized the handle of the lasagna lid. He jerked it off the food just like Jimmy had done, but his right hand clawed into the lid's concave bottom where it found his compact featherweight Caspian .45. He ripped it from its magnetic catch as his eyes swept the cons and evaluated their alertness and weapons one last time. Nothing had changed. Once again he held the power of life or death in his hands. Once again he was light years ahead of his adversaries. His last thought before pressing the trigger was about Danny and how angry he'd be.

Nathan extended his arm slightly and shot Jimmy, whose head was still turned, precisely through the right elbow. It was within a foot of contact distance and the shot shredded the arm. No need for a second, he thought, the troops on the other side of the door will be all over him in seconds. Still holding the .45 in one hand he shifted to number two, the con on the desk. He'd realized what was happening by now but hadn't had time to begin to move his rifle. The muzzle up hold was obscuring the entire right arm, so Nathan shot him once in the left shoulder. He tried for the heavy bone at the joint and could tell he'd connected as the shock opened up the right side target and his third round blew out the man's other shoulder sending him rolling from the desk. Being the last, the con with the knife was more aware than any of the others. His mind had caught up to what his eyes could barely follow but his body hadn't received notice yet. Nathan sent the fourth bullet through the con's leg, five inches above the knee. It expanded when it contacted flesh and shattered the femur as it coursed through the leg. The man fell where he stood.

Then Nathan dove to the floor and rolled into the corner as a black human spring uncoiled through the door and into the room with the force of a tornado.

Later that afternoon at the debriefing everyone involved in the operation watched the incident repeatedly on tape. Nathan and Kim weren't there. Kim had called in the results to Danny as she was required to do and he had ordered them both back to Tucson on the next available flight. The camera that had been planted into the room where the hostage taking had occurred had caught everything in its all seeing eye and although the perspective was somewhat off because of the wide-angle lens, the event was still there for all to watch. It was Tom the technician who noticed it first.

"Watch the tray after Nathan lets go of it," he said.

"Why?"

"Just watch it." He played the tape again in slow motion and fifty pairs of eyes watched intently.

"What?"

"I didn't see anything either."

"What are you talking about Tom?"

Tom leaned back in his chair. He'd watched it three times since first noticing it but there was still unbelief in his voice. "I'll play it again," he said. "Watch the tray. He shoots them all before the tray hits the floor."

CHAPTER ELEVEN

Nathan and Kim took a commercial flight back to Tucson, but George wasn't waiting at the airport to pick them up, it was Danny. He was cool and polite as he helped them with their baggage and tossed Kim the keys to the Suburban. He climbed in beside her and twisted in his seat to face Nathan as Kim negotiated out of the airport and onto the open road.

"What happened this time?" was all he said. Nathan saw dark circles under his eyes when he took off his sunglasses.

"Everything went pretty much the way we planned it," said Nathan. "I suppose Kim filled you in on all the details."

"Uh huh."

"The meowing speaker that the snipers lowered into position outside the window worked great. Everyone turned and looked. It gave me lots of time and as a result I was way ahead of them." He paused studying Danny and concluded he might as well go the rest of the way, Danny would take it there anyway. "I hadn't gone into the room planning to disable them Danny, but there was a point, probably about the time I kicked off the safety on the Caspian, that I realized it was all I could do."

"What do you mean, 'all you could do'?" asked Danny harshly. "Do you mean you couldn't bring yourself to kill them?"

"Yeah," said Nathan. "That's exactly what I mean. When . . . "

Danny cut him off. "Then you're no good to me Nathan and you're no good to anybody in this business. You're out of here. It's over. You can pack your stuff at the ranch and I'll get you a ticket home. It was a mistake to pick you."

Kim reached over and laid a hand on Danny's arm, stopping his tirade. "Let Nathan finish," she said.

Danny faced forward and stared thin-lipped at the traffic while Kim drove. Nathan took a deep breath. "I can't believe you don't get it Danny. I had all three of them dead to rights, over the barrel, flat out beat. Killing them wasn't necessary. They didn't stand a chance. You know what my reaction times are like; I'm the fastest human on the planet. A flipping freak of nature, you said it yourself."

Danny didn't turn around. "It was a lie."

There was no sound in the Suburban. Kim's grip on the steering wheel turned knuckle-white and she waited for the explosion. Danny's words reminded her of an evening many years ago in an IDF barracks when the sound of a hand grenade spoon clattering across the floor had killed all the noise in the room. She barely had time to roll onto the floor, taking her mattress with her while thinking this is not the time or place for that sound. Nothing good can come of this.

"What?" said Nathan.

"It was a lie," Danny repeated. He looked Nathan in the eye. "It was a lie. We pulled that same scam on the other candidates too. We told everyone they had the fastest reaction times in the world and then warned them not to tell anyone else or get kicked out of the program. We wanted to see who would actually believe it. I had to know who believed in their own abilities. If you don't have self-confidence in this game you're dead before you start. You're reaction times aren't materially different from anyone else's. It was a lie."

Nathan fell back in his seat and stared out the darkened side windows. Late afternoon in Arizona had produced a brewing thunderstorm in the distance. The tops of the thunderhead rolled and blazed white in the afternoon sun while the bottom showed the dark blue/black of impending rain and the promise of jagged lightning.

Kim broke the silence. "Nathan, it doesn't matter what was said. You don't need anyone to trick you into believing you're good, or even the best in the world. That's a fact now, you've proven it. We all know it, and how it came to be doesn't matter any more. Danny is just concerned that you might not be able to kill someone if it were necessary."

"He's had to, twice. Two strikes. Can you tell me why I shouldn't call you out, Nathan."

"Yes, I can," said Nathan. "Kim and I talked about it on the plane. Do you remember those two lawyer-agents that you brought in to talk about legal justification, use of force, that kind of thing? They said a person can't legally use deadly force on someone if there's a viable lesser option. Okay, that's the law and it sounds good to me. Personally, morally, I agree with that and it's how I've felt both times. I'm new at this Danny, and still learning, but as I'm lining up on these guys my conscience is telling me I can't kill them because I have a lesser option available."

Danny shook his head, opening his mouth but Nathan cut him off. "Every good cop does the same thing, Danny. The difference is they don't have my abilities. They all have roughly the same competency and so the action that is legally and morally correct for them to take is going to be the same for all of them. Get this through your head, Danny, I'm different!"

"Okay, you're different," said Danny, the anger still in his voice. "I'll allow you that. But can you guarantee me that you can kill someone when you have to? Can you guarantee me that one of your fancy shots won't miss and you'll get someone hurt or killed as a result?"

Nathan conceded. "No, of course I can't guarantee that. All I can guarantee is to judge each situation as it comes along and do my best with it."

They drove on in silence. The thunderstorm was moving fast and they caught the edge of the rain. Kim turned on the wipers and their rhythmic slapping provided welcome relief from the stillness in the vehicle. The storm either took a different course or she had outrun it by the time they got to the ranch. It was dry there but the clouds were visible in the distance.

Danny extracted a sheaf of papers from his portfolio as Kim brought the vehicle to a stop. "He's off operational duties for ten days," said Danny, pointing his thumb back at Nathan and giving Kim the papers. "The Secret Service is starting an Executive Protection course in Quantico after the long weekend. You're both booked to take it. The details are in here. Be there. Take some time off and come back ready to work on the 18th. I have meetings in Washington and I'm going to spend some time with my family." He ignored Nathan.

* * * * *

Mr. Kent looked up as his secretary, Jenny, ushered Danny Forbes into the office. Extracting himself from behind his desk he immediately went forward to shake hands.

"Good day Mr. Forbes," he said. "So good to see you again."

Danny exchanged pleasantries with him. This was his first time in Mr. Kent's office and he was impressed. He'd been in government service long enough to recognize that a corner office with large windows, like this one, meant you had arrived. Large enough to hold four standard government offices it was decorated in a purely British fashion with oak paneling, leather and antiques. And not just British, thought Danny, but old world colonial British. Correction, colonial hunting gentleman of the upper classes, British. But then Mr. Kent did seem to fit that British tradition. One could easily imagine him, a man in his sixties, in a pith helmet and grasping a double rifle stalking game in the wilds of Africa. The room fit.

"Do you like my little sanctuary?" asked Mr. Kent. "I realize it's not normally what one sees in corporate America."

There was something about him that put people at ease in an instant. Perhaps it was the accent and the grandfatherly face. "Very impressive," said Danny. He wondered how he managed to get away with having a Zebra skin on one of the paneled walls. It must drive the bunny huggers in the building nuts.

"You're wondering how I can do this in a 'government' office," said Mr. Kent.

"Definitely."

"The trick is to have an employer who wants your talents badly enough to allow some eccentricities and then to pay for them yourself."

Danny nodded, still looking around the room. Mr. Kent had arrived on scene once The B-Zone Project went international, ostensibly as a combined representative of Interpol and an anti-terrorist office within the United Nations. The Director had brought him down personally and introduced him.

"Give Mr. Kent every co-operation," the Director had said pointedly. "It's important to me."

So Mr. Kent had entered the loop, establishing a presence at all the top level briefings as well as being on the receiving list of Danny's progress reports. At first he'd said little in the meetings but his apparent interest and participation grew as the project progressed. The appointment today was a first. Mr. Kent had called him, requesting a meeting in his New York office three blocks from the UN building. At least Danny had been heading to Washington; it allowed him to merely make the New York stop first.

Mr. Kent lifted a file folder from the scrupulously neat top of his walnut desk. Danny was able to read the tab, *Project B-Zone – After Action Reports*. He suspected the few papers in the file were his reports on Nathan's active jobs so far.

"Come, sit down with me won't you?" Mr. Kent ushered Danny away from the desk and window to a sitting area framed in by a small bar and an extensive book collection. "Could I offer you a drink?" he asked. Danny declined. "Very well then, shall we get down to business Mr. Forbes. I see your people have seen some action." He held the file in his lap unopened.

"Yes sir, they have," said Danny.

"As I recall from your original briefings you had not expected this amount of activity so early in the project?"

Danny nodded. "That's absolutely right. So far my activity predictions haven't been accurate at all. I had originally anticipated our candidate to go active on five to ten percent of the projects he was sent on. It's turned out to be two-thirds. But we're evaluating a small sample so far and I believe what's happening is nothing more than a statistical anomaly. I still believe my projections will be correct over the long term."

"He has done very well so far," said Mr. Kent. "I congratulate you Mr. Forbes. This is really top notch work on your part and seems to have much potential." He tapped the file in his lap. "You have done precisely what you claimed you could do, extract skills from competition and apply them to law enforcement. You are a man of vision, a quality sadly lacking in our world.

"You know we have a chap in the UK who was, at one time, a champion rifle shot. He too had a vision. He believed that if he took what he had learned from competitive rifle shooting and applied that knowledge to building sniper rifles for the military and law enforcement a superior product would result. And, you know, he was right. He currently owns a firm that supplies professional users world wide with tactical rifles. Someone with vision much like yourself."

"Thank you sir," said Danny, the praise making him uncomfortable but proud at the same time.

"Anyway, enough of that Mr. Forbes. Suffice it to say, you have made a believer of me. Tell me now, how is Mr. Burdett adjusting to his new role?"

"I think he's still exploring it," said Danny, glad to change topics. "He's moving from the competition shooting world into the law enforcement world and that's a major shift."

"Yes. Quite. I'm sure it is. Tell me, do you intend to allow him to continue shooting competitively."

"Yes I do. I think it's important he remain, at least to some degree, within that environment and community. Equipment and technique continue to evolve and anything new will be developed and learned there first. Because of security concerns I've instructed him not to win any major matches. He doesn't like the idea, but the compromise we've worked out is he can shoot to the fullest extent of his capabilities on several stages at any match. The rest he has to throw. That'll give him the benefit of competition without the risk of becoming a star."

Mr. Kent chuckled. "I imagine he will develop a bit of a reputation if he does much of that."

"I expect he will," said Danny. "He'll become known as a crash and burn artist. I suspect 'doing a Burdett' may become a new phrase in that sport, but he's willing to live with it. He knows what his abilities really are."

Mr. Kent was about to say something but stopped himself and paused for a moment before carrying on. "I sense there is something else Mr. Forbes. Something you're not sure of yourself and it surprises you, something that makes Mr. Burdett very different. It's not in any of your reports or in what you've told me, but it's there nonetheless. Am I correct?"

Danny felt like someone had pried open his skull and looked inside at his thoughts. He shrugged, hands apart. "Well, yes. Sure. Everyone is different. No one is totally predictable."

"Come now, Mr. Forbes," said Mr. Kent. "I understand that, but there's something else here?"

"Burdett's still improving." Danny paused to let Mr. Kent digest that piece of information. "I had expected that by now he would've plateaued. He hasn't. He's still working hard at his skills and although the improvement rate has slowed, his abilities are still showing a steady methodical improvement."

"Amazing," said Mr. Kent. "Amazing." He seemed to be probing his own thoughts as he fingered the file in his lap. "I do have one concern," he said, picking both reports from the file and signaling a change of topic. "Mr. Burdett's first two actions are interesting. I had some of our people review the video segments available to us and everyone is highly impressed by his technical skills. Comments such as 'unbelievable,' 'super-human' and 'staggering' were the order of the day. He certainly is a skilled marksman."

"So what's the concern?" asked Danny.

"I'm getting to that ... I'm getting to that," said Mr. Kent holding up one hand. He leaned back in his chair and hesitated as if to add emphasis to his words. The leather and oak creaked as his weight shifted.

"Now, you must understand that these incidents have been reviewed by some of the best people in the business." He swept a hand in Danny's direction. "People not unlike yourself Mr. Forbes. They all agree that Mr. Burdett would have been justified in killing all the scoundrels he's encountered so far. Additionally, killing them would have posed less risk to the outcome of the operation. In all the proposals and reports I've reviewed on this project, I don't recall any discussion about this bizarre shooting technique of his. Is not our intention to deploy a shooter like him against people who must be neutralized? If that requirement is not there – we do not use that degree of force. Do you agree Mr. Forbes?"

"That was our original intention – I agree to that extent. Your comments remind me of a question Nathan Burdett asked when I first told him the truth, he asked me if neutralize meant kill. I told him in the real world it did and he accepted that at the time. His skill, however, is rewriting our own rule book for us. Without our permission I might add."

"Is there a reluctance to kill?" asked Mr. Kent pointedly.

Danny hesitated before answering. He didn't like this conversation any more. "No, none that I'm aware of," he lied. As soon as the words were uttered he suspected Mr. Kent knew them to be lies.

"I see." The reports went back into the file, but not until the sheets of paper were precisely aligned. "That is encouraging. I would hate to see unnecessary risks taken and injuries occur because Mr. Burdett has some difficulty in performing his job."

"That won't happen," said Danny.

"I'm pleased to hear that," said Mr. Kent.

He knows I'm lying, thought Danny. And he knows that I know. So we both know, but we'll play the game nonetheless. "If I perceive a problem I'll report it," said Danny.

"Certainly. I'm sure you will. If he did have such a problem, theoretically speaking of course, how would you go about helping him . . . " he pursed his lips searching for the right word, ". . . helping him overcome this personal obstacle."

"There is no problem," repeated Danny. "He's a young man with a high moral standard who won't kill unless it's absolutely necessary. His abilities give him more leeway in making that decision than anyone I've ever known."

"I see," said Mr. Kent. "Is he capable of seeing the big picture?" he asked.

"I don't know what you mean?"

"Suppose he were . . . ?" Something stopped that train of thought. "Never mind," said Mr. Kent waving it off with a toss of his hand. "Mr. Burdett is a teachable young man and responds well to training does he not?"

"Yes he does."

"Of course, but that's a recurring theme in your reports isn't it?"

There was a chill in the room. Mr. Kent tried to warm it by discussing other aspects of the project and leaving that topic behind. He only partially succeeded. Danny eventually looked at his watch and politely took his leave, making it as far as the door.

"One last thing before you go Mr. Forbes. Would you please have your office send over Mr. Burdett's complete personal file? I confess that we don't normally require information that detailed on any project but Mr. Burdett is of great interest and it would be of assistance to me I'm sure."

Danny stiffened. "No," he said. "I don't think that's necessary or appropriate. I understand that the project is international now, and I accept that your position in Interpol and the UN means you have an interest in it, but the people are mine. I'm sorry Mr. Kent, I'll extend every courtesy I can but I can't give you personal files. Good day, sir." He turned and left, closing the door with slightly more force than necessary.

Mr. Kent waited a few moments to be sure Danny had passed by his secretary before buzzing her. "Jenny would you call the Director's office and have them send over Nathan Burdett's personal file . . . . Yes, The B-Zone Project. . . . That would be fine. Thank you, my dear."

217

CHAPTER TWELVE

After the killer brought in to eliminate Nathan Burdett had himself been killed, the Riders temporarily withdrew in anticipation of the heat that would result. They noted an increase in police drug raids, at least that's what the warrants said, but preparations had been made and little was found. Once it was safe they started looking for him again.

But now he and his family had really disappeared. That made Red's temper worse than ever. Not so much as a sniff of Burdett for months. Even the slut they had wormed into a job at the police computer center couldn't come up with anything.

Then he got the phone call. It was a jerk he ran into several times every year, especially when the Riders did their public relations projects, like the charity bike rides. He hated those things. Ferrying stuffed animals to a bunch of ungrateful snotty kids was a waste of time. But the boys upstairs said 'do it,' so every year it happened. Last year, once the media left, they put stuffed animals under the rear wheels of their hogs and spun out on them. Man, could those critters fly! Now *that* had been fun. The worst thing about those projects was guys like this sniveling weasel who hung around and tried to help. Mostly though, they just idolized the Satan's Riders, dreaming of the day they too would be allowed to join. Now that was a joke. A 'wannabe' was all this bozo would ever amount to. He had about as much chance of becoming a member, as Hell freezing over and the devil taking up figure skating.

"Heard you're looking for Nathan Burdett," the caller had said.

"Maybe," Red didn't like getting these calls at home. He had to assume the phone here was wired.

"I heard something the other day that you might be interested in," the man said, in his usual boot-licking voice.

"Go ahead." Best not to say too much. That's what their lawyer told them to do when not sure who's talking or who's listening.

"Burdett's mother's birthday is coming up and he'll be back in the area."

Red didn't reply right away, he chose his words carefully. "Yeah, so?"

"So he'll be showing up at his gunsmith buddy's shop next week, Saturday the 15th. Sometime in the evening. Probably not till after dark. Do you need the address?"

Red wanted to ask him how he knew all this but he couldn't. Again he chose his words carefully. "Never heard of him," he said, hanging up the phone and immediately leaving the house.

"What do you think?" asked Pete. "Is it legit' or is it a set-up."

"I don't know," Red replied, making a right turn onto 3rd Street. "I don't know what to think." They were driving around downtown in a random pattern taking advantage of the privacy in Red's Dodge pick-up to discuss this new development. "We've sure put the word out everywhere. Maybe something's finally clicked. On the other hand, Burdett's got a lot of cop friends."

"So what do we do?"

Red stopped at a light and waited for the pedestrians to cross. A pretty girl in a short skirt got a little extra attention. She straightened as she noticed them, especially the disfigured face behind the wheel and walked faster as a result. The target of the gaze was obvious so Red flipped her an obscene gesture to hurry her across the street. "I've got an idea," he said. "It'll give us a chance to grab him without committing to anything if we smell a rat. We'll hang back and if he shows, his carcass is ours. It's hard to believe we might finally get him." He tried to smile but the scarring on his face made it lopsided.

* * * * *

Load, acquire the target, press the trigger. . . another bike exploded. Load, acquire the target . . . someone ran up to the bike he was sighting on and tried to drag it from the line. Was he crazy? A gas tank blew from the heat of the fire and he saw the man knocked backwards by the blast. His long hair burst into flame and then his clothes caught fire as well. Leaping to his feet he fought blindly against the flames. Nathan clearly heard screaming above the racket of the still booming music.

As Nathan watched, he came to the realization that the scopes' cross hairs were centered on the struggling man's back and that his finger had taken up at least two pounds of weight on the three-pound trigger. He added one more pound, the Ruger punched back at him as the bullet streaked forward, no longer under his control, and he waited to wake up.

Kim looked down at the young man sleeping in the airplane seat beside her. His eyelids showed the twitching indicative of REM sleep. He was dreaming. Good dreams or bad dreams she wondered. She was concerned and there was reason for it. A battle was going on inside of him, she'd seen it ever since they came back from Attica. Danny's tirade had started it. He had been quiet and morose while on the course, had made too many dumb mistakes and then refused to talk about any of it. Something had to change or he wasn't going to survive. That would be too bad. He was genuinely a nice person, just a little naive.

Something was wrong – he wasn't waking up. The Nosler passed two hundred yards, still climbing. This wasn't how the dream went, he was supposed to wake up now. Three hundred yards and just beginning to level off. This wasn't right. Nathan didn't want to see this. At 411 yards the bullet reached apogee and started down. He didn't want to watch but he couldn't tear his eyes away from the scope. One hundred and fifty grains of lead, gilding metal and polymer hurtled past six hundred yards at more than twice the speed of sound. Wake up. Wake up now! Seven hundred yards and Nathan's screams were cut short by the impact. He saw the hit. A geyser of dirt and dust tossed up as the bullet buried itself. Buried itself a foot to the right of the burning figure. The wind caught the dust and blew the plume further right. Then he felt it on his face – the wind, blowing in from his left, an authoritarian gust of a breeze, a night visitor moving through the bowl, rearranging whatever was in its power; leaves, dust and bullets. Gone into the Rockies. The only thing left to show for its presence, a bullet blown off course.

"Welcome back," said Kim as Nathan stirred beside her and opened his eyes. "The pilot just throttled back the engines to begin descent."

"I missed . . . ," Nathan mumbled through the receding fog of sleep.

Kim heard it and cringed inwardly. Something from the dream no doubt and it didn't sound encouraging. "What did you say Nathan?" She closed her magazine hoping he'd talk.

"What? . . . Oh, nothing Kim." He massaged his face with his palms and finished by smoothing his hair back. He sat erect and looked out the window away from Kim. He'd missed, hadn't been paying attention to conditions and the wind came up. The sparks from the fire would have told him of the change if he'd been watching. But he hadn't been – and so he missed. Saved by the wind. Wasn't that a kick in the head. Nathan took a deep breath. He'd been saved by the wind.

At least now he knew how the dream ended. Had there been a puff of wind that night? He couldn't consciously remember one – but he'd been doing this long enough that maybe, just maybe, something had registered in his subconscious and this was his mind's way of processing it. If the Ruger had fired this is what would have happened. He liked that explanation, turning it over in his mind several times and then grabbing onto it. With it came a feeling the dream was over now, that it wouldn't be back.

Nathan and Kim's Northwest Airlines flight approached the Calgary International Airport on Friday the 14th of August. The window seat and the long circling approach allowed him to see far enough into the western mountains to pick out areas of the wild land he had once hunted. That seemed so long ago, everything had changed since then. He couldn't help but wonder what would have happened if he had stayed here and kept his EMT job. What if he had told Danny to stuff it? But he hadn't and he knew better than to dwell on 'if onlys' and 'I should haves.' Besides, when he asked himself if he had made the right decisions in the last year the conclusion was always yes. Well, except for shooting up the Riders.

Nathan was looking forward to a weekend at 'home.' They'd finished the Executive Protection course and Kim had agreed to fly to Calgary with him. He felt like talking now.

"I should've let you have the window seat," he said. "You've never seen this part of the Rockies."

"I'll take it on the way back to Tucson," replied Kim. "Besides, I'll see them from the ground. Naomi is taking me to Banff and Lake Louise."

"She's been at the Consulate long enough to know her way around this part of the world?"

Kim nodded. "Three years as administrative manager at the Calgary Israeli Consulate. And it's been more than four years since I've seen her, so I'm looking forward to it. Like I told you, we were good friends in University."

Nathan pulled his Daytimer from the inside pocket of his sports jacket and extracted a worn business card. It said 'Bob's Gunsmithing' on the front along with all the other usual business details and on the back was a small map showing how to find the shop. "This is my friend Bob's business card. You've heard me talk about him and you gave me Frankie's message?" Kim nodded. "I'm going there for dinner tomorrow evening and I'd love for you to meet them. They live in a beautiful little spot out in the country near where my family used to live. I'll be hanging around there. I'll write my mother's phone number on the back too, so you can get in touch with me there if you need to. And of course you have my pager number."

Kim smiled patiently, taking the card. "If I need to reach you I will. But I haven't seen Naomi for a long time so I suspect I'll be spending the entire weekend with her."

They picked up their luggage together and Nathan walked with her to the cabs lined up outside the terminal building. "Meet you upstairs in front of the Northwest Airlines counter one hour before our return flight on Monday," Kim said before she closed the cab's door. Nathan watched the car pull away and merge into traffic, he couldn't help feeling disappointed she hadn't taken the opportunity to meet his family.

223

Readjusting the grip on his own bags he walked off to find the car rental booths.

Fifteen minutes later he drove a Grand Am off the airport property, took two quick exits and checked for tails. Nothing attracted his attention so he pulled into the parking lot of one of the numerous courier companies occupying the light industrial area around the airport. His bags were in the back seat and it took him only a short time to find the Para-Ordnance P-10 stashed there. Threading the holster through his belt secured the gun behind his right hip while the jacket he wore adequately concealed it.

It was his mother's birthday today and they were going out for dinner. When she got off work Nathan was waiting for her in the alley outside the Calgary Police Service downtown headquarters. She felt the Para-Ordnance through his jacket when she hugged him but didn't say anything even though her hand hesitated on the lump for just a moment.

Nathan noticed the different touch. "A tool of the trade, Mom," he said. "You should be used to them, considering where you work."

"I guess I'm just not used to my son carrying them," said Emily Burdett. "I was getting used to you being an EMT and now you're a policeman. Sometimes things change too quickly for an old lady."

"You're a lady but you're not old," said Nathan, taking her by the arm. "Tell me how you've been doing and where you want to go for dinner."

He ushered her into his car and negotiated the vehicle into the Friday afternoon rush hour. "Todd and Louise are going to join us at the restaurant," she said.

"Wonderful," replied Nathan, surprised and pleased at the prospect of seeing his sister and brother-in-law again.

Their dinner together proved to be excellent, both in terms of the food and the company. The family stayed late into the evening, talking about all the things families discuss when they gather after long absences, but they didn't talk about Nathan's job. Todd had intended to ask him about it. All he knew was that Nathan had been hired on as a firearms consultant to an international law enforcement project and the word in the family was not to ask him about it. He'd been thinking about doing it anyway but as he talked to his brother-in-law he became aware of a difference in him. He had changed in some ways.

Todd noticed that he made a point of sitting so he could see the door and he examined everyone that came in or walked by their table. In fact his eyes never stopped moving, even when having a direct conversation with one of them his eyes roamed the room. It was as if he wanted to be aware of absolutely everything that was going on around him. What Nathan was seeing or what he did with the information that was being collected, Todd had no idea, but it was a new behavior pattern and it made him apprehensive. Todd decided to leave it alone.

The next day Nathan made a point of looking up Paul, whose leg was improving and who had recently been upgraded to desk duties. Paul saw the same changes that Todd had. Paul, however, commented on them.

"So you've seen the elephant," he said.

"Danny tell you?"

"No, I never see Danny any more. He just used me to check up on you, remember?"

"How'd you know?" asked Nathan.

"Oh . . . it shows. Reading people is part of this business." He paused. "Tricking people into admitting stuff is another part."

Nathan cuffed him on the back of the head.

"Hey, don't pick on a cripple!"

"I'll break your other leg if you try that on me again," said Nathan laughing.

"Then don't fall for it again," Paul countered. "You obviously made out okay."

"Yeah."

Paul waited to see if that curt answer was all and when nothing else was volunteered he decided it might be appropriate to change the subject. "By the way, what are you shooting? Get to try any neat stuff lately?"

"Always trying something new," said Nathan. "But still staying with the .45 in a 1911 design."

"No new wonder guns?"

"Not here. We've tried them but they don't have the accuracy or the shootability I need and because the aftermarket parts and gunsmithing knowledge isn't there to support them," he spread his hands and shrugged, "they can't be easily brought up to what I need. Good general purpose guns, but from my perspective give H&K and Glock a hundred years, if they're still around then I'll look seriously at them."

Paul laughed. "What kind of ammo do you like?"

"I'm shooting pretty much whatever the Bureau tests and checks out as okay for accuracy and expansion. Mostly Remington. That was a surprise to me. I got one lot of Winchester last month that also shoots well. I loaded some in a C-More sighted SVI match gun two weeks ago and went out into the desert jump shooting jacks. Talk about red mist! Great practice too."

"Danny still making you reload?"

"Not any more. I still do quite a bit though, I feel more in touch with a gun if I shoot reloads through it at least some of the time. It's as if I understand it better, how it operates, what it likes, what makes it choke, even if it operates one hundred percent with factory ammo. Does that sound weird?"

"Not to me, grasshopper," said Paul in a none too believable Chinese accent. "Being one with gun bring peace and harmony to inner being."

Nathan laughed as he clasped his hands together and bowed at Paul in response.

He's comfortable with technical matters noted Paul, keeping the conversation there, waiting for Nathan to signal a change.

"Been out to Bob's place recently?" Nathan eventually asked.

"No, I haven't," said Paul. "With this desk job I can't make the excuse to go out on patrol that way any more. Are you going to stop and see him while you're in town?"

"Absolutely," said Nathan. "That's part of why I'm here. Kim passed on a message from Frankie asking me to come up and see Bob. Seems he's been under the weather for a couple of weeks and needs cheering up. I'm not supposed to phone, just show up unannounced for supper and surprise him. It'll be fun."

That evening as the sun was setting, using the last of its fire to highlight the jagged shapes of the Rockies, Nathan drove northwest out of Calgary on 1A. The road he traveled and the sights he saw were all familiar and the feelings he'd experienced on the airplane yesterday came flooding back to him. Coming home was why the dream had resolved itself, he knew that now. Not that it made much difference, it was one of those nuisances you lived with, that's all. So much had changed that nuisances like it were inevitable. At least he hadn't changed. Everything around him maybe, but not him.

There was heavy traffic on the road through Cochrane and then very little after he turned down the county road that led to his old home. Shortly after turning off the highway, he passed a pick-up backed onto a little used approach leading to a large empty pasture. The two occupants were changing a tire. Their headlights shone across the road and illuminated Nathan's face as he slowed and looked without stopping. They didn't appear to need help.

They had been hiding in the trees below Bob Coombs' house since mid-afternoon. Except for the bugs trying to eat them, everything had been quiet. The traffic on the road out front was light and the old yellow dog lying on the deck hadn't moved the entire time. At one point, as the sun was setting, they had caught a flash of reflected light from the hills above the old Burdett place but they never saw it again and nothing moved up there now except a deer that trotted out of the timber and over the crest of the hill.

Red's cell phone buzzed quietly. "Yeah," he whispered into the mouthpiece.

"We got him. Just turned off the main road heading your way. Driving a green rental Grand Am. Looks to be alone. You got ten minutes max."

"Good. Stay where you are. Don't come in till I call." He pressed the 'End' button and pocketed the phone. "Payback time," said Red to the five men with him. "Let's go."

Red's biggest concern, the dog, had just been taken into the house, probably to be fed – lucky break for them. Darkness was descending as they moved through the trees. To the men outside there was sufficient light by which to see and maneuver but to those inside the dwelling and surrounded by artificial light it appeared to be fully dark outside. Moving more quietly as they neared the house Red signaled three armed men around to the front door. He crouched at the back with the others.

The shop doorbell buzzed and Bob got up from watching the evening news. "I'll get it," he said to Frankie, who was just finishing the dishes. When he opened the door, being a gunsmith, he noticed the sawed off pump shotgun before he really took note of the seedy individual holding it. He was about to give him his standard 'get that illegal gun out of my shop right now' lecture along with his 'and watch where you're pointing it too,' when the realization he was in trouble came to him. The two other armed men who appeared from the sides of the open door clinched it.

He raised his hands slowly, "Tell me what you want, no one has to get hurt."

The man nudged him with the muzzle of the gun and as he shuffled backwards he heard noises from the rear of the house. Frankie screamed. The concussion of a gunshot filled his ears.

Bob half turned toward the sound but then pivoted back to the three men, now fully in the shop. "Hey . . . "

The biker in front clipped off his words by straight arming the flat side of the shotgun's receiver into Bob's face, sprawling him backwards onto the floor and against the low table. "Shut up," he said, motioning to the other men to leave. "Go check the rest of the place. You . . . " the muzzle indicated he was speaking to Bob again, "Don't move and don't say nothin'."

The taste of blood filled Bob's mouth and he was trying to stem its flow from his nose when another man came into the shop and looked down at him. Through the daze that still swirled before his eyes the gunsmith saw the disfigured head look quizzically at the shotgun wielding man standing over him.

"I had to stroke him," was the answer.

The scarred head nodded and called back into the house. "Bring the woman in here."

Frankie appeared, pushed ahead of the men. She ran to Bob and knelt beside him crying.

"Are you okay?" she sobbed. "They shot Sandy."

"I think my nose is broken," said Bob as he put an arm around his wife. He'd never thought it would be a relief to hear his dog had been shot.

"Okay, Grandma. You first," said the scarred man. He grabbed her roughly by the arm and jerked her upright. Another man used duct tape to secure Frankie's hands behind her. Bob was next. They seated both on the floor in the center of the shop, backs to Bob's lathe.

They're in a hurry thought Bob, and they haven't asked for money or guns. What gives? Then, abruptly, they all disappeared from view, except for one who stayed to guard them. In the dim light there was no conversation and only the occasional soft sounds of men shifting positions as questions outnumbered answers. But within two minutes they heard the crunching of gravel and saw the glow of headlights that indicated a vehicle was parking in front of the shop.

Nathan planned on ringing the shop doorbell, that way the person opening the door would surely be Bob and the best net surprise could therefore be extracted. He pushed the button, still thinking about what to say when the door opened. His thoughts were cut off when he too saw the muzzle of a shotgun first, then the biker holding it and beyond that, Bob and Frankie seated on the floor with an armed man standing over them.

"Well, well, look who came to visit," said the man with the shotgun.

For a fleeting second Nathan thought of feeding him a .45 hollow point but abandoned the idea as another man with a Mini-14 stepped around the corner of the house on his left.

"Step in," said the holder of the shotgun. "Real slow." Nathan did as he was told. He heard the man from outside come in behind him and close the door. That made four men in the shop now. Riders! He knew what this was about, they wanted his hide. Play dumb and keep thinking he told himself.

"What's going on here?" he asked.

A powerful man with a scarred face and scalp stepped around to face Nathan. He transferred a six inch barreled Smith & Wesson revolver from his right hand to his left as he walked up to Nathan. "What's going on is payback," he said, driving his right fist into Nathan's stomach.

Nathan doubled over and fell to the floor. He heard Frankie gasp before spasms of pain briefly blocked out the events around him.

His attacker, about to kick him as he collapsed, caught a glimpse of blued steel and brown leather. "He's got a gun under his coat," he yelled. The revolver came back into his right hand and he stepped back covering Nathan, at the same time indicating two of the others should take it away from him.

They pounced on him like feral dogs and pulled the .45 from his belt. One hesitated, then added two heavy booted kicks to Nathan's back before moving away and tossing the Para-Ordnance to the scarred man.

"Get him up."

They lifted Nathan and he staggered back to lean against the wall. The scarred man glared at him while he punched a number into his cell phone. There was a pause, "We got him, come on in. Stay outside though and watch to make sure we're not interrupted. One out front and one in the back. We'll let you know when we're done." He snapped the phone shut still looking at Nathan, who was starting to catch his breath, examining him like a cat might a pinned mouse. "You're the punk who shot up our bikes," he snarled. "And now it's time to settle that score."

"What about them?" gasped Nathan nodding toward Bob and Frankie. "They didn't have anything to do with it."

"Maybe so . . . maybe not. I don't care. We used them to get to you and they're friends of yours, so that settles it for them. I don't have any particular beef with those two so I'll make it quick for them. You're going to *want* to die . . . just like I did," he added. Then he noticed the puzzled look on Nathan's face.

"They call me Red. They used to call me that because of my red hair. Which as you can see ain't there no more." He tapped the stainless revolver's barrel against his bare skull. "Now they call me Red because that's the color my face is – forever!" He was nose to nose with Nathan now, reeking of stale booze and jabbing him in the chest with the revolver's barrel as he spoke. "One of your cute gas tank shots did this to me."

Nathan fought a rising panic and tried to get his training to kick in. The man was venting and that gave him time. Nothing would happen until he was through or before whoever he'd called showed up. Red delivered two vicious slaps to Nathan's face and continued ranting until they heard the sound of a vehicle pulling up outside. One of the bikers peeked out a curtained window. "Its Mack and Joey," he said.

"Good," replied Red.

Two more bikers appeared at the doorway leading into the house. "Mack and Joey are setting up to watch the outside," one of them said. "What do we do now?"

"Move Burdett over by the old timers, sit him down and watch them all. We're going to collect our bonus first." Red walked to where Bob sat on the floor. "Okay old man, we're going to take every gun you've got in the place. How do we do it? Do you give us the safe combination or should we beat it out of you?"

Bob saw no point in taking a beating so he surrendered the combinations to all three safes. With all three open the Riders began building a pile on the floor by the shop door, each gun tossed carelessly and landing with a clatter that made Bob wince. He was going to have some unhappy customers – if he lived to see it.

When Bob's personal Browning Superposed landed on the pile the shop air compressor abruptly kicked in and started chugging. That was normal enough since Bob had not yet turned it off for the evening. On a normal day people wouldn't have noticed, but in the tense atmosphere that filled the shop everyone jumped. Bob feared the gunman watching them would inadvertently pull the shotgun's trigger. "It's just the air compressor," he said. "It kicks in automatically whenever the pressure leaks down to 90 PSI."

"Shut up, I know about air compressors," snarled their captor.

The compressor had been running for five minutes when Bob heard a soft thunking sound, rapidly repeated and almost lost in the noise of the running machine. So faint he wasn't even sure he'd heard it and sounding like something he hadn't heard in a long time, there was no direction to the sound and it could have come from anywhere. He couldn't tell. Then he heard it again. He knew every strange noise or hiccup this compressor was capable of making, he'd heard them a thousand times. All the other shop noises he knew as well, but this sound didn't fit.

He was scared, but had hope too. He looked at Nathan, who gave no indication he'd heard anything.

When the pile of guns was complete Red instructed his laborers to collect ammo. Gathering every round they could find took another fifteen minutes. The smashing noises coming from inside the house told Bob they were searching there also, and by the time they stopped, Bob had to admit their thoroughness.

The bikers were standing over their loot evaluating the pile when Nathan spoke up in loud voice. "I hope you're going to fill out the appropriate government paperwork on all these guns your acquiring." A roar of laughter answered him and then Red swaggered over to where the captives sat.

"The only papers getting filled in here are your obituaries." The bikers laughed again. "Pete, you're a pretty good man with a torch. You think you can light up this old man's welding rig for me? We'll start by burning pretty boy's hair off."

"If he's got gas, I can light it," said Pete. He walked past the captives to the corner of the shop and came back towing a hand dolly with Bob's oxyacetylene system.

"No. Please. You can't do this," pleaded Frankie as Pete wheeled the cart past her.

Pete didn't break stride as he reached down and slapped her viciously across the face. "Shut up." Bob kicked out at him and sent the biker sprawling against the drill press. He bounced back and punched Bob in the mouth. Frankie began sobbing.

"Leave it!" yelled Red. "It's time we killed them anyway. We don't need them anymore." He turned to Nathan, a lopsided smile spreading across his face. "We could make Burdett watch." He hadn't thought of that before but he liked the idea. Anything to inflict pain on Burdett was a good idea. The ringing of the shop phone interrupted his thoughts. "Let it ring," he said. "Don't answer it."

"Rick, I want you to off our two senior citizens here. You're new and it's time you earned your colors."

Bob's answering machine cut in then and his taped voice came over the small speaker sounding raspy and out of place as he did his best to sound cheerful and encouraging to a potential customer whose call he had not been able to take. ". . . Just leave your name and number and a brief message after the beep." The beep sounded and the room's occupants heard a female voice.

"Good evening Satan's Riders. This is Hell calling. I thought you'd like to know that your reservations here are confirmed. Occupancy is mandatory unless you turn your guns over to your prisoners and surrender. Do that and you may live. By the way, we are an all-smoking establishment." A loud click indicated the caller had hung up. For a moment the only sound in the shop was the whir and click of the old tape machine as it stopped.

"What the . . ."

"Who was that?"

"Quiet! Pete! Check the front."

Pete ran to the shop door and opened it slowly. "Mack. Hey, Mack you . . . " The door stopped against something solid but Pete had it open far enough to get his head out and look down. He pulled back, slammed the door and threw the deadbolt. Pivoting away from the door he looked in horror at Red. "Mack's dead. He looks like he took a whole clip in the chest."

"Check the back," said Red. The two who had come in from the house ran back, turning off the interior lights as they went. One came back almost immediately.

"Joey's dead on the back step by the dog. It's a toss up as to who's got a bigger hole in 'em. What's happening Red?" The man was pale. "We didn't hear nothin'."

"Get back in the house and watch the outside," yelled Red. He stuffed the revolver into his waistband as he walked over to Nathan. "I'll find out what's going on here," he said, grabbing his lapels and jerking him up off the floor. The shop shook as he slammed Nathan into the wall beside the Colt cowgirl poster, pinning him there.

"Enough games!" He roared, foam forming on the sides of his mouth. He slammed Nathan against the wall again. "Who's out there? Did you call the cops somehow?" He slapped Nathan as hard as he could, once on each side of the face.

Nathan blinked his eyes to clear tears the stinging blows had generated but he said nothing, he was too scared.

Red took a step back and shouted to the others. "Pete keep watch out that back window. You two bring his friends over here where Burdett can see them."

Nathan watched as two bikers dragged the Coombs' to their feet and stood them eight feet to his right. Frankie had a Glock pistol leveled at her head and Bob was on the receiving end of a Beretta. Red was within touching distance to Nathan's left, the revolver still in his waistband.

A biker appearing in the doorway to the house interrupted whatever Red was planning. "Hey, Red, get in here, I see something moving out back."

"Watch him," said Red to the shooter holding Frankie. Pulling the revolver from his belt he ran off into the house. "I'll be right back," he called over his shoulder as the door closed behind him.

Nathan shifted slightly to his right and faced the two men holding his friends. Both the Coombs' were bleeding from the hits they'd taken and Frankie still sobbed quietly. The biker holding her pointed his Glock directly at Nathan now, arm bent, holding the gun loosely at waist level. He was ten feet away.

Nathan shifted his gaze to Bob and when their eyes met, saw agreement there.

The man covering him with the Glock wouldn't be able to keep his eyes on him constantly, there was too much going on, too much tension in the room. Besides, he wasn't disciplined enough. Eventually he'd look elsewhere. When he did, it'd be an edge, razor thin, but the best he'd get. Red would be back soon and then the odds would deteriorate further.

It was time. Six months ago he had dealt himself a hand in this game with the Riders, a seven hundred yard hand and now he was reaping the consequences of it. This wasn't what he wanted but because the past couldn't be undone it was what faced him . . . at least six bikers inside, all armed, with two no-shoots to keep out of harm's way. The gun would be there, loaded and ready to run, it had to be. He had never fired the Colt before, that meant learning it in process. Probably ten rounds, he thought. Bob usually didn't load ten plus one . . .

Nathan was watching the man's eyes when he heard Pete moving around the corner and metal clinked on metal. Frankie's captor turned his head to look and in Nathan's mind a buzzer sounded. He drove his own right hand through the center of the Colt poster where he scooped Bob's 'Ace-in-the-Hole' 1911 from its shelf, thumbed off the safety and brought it to bear on the nearest Rider. Action beats reaction every time thought Nathan, as he sent 230 grains of Bob's favorite, Speer Gold Dot, into the base of the man's brain. Shifting the gun slightly to the right gave him a view of the other biker's eyes over the front sight. For a moment panic gripped Nathan when it seemed that his gun's slide had not returned to battery. Just as quickly his subconscious reminded him, unlike the guns he was accustomed to, this was a 1911 with a normal cycling speed. He waited for the slide to slam home and when it did, delivered the same shot to the man holding Bob. If the killer had been totally keyed and watching for Nathan to so much as twitch he may have shot Bob before Nathan fired. He wasn't though, and seeing Nathan's movement his instinct had been to try and bring his gun to bear on the threat. The muzzle began its movement toward Nathan but never made the intended journey.

Both Riders crumbled as Nathan wheeled to his right to engage Pete around the corner. With pistol up and eyes looking over the top of the slide his left hand had moved up into a support grip on the turn and now felt the extended magazine that told him there was indeed a ten rounder in the gun. He'd seen Bob move also and heard him shoulder Frankie onto the floor as his eyes found Pete at the rear wall. Fully turned, facing Nathan and looking for the reason for the gunfire, his shotgun was coming up in anticipation. From his barricade position at the corner Nathan acquired a single sight picture and triggered a double tap into the man's chest.

That part of Nathan's shooting brain that automatically evaluated his shots told him one had hit the shotgun's receiver. Cursing his sloppiness in looking at the gun and not the target he fired again, a single insurance round into the standing man's forehead. Just to be sure he told himself. Then he spun left to face the doorway into the house, hearing behind him the ringing sound of ordnance steel striking concrete as the falling biker took down Bob's barrel rack on his trip to the floor.

Five shots gone, thought Nathan, and three killers left. Pounding footsteps approached and the door to the house burst open. He didn't have time to take cover but neither did the biker who appeared in the doorway. Nathan shot him once. The hollow point coursed in through the man's open mouth, expanded in reaction to flesh and bone and blew out the medulla as it exited. He caught a glimpse of Red dodging out of the hallway and into Bob's office as he fired.

The biker in the doorway fell and lodged it open with his body. Red had disappeared. Nathan sprinted through the open door, wanting desperately to bring the fight to the remaining killers before they had a chance to think and consolidate and do anything other than feel fear and uncertainty. Ten seconds was all he had before they started getting their heads around what was happening.

Red had slammed the door after dodging into the office so Nathan ran past. Anyone who came in that door he'd have cold . . . save him for later. The corpse in the doorway was not the one who had told Red to come look at something 'moving out back.' That meant his next target was probably to his left where the deck's sliding glass doors gave the best view of the backyard. The man would, by now, have his attention focused on where the hallway opened into the room, trying to sort out what was happening. He'll be looking high though, where people normally appear, thought Nathan, as he dropped to the floor and slid around the corner, leading with his .45.

Target number five was there, squatting back against the wall, his knees and gun arm silhouetted against the glass doors, body hidden in shadow. Nathan wished Bob had put night sights on the gun. He had no sight picture as he resorted to point shooting and double tapped into the darkness where the man's torso should be. The biker's shotgun roared in response, splintering wood and drywall over Nathan's head. Nathan knew he had two hits but couldn't tell how good they were as the muzzle flash illuminated a mixture of horror and puzzlement on the biker's face. It also gave him enough light to acquire a sight picture as he indexed on where the man's head had been a heartbeat ago. He triggered one more shot and heard him hit the floor with a solid thump that told Nathan he was now free to turn around and deal with the threat in the closed room behind him.

Nine shots fired. One bullet left and one killer left. Now, he thought, would be a good time for a reload. Too bad he didn't have one.

Still on the floor, he heard the office door open behind him. As he started to roll over in response, the concussion of a .357 Magnum slammed into his face, its bullet blasting the empty floor where a moment ago he had been positioned. His own .45 was already tracking upwards as he rolled onto his back and the front sight, like a living being with a will of its own, located the route to the base of the scarred skull. Nathan fought to tear his eyes away from the gun muzzle pointing at his chest and instead to seek his own target. Aware, as he struggled, that the cylinder of the revolver was beginning its turn as Red applied pressure to the trigger in a double action stroke. There was no conscious thought as Nathan pressed the trigger of the big .45. His ears were sufficiently overloaded by now that he never heard the shot. The muzzle flash and the recoil told him his last round had fired and the cavernous hollow point was on its way. Yet, in the slow motion world that now existed, the revolver cylinder kept turning. It completed its turn, bringing the next live round up and locking it into place ready for the hammer fall that would launch the bullet. As he watched, the hammer fell. It appeared to be a slow dreamlike movement, the firing pin arching forward with agonizing slowness, reaching for the primer, eager to complete its mechanical mission and snuff out Nathan's life. He was bracing for the impact when he realized it was not tachypsychia that made the hammer's forward motion seem slow. The finger holding back the double action trigger was merely relaxing and the hammer was being lowered with it. As strength evaporated from the man's muscles the vacant look of death invaded the eyes and he started to sag. The shiny Smith & Wesson slipped from his hands, landing on Nathan's legs. He twisted out of the way as the killer collapsed to the floor.

Nathan stood up, looking down at his gun, the slide was locked back on an empty magazine. Tossing it aside he rolled over the dead man and found his own P-10 in one of the pockets. A press check ensured it was still loaded and then he ran to find Bob. The two cleared the remainder of the house, insuring no surprises lurked in the shadows. Nathan's hearing was returning as they gathered back in the shop where Frankie was trying to get herself together.

Nathan unlocked the shop door and yelled into the night. "Okay Kim you can come out now. It's over." He tried to control his shaking hands while he waited for her. The adrenaline was flushing out of his body, but that took time. Grabbing the P-10 with two hands and trying to crush it helped. Bob was comforting Frankie.

Half a minute later Kim stepped through the door. An MP5SD was slung over her head and right shoulder. She wore black jeans and a dark leather jacket, her right hand remained on the submachine gun's pistol grip, finger extended along the black plastic frame just above the trigger. Bob saw the gun and nodded. "I was right," he said to no one in particular. Nathan stumbled through an introduction.

"Care to tell me how you got in on this little shoot-em-up?" he asked Kim, looking enquiringly at the MP5. He still had both hands on the P-10. Alternately squeezing and relaxing them.

"Naomi came down with the flu this afternoon, so I checked out one of the consulate cars and came to find you. Thought I'd take you up on that invitation to meet your friends." Kim was wandering around the shop, stepping over and around the dead bodies. "I was following the little map you gave me and drove by just in time to see those two goons outside arrive and get out of their truck with guns that didn't look like deer rifles. I drove by, parked, got this out of the trunk," she held up the MP5, "there's one in every official diplomatic trunk you know, and came to help you. Just in time it looks like."

"That was you on the phone?" said Bob.

"Yeah. That was her," volunteered Nathan.

"Me and my trusty cell phone," said Kim.

"I take it you've used that trusty cell phone to dial 911?" asked Nathan.

"I have indeed," she said. "I would think they'll be here soon." She had gone full circle around the shop and walked down the hallway of the house as well. The room was starting to fill with the heavy damp smell of blood as growing pools of red grew around the bodies of the dead. She stopped beside Frankie and put an arm around her shoulders. "Why don't we all go outside and try and find someplace that isn't quite so messy?" she said.

"I think I'd like that," replied Frankie. Kim took her by the arm and the four of them walked outside.

Kim gave Frankie back to Bob. "I'll run and get my car," she said as she tucked the silenced MP5 under her arm and trotted down the road toward the trees.

"Now that's quite a girl," said Bob watching her leave.

"Yeah . . . she sure is . . . sure is." Nathan's mind was somewhere else. "Bob?" he said eventually.

"What?"

"When you double action the trigger of a Smith revolver what would you estimate the amount of trigger movement to be between cylinder lock-up and hammer fall?"

"Huh?" Bob stared at Nathan incredulously. Where had this come from?

"You heard me. How much trigger movement would you estimate between cylinder lock-up and hammer fall on a double action pull?"

"Come on Nathan. You know the answer to that as well as I do. Not very much."

"I know that. But really now . . . exactly how much do you think it is?"

"Exactly?" said Bob. "I'll tell you exactly. Not very *damn* much."

Nathan looked at his friend. "Yeah. That's about what I thought it was too," he said, looking around for someplace to sit down. He could hear sirens in the distance.

EPILOGUE

The phone on Mr. Kent's desk warbled the tone that indicated his private line. Because he was reading in one of the chairs in his office's sitting area it was necessary to get up and walk to the desk. He lifted the receiver, punched the flashing button and asked for the appropriate security code.

"Bravo-Zulu three," said the caller.

"Go ahead," said Mr. Kent.

"It's over."

"Outcome?"

"Burdett neutralized six bikers. He's unhurt, no collateral damage and no complications observed."

"Superb," enthused Mr. Kent slapping a palm on the polished walnut of his desktop. "Absolutely superb. Outstanding. He came through. Six you say? And all neutralized?"

"Yes, sir. B-Zoned every one."

"Mr. Burdett is most definitely a talented individual. I've never seen an asset like him."

"Nor I, sir. Never."

"Would you agree he's ready?"

"Yes. Tested and ready."

"Very good. By the way . . . excellent work. Sterilize and come in." He hung up the phone and straightened the ivory penholder on his desk. The phone cord had moved it out of place when he'd picked up the handset. Returning to his seat, he opened the book again and contemplated where he'd left off before being interrupted. He read late into the night.

Enjoyed B-ZONE?

Be sure to read other novels by Al Voth, including:

Mandatory Reload – The sequel to B-Zone
ISBN 0968505015

Available from all major booksellers or from the publisher
Trigger Press International
Box 3713
Spruce Grove, AB
Canada
T7X 3A9

www. triggerpress.com

ABOUT THE AUTHOR

Al Voth, like many of his generation, grew up on a family farm and began a lifelong interest in firearms by hunting small game with a single shot .22 caliber rifle. After graduating from university with a degree in sociology, he began a career in law enforcement and has never left that field. This included work as a patrol officer and nine years of service on an Emergency Response Team. Along the way he has won numerous awards in rifle and handgun competition, usually building and modifying his own match guns in the process. He currently works at a forensic laboratory as a firearm and toolmark examiner and still shoots competitively and hunts as much as time permits.